H.B. LYLE

The Year of the Gun

HODDER

First published in Great Britain in 2020 by Hodder & Stoughton
An Hachette UK company

This paperback edition published in 2021

1

A CIP catalogue record for this title is available from the British Library

Paperback ISBN 978 1 473 65551 5
eBook ISBN 978 1 473 65550 8

Typeset in Plantin Light by Palimpsest Book Production Ltd, Falkirk, Stirlingshire

Printed and bound in Great Britain by Clays Ltd, Elcograf S.p.A.

Hodder & Stoughton policy is to use papers that are natural, renewable
and recyclable products and made from wood grown in sustainable forests.
The logging and manufacturing processes are expected to conform to the
environmental regulations of the country of origin.

Hodder & Stoughton Ltd
Carmelite House
50 Victoria Embankment
London EC4Y 0DZ

www.hodder.co.uk

'Lyle's series of thrillers featuring Wiggins, once one of Sherlock Holmes's Baker Street Irregulars, are coming on splendidly . . . Skilfully mixing real history with action sequences worthy of Lee Child, this is historical crime-writing at its best'
– John Williams, *Mail on Sunday*

'Full throttle, highly entertaining historical hokum, delivering entertainment in spades'   – Myles McWeeney, *Irish Independent*

'Lyle's unique blend of real history, inventive storytelling and characters borrowed from Conan Doyle is exhilarating . . . an action packed historical thriller . . . This is a series I hope will run and run'   – *New Books Magazine*

'The third outing in H.B. Lyle's engaging series of historical thrillers . . . The story rattles along at pace, the characters are engaging and the fight scenes burst with action. But Lyle's great strength is in his depiction of time and place; from its stinking tenements, where babies cry from hunger, to its sinister docks and upmarket brothels, the Edwardian city – then still part of Britain – is brought to life in all its squalid, magnificent glory'
– *Financial Times*

'A bruising, gritty and very entertaining adventure amid the slums and salons of 1912 Dublin, a city about to explode'
– Ed O'Loughlin

Also by H.B. Lyle

The Irregular: A Different Class of Spy
The Red Ribbon

For R and E, and, as ever, Annalise

Tyrone wished they'd let him carry a piece. But Meath said no way, and Little Patsy had just laughed in his face. He hated running errands without a gun.

He came out of the bar onto the street. It was nearly midnight. He looked about him, saw no one. The sounds of laughter, singing, drunkenness filtered out of the door behind him. Still serving, and they would for a while yet – especially now Patrolman Hennessy had stopped by for a few. He shivered slightly against a sudden chill. It was warm, but something about this errand had got into his bones. Little Patsy had been jumpy all evening and when he'd ordered him out to the neighbouring Hudson River docks to pick up a package, Tyrone had initially felt relief. Just to get out of that bar, with that Meath tapping his feet and snorting off the table, and Little Patsy pointing and laughing and red-eyed, was enough to make him nervous. But now, out on the street, the relief dissipated and the fear returned. Working for Little Patsy Doyle was all about the nerves.

He set off at a jog. He did not look around, like an act of faith or something. It was strangely quiet. He expected the death train down Tenth any minute, but he couldn't see or hear it in the midnight black. He hurried across the wide road and out towards the docks. A number of unlit warehouses were ranged along the street, and he headed towards a gap between two. It was even darker down here, dark like he imagined the countryside to be, though he'd never set foot outside of Manhattan, save one or two trips to the Bronx with his mama when he was knee-high. When he looked up, he could even see the stars. It felt like it must be the only place on the island this dark. He knew every inch of the island and little else besides.

His heart began to race. He could sense someone at the end of the alley, behind him, but he didn't want to look. He stopped instead at the address Meath had given him for the Little Patsy pick-up. A small wooden door cut into the side of the alley, it looked like it hadn't been opened in years. He raised his hand to knock—

'Tyrone,' someone shouted, in an English accent.

A shape appeared at the end of the alley – the Englishman for sure. Tyrone made out the raised hand, the aggression in the voice, and he ran.

The alley opened out onto a wide pier and Tyrone hurtled across it, his heart beating fast. He could outdistance the Englishman, but in that instant he ran straight on – away from any exit and out onto the long, empty pier. It was a cargo pier, not for the big liners that docked upriver. A smugglers' pier, dark as death and just as frightening.

His mind raced. 'Right, left, right, left?' he chanted to himself, looking for a gap in the cargo. The Englishman shouted again, closer than he thought.

Suddenly, the pier ran out. He glanced out quickly into the darkness of the Hudson River, then back around, and wheeled to the right-hand edge. He thrust his hands into the air and whispered, 'Don't shoot.'

The man came closer. He moved like a cat. A cat with a gun.

'Don't do it, Englishman,' Tyrone said.

'Speak up!'

'Please, don't kill me,' Tyrone shouted. He wailed and hollered into the wind-whipped night. 'This . . . this ain't your battle. Please help. Help, Lord, help,' he cried at the top of his voice, along the pier to the warehouses, the choppy river-sea at his back. 'Please, Englishman, have mercy.'

The Englishman nodded slightly. 'The name's Wiggins,' he said, and fired twice.

2

'Unsinkable, my arse.'

'It's got the ballast, so it has, John Coffey. The good ship *Coffey's Arse*.'

'Wheesht, you, and pour another.' The young man laughed and pointed at the bottle.

Wiggins sat in a circle of six or seven men playing cards around a table improvised from luggage. They were in the mixed third-class saloon of the RMS *Titanic* as it steamed north from Cherbourg to Ireland on its second night at sea. Someone played a violin. A bodhrán marked the beat. Men and women danced. Drink ran free.

A rat-faced man sat next to Wiggins. He had sharp eyes and a scorched cheek. He threw his cards down in anger, then turned to the winner, Coffey.

'What-the-hell-you-know?' Ratface said. He strung his words together at speed. Wiggins didn't have a handle on American accents, but he guessed New York. 'This ship'll never sink. It's in all the papers.'

'Ach, I'm not saying it will sink. But it might.'

'And who are you?' the American scoffed.

Wiggins leaned forward. 'You're one of the engineers, ain't you?'

Coffey looked up, surprised. 'True, I am. But only until Queenstown.'

'Are we playing cards here?' The American scowled as he tossed around another hand. 'Because some of us here aren't by way of enjoying being taken for money.' He glared at Wiggins, who had a handy pile of coins to his name.

Wiggins pointedly ignored him. Instead, he eyed Coffey. The young man was broad, almost fresh-faced, but he had calloused hands and the beefy upper arms of a manual labourer, not an engineer. Wiggins had said that to flatter the man, for it was clear he worked in the furnace (coal splatter all over his trousers) – he was a fireman, off shift. Still, he did work on the ship, and knew more about it than anyone there.

'Why do you say it's sinkable?' Wiggins asked.

'Any ship is sinkable. It's a question of physics. If it takes on enough water below decks, it will go down.'

'But what about the isolation system?'

Coffey shrugged. 'It's not going to sink, surely. But if the water gets in . . . Look, if you put a hole big enough into the hull, say here or here . . .' he gestured with his hands '. . . then it doesn't matter what all else you've got. Same principle for a skiff, a yawl or a dinghy. You're going down into the deep and you don't come back.'

Coffey's friend raised his eyebrows. 'It would have to be a pretty big hole.'

'Ach, now you're being filthy.' Coffey flicked a cigarette at his friend and laughed.

They settled down to play the hand. Wiggins's mind drifted, what with the bottled beer and the half-empty flask at his hip. The saloon heaved with people, even at this late hour, still jolly, excited. Young children ran wild, their mothers smiled, their fathers drank. They were all going to a better life in America, they thought. The great capitalist experiment out West: no kings and queens and emperors to take the spoils, no aristocracy to bleed the workers dry. Wiggins wasn't so sure. He didn't know much about New York, but he knew the only solution to poverty was money. And *that* was never free.

New York. He guessed she was there. It'd been almost three years since he'd seen her in London, his Bela, his love, his life, his betrayer. Bela, killer of his best friend, Bill, architect of terror, breaker of his heart. Bela—

'Whoa!' *CRASH!*

The rat-faced American had launched himself at Coffey. 'Cheat!' he cried, upending the table. He grasped Coffey by the lapels, pulled him up. The saloon was in uproar. Shouts and screams, smashed glass.

'See here,' Ratface pulled cards from Coffey's sleeve, 'that pot's mine. It's all mine.' As if out of nowhere, Ratface now had two or three friends. Large men, in American clothes, crowding Coffey, blocking the view.

Wiggins put his hand on Ratface's shoulder. 'Watch it, Ratty.'

Ratface swivelled. Wiggins glanced at his heavies, reset his feet. 'Jack of spades, three of clubs, ace of hearts? You should know – you had them all in there.' He tapped the man's breast pocket.

Ratface glared, then tilted his head.

Wiggins met the first heavy's chin with the flat of his palm. He jammed his foot into the knee of the second man, then turned, only to find a revolver in his face.

'I'll take *your* money, too.' Ratface showed his teeth, just above the Colt's sight. 'Welcome to America.'

Wiggins raised his hands slowly. 'We ain't there yet. No need for a shooter here, mate.'

'There's always need for a gun.'

Wiggins took a breath. Coffey and the other players had slithered off into the crowd. Ratface had a gun and three heavies. And he looked like a man who would use it. On the other hand, all the money Wiggins had in the world was sewn into his waistband. Ratface would know that, too. He'd have to take care to get it right, to—

'Aahh!' BANG BANG.

Wiggins grasped the gun muzzle in his left hand while flooring Ratface with his right. Gunshots peppered the ceiling as he wrestled for control of the weapon.

Finally, he staggered back, gun in hand. 'You want some?' Wiggins shouted theatrically at the prone Ratface. 'Then use your bloody hands.' Bullets clattered to the floor as he emptied the gun. 'Come on, then! And no bloody gun— *oomph!*'

A great force smashed into his back. He flew to the floor, pinned by the weight of at least three men.

'Gun gun gun!' someone shouted.

The gun was pulled from his grasp. Handcuffs pinched his wrists.

'It ain't loaded,' Wiggins said.

'To the master-at-arms, now!' The voice, a bass Lancastrian, boomed close by.

Wiggins was lifted to his feet by two burly sailors, twisting his arms behind him as they did so. A startled crowd watched, mothers herding away their children, men looking on in fascination. The gunshots had rattled around the saloon with such shocking loudness that a hushed awe had settled on the people in the packed saloon. They looked at Wiggins with surprise and pity. There was no sign of the rat-faced American or his people, or Coffey. The entire game – the cards, the coins, the improvised table – had disappeared and all that remained was Wiggins, holding a gun.

The Lancastrian and his two heavy-handed helpers hustled Wiggins through the crowd, then down narrow, tilting corridors.

'It ain't what it looked like,' Wiggins said, once he'd been pulled into the master-at-arms' cabin.

'You stink of booze, lad,' the Lancastrian said.

'I always stink of booze.' He grinned. The Lancastrian did not.

'No use. The King's on duty. Baily'd be a different matter.'

Wiggins found out what this meant shortly afterwards, when a short, clear-eyed man marched into the cabin.

'You were armed?' he said to Wiggins without preamble.

'Who are you?'

'Master-at-Arms King. You were armed?'

'Like I said, it weren't mine. I fucking hate those things.'

'Language! You filthy beast.' King turned to the Lancastrian. 'Put him off at Queenstown.'

'You tossing me over?' Wiggins gasped.

'As per the ship's regulations. We drop anchor in three hours.

Make sure he's on the quay – with your own eyes, Anderson, you hear me?'

'Aye aye, sir.'

The great ship, a city of the sea, anchored far out of Cork Bay. Master-at-Arms King had deemed Wiggins dangerous and had shackled his wrist to the bed. When it was time, Anderson pulled him from the cabin and marched him, like a criminal, through the crowded corridors and out onto a tender bound to the *Titanic* by great swaying cables.

Anderson pushed him onto the deck of the small steamboat and held him firm. A few other passengers stood about, looking towards the coast. Not many getting off the most famous ship in the world. A buzz rippled through those that saw him, as if he was a cricketer, or a famous actor.

'You're notorious, lad,' Anderson muttered. 'The man that lost his berth on the greatest-ever ship, all for carrying a gun. Small cock, is it? Like to handle a hard piece?'

'Is that a proposition?'

Anderson scowled and spat into the sea. Wiggins glanced along the rail. John Coffey, the card-playing fireman, caught his eye, then turned away, hiding in his coat. The boat chugged around the headland just then and a town came into view. Streets zigzagged up a green hill above the dock, topped off by a large church. The quayside thronged with people waiting to board. A Union flag jagged red, white and blue against the dark grey sky. Bunting fluttered like a string of stamps. 'Queenstown,' Anderson said.

'You're wasted below decks. You should be on the bridge.'

'Shut it.'

On the *Titanic*, Wiggins had become a celebrity. But here, on the packed White Star quay, no one gave him a second glance. Bodies hustled to get aboard two small steamboats that waited at the quay amidst a mountain of luggage and cargo. Excitement, almost glee, radiated from the throng. A young man scampered past him and onto the deck, carrying nothing but a set of bagpipes.

Wiggins looked back to the tender and wondered whether it could get any worse. The young man started to play.

'You wanting a bed?'

Wiggins turned. John Coffey stood before him, shielding his eyes. 'I'm wanting to earn a passage to New York.'

Coffey shook his head. 'I am sorry, so I am. That Yank was a sore loser.'

Wiggins shrugged a canvas bag over his shoulder. Some passengers started to sing along to the pipes.

And Ireland, long a province, be

A nation once again.

'Christ,' Wiggins muttered.

'This is the rebel county, Englishman.'

'I ain't English. I'm London.'

A nation once again,

A nation once again.

And Ireland, long a province . . .

'There's nothing here for yous, man, all the same. Yous best get yourself to Dublin if you want work.'

'Do they sing there and all?'

Coffey laughed. 'Not as grandly as us Cork men.' He thought for a moment. 'Listen, I owe you.'

'Ten quid's worth?'

'I thinks I know a man as could give you a lift.'

'To New York?'

'To Dublin.'

Green leprechauns danced down Sackville Street. Jaunty yokels called out 'to be sure, to be sure'. Emeralds fell from every tree and nestled among the shamrocks. Nuns tutted, priests grinned. Dark and devilish swains kissed the Blarney Stone and made their sweethearts swoon. Oh for Ireland, green and bonny land.

Wiggins had not kissed the Blarney Stone. He did not see leprechauns, or jaunty yokels, or even the hint of an emerald. He kissed the top of his pint, a thick yeasty cream, and drank deeply. The whiskey chaser on the bar represented almost the last of his money. He reasoned that when he was low on cash, best to save the last of it for drink – who wants to be sober when they meet their maker? He downed the short.

The clock above the bar read 11:55. 'Is that right?' Wiggins gestured at the barman.

'In a hurry, are you?'

'Time for a short before noon, I reckon.'

Another whiskey appeared. Wiggins took it in one swift shot. John Coffey had set him up on a cargo train to Dublin from Cork. He'd also given Wiggins an introduction of sorts, to a man named Lynch. 'He's got fingers in a lot of pies, I am thinking, Mr Lynch. But he was a Cork man once, and I hear he does well now, up there in the big city. He is not afraid of the English,' Coffey had said with a smile. 'And he is not afraid of the law either, so I am hearing. But tell him John Coffey knows you – that's the Coffeys of Chapel Street.'

Wiggins had got the train up to Dublin, squished into the guard's van thanks to Coffey's cousin. He'd arrived earlier that morning and had taken a walk along the Liffey. Long, wide quays stretched all the way into the city, culminating in the bustle and industry of the Guinness Brewery quay and its jetties. Fat barges drifted off the quay laden with barrels, men stripped to the waist rolled many more across the cobbles, dray carts and lorries driven to and fro, all sloshing and banging with porter. A few folk – tourists, Wiggins guessed – looked on at the sight of the enormous brewery doling out its beer to Ireland and the world. The big barrels, easily up to Wiggins's hip when on end, bumped and rattled across the cobbled quay. The draymen hauled the barrels up onto motorised lorries or carts, or left them waiting for the next barge to draw close. It was enough to make a sober man thirsty, and Wiggins was not a sober man.

Which was why he found himself at the pub, with no intention of finding the Lynch fellow, or starting work at all, any time soon. Wiggins always reasoned that the best place to take the temperature of a town was to take a taste of its beer – certainly in Britain – and if not beer, then whatever it was the locals drank to make them forget where they were. That was how to know a place. Besides, Wiggins had spent the last year trying to escape work. Captain Vernon Kell, head of the Secret Service Bureau, was all work. He didn't need another boss in a hurry.

Bottles ranged the shelves behind the bar, like shells. A large sign read: *Finest Old Dublin Whiskey 20/- a gallon.* Cigarette and pipe smoke clouded the ceiling. The wooden bar smelled of wax. Outside, church bells rang. 'I thought you said that was right?' Wiggins glanced at the clock.

'It will be by the time St Paddy's has finished.'

He worked at the rest of his black pint. Work. For the last year, Kell had ballooned the Bureau's activities and personnel. But it had become nothing but administration. All paper and files and starched collars. Kell had begun compiling dossiers on everyone he could, and in the end Wiggins had wanted no more of it. He was done with starch and uniforms.

A year earlier, Kell had promised him the price of a berth to New York, on condition he would return to fight the Germans, should it come to war. Kell was convinced that war with Germany was inevitable, though no one else – as far as Wiggins could see – took any notice. For his part, Wiggins had not told Kell why he wanted to go to New York. He hardly knew himself, other than a name – a face – he couldn't forget.

'Again.' Wiggins tapped a coin on the bar.

'The large or the small?'

'Funny.'

The doors burst open behind Wiggins and a man marched up to the barman. 'Have you got it, Rooney?'

'Good day to you, Mr Hannigan, I'm sure.'

Hannigan stretched his mouth in a grin. His eyes stayed steady. 'Ach, don't be carrying on all hysterical. The OC is on the walk, that's all. I'd hate for him to give you the black mark.'

Rooney ducked behind the bar. Wiggins wasn't fooled by the banter. He felt Hannigan's eyes on him and turned.

'You buying?' Wiggins said.

Hannigan hadn't taken off his cap. He wore a long coat that

almost tipped the ground. His skin was smooth and brown, impervious to rain and sun, beaten and unyielding. He stared at Wiggins with a bright, dark intelligence. He reminded Wiggins of a Limehouse Lascar. As Wiggins spoke, all the fake levity of the exchange with the barman drained from Hannigan's face.

'Ha!' he barked. 'An Englishman taking money from an Irishman? Who'd have thought?'

'Not money. Drink.'

Hannigan stared levelly once more, but said nothing. Rooney the barman reappeared. He handed Hannigan an envelope. 'Will himself be coming by?'

'No.' Hannigan hadn't taken his eyes off Wiggins until this point. But then he nodded at Rooney. 'He's walking with Fitz today. I'm needed for a barntackle.' He turned back to Wiggins. 'That's Irish for a friendly conversation. With violence.'

'And there was me thinking you was just a shit shoveller.'

The barman gasped. Hannigan clenched his fist, leaned forward, then stopped himself. 'I haven't done that in a long time, Englishman. I deal with shit of an entirely different kind now. And if you're not out of Francis Street by tonight, I'll deal with you too. See-ho?' He walked towards the door then, slow and boiling.

The barman said nothing. Wiggins sipped his drink. His glass gently tapped the hardwood bar. Two old men sat at the far end of the pub, gazing at their pints in silence.

Eventually, the barman spoke. 'How are you knowing that about our man there?'

'His history in shit?'

'Well, I wouldn't . . . Well, yes.'

'If the cap fits . . .'

'You shouldn't be talking to Hannigan like that. I'd say that was enough for you here.'

Wiggins tipped the last of the whiskey down his shirt front as he teetered. He looked at the clock, and nodded.

He swayed out of the pub and along Francis Street. Small, dirty alleyways opened off either side of the road. They stank of poor.

Wiggins knew that stink, back from the East End of London, from his home in Paddington back in the eighties, down the Jago, but he hadn't felt it this bad in years. Dublin was poor.

He checked his watch again just as he reached the corner of Coombe Street, then began a slow promenade. He felt a bit drunk. The fusty grey air didn't help, nor the poverty stink, the piss and the shit, mingled with the high, yeasty, malty, hoppy stench of the big beer factories that dominated the horizon to his left. It reminded him of the Horse Shoe Brewery on Tottenham Court Road, only more so, much more so, what with the shit in the Liffey and the mouldy, damp, misty air that wasn't rain but wasn't clear and made your very bones wet under the skin.

The weather hadn't deterred the traffic – booze carts, trams, a general busyness that reminded him of parts of London on a Sunday. But as he turned away from the river, the traffic stilled. He checked the street signs and ambled on. A man selling Lipton tea from a wooden box on wheels veered towards him until he saw Wiggins's glare.

Just then, coming south, a brisk man in a tweed suit and green felt hat walked down the street towards him. He barked commands at a young man by his side. The tweed man waved his hands this way and that. His cufflinks shone brilliantly against the grey, his shirt dazzled white, the three-piece as sharp as a crease. The boy shambled beside him, a scrap of a thing, wearing his clothes like a bag. Wiggins swayed out of their way.

'I tell you, Fitz, it's business, you hear?' the tweed man said. He flicked his eyes at Wiggins as he said this but didn't break stride. Wiggins glanced back and hesitated.

As the two reached the corner, three large men with hats pulled low stepped out in front of them.

'Hey, what are you about?' the tweed man said, stopping.

Another two men came rushing across the street towards them, clubs drawn.

'What's this then?'

The first three grabbed him about the shoulders. Another punched down the younger man's protests.

'Off me now. You know who I am? Fitz, Fitz! Get Vincent,' the tweed man cried, holding up his fists.

He took a heavy slap around the face, and a punch to the gut. The men began to haul him away, leaving one to boot the younger man, Fitz, on the floor.

As the thug drew back his boot for a second go, he reeled away with an agonised cry. Wiggins's knuckles sang with pain. He didn't need to punch him again. As the thug tumbled to the floor, Wiggins wheeled and smashed his palm into a second attacker's throat.

'What's this?' One of the hatted men let go of the tweed and turned in confusion.

Wiggins smashed his head against the wall. His heart pounded with booze, adrenaline and bloodlust. A fourth man jumped on his back, but Wiggins angled his hip and threw him over his shoulder in a bone-juddering thud. Bartitsu never leaves you, he thought in a flash. The old detective's time in Tibet not totally wasted.

A hand raked his eyes from behind, pulling at his nose. *Act, don't hesitate.* He reached back and took a handful of bollocks. In the blur, the young man's voice wailed out, 'Sir, sir, let's gawn. It's the DMPs.'

Wiggins tangled the balls in his hand, his nose still caught. The first man got up and punched him in the chest like a hammer. He went to try again, but Wiggins swung his boot into the on-comer's kneecap. He crumpled, screaming filthy. The air was full of whistles and shouts. Wiggins glanced around and caught a haymaker flush on the cheek. He stumbled, but let loose a straight left as he fell.

Out of nowhere, an open lorry had appeared and the attackers jumped into the back. Wiggins tried to grab the last of them, but a great pain seared across the back of his head, a truncheon flashed, then another. The shouts and whistles faded, and then it was light no more.

Wiggins woke. A distant clanging sounded in his ears, far off, every few seconds. A bitter cold gripped him. His left eye throbbed, his head swam. He opened his good eye in a crusty slit.

He could see almost nothing. A faint milky oblong shimmered in the far distance. The clanging continued, like an iron bar struck against a rail. He lay on his back on cold, moist stone. His knuckles tingled. He checked his teeth one by one, an old street fighter's routine that never left you. And then he closed his eyes again.

Vague images flashed in his mind: a huge policeman dragging him along the ground, a boot in the face, being hurried along a dark stone tunnel through a wet mist. Inside or outside, he couldn't tell. He remembered, too, the thrill of fear – he'd been in a fight one moment, and the next he was in the God-knows-where and the God-knows-what. Alone. There was no one here to cry foul. These coppers or soldiers, if that's what they were, could dump him in the river or do all of anything else and no one would ever know.

He stilled his breathing and shifted up on one elbow. A sharp smell of iron, tinged with damp, clung in his nostrils. His blood. Or someone else's. The clanging stopped. It was replaced by the sound of heavy boots nearing. The oblong of light went dark for a moment.

'You broke a copper's jaw,' a thick, heavy voice said. Wiggins made out a huge silhouette against the light of the door. Another figure moved behind.

'Ahh . . .' Wiggins could only croak, his mouth glasspaper dry.

'Shut it.' The large man glanced back and added, 'Is it all clear?'

'It's all clear,' a flat voice returned. Wiggins suddenly thought that he might never come out.

Wiggins could only croak. 'Wha—'

A huge paw swiftly grabbed his collar and lifted him half off the ground. Silenced, Wiggins waited for the punch.

Instead, the man dragged him across the flagstones, shouting at his mate to help. Wiggins tried to call out, but the brute crunched the back of his head against the stone floor.

He came to in a pitch-black alley. Or rather, he came to as he was hurtled along the alley. Three men now carried him through the rain. Windows rattled in the wind. Wiggins could barely see in front of him, he could just hear the grunts and gasps of the men carrying him. They burst out into a wide-open space, barely lit. Wiggins could feel the wind, the rain slashing his upturned face and cheeks. He kept his body limp, his only chance.

'Quick, man,' the leader hissed. 'There, back of the bridge.'

'Gis the hood.'

They hurried onwards, into the wind. He guessed they were going to throw him in the river. It was only then that Wiggins realised, with a sudden, sickening horror, that his hands and legs were bound.

3

'Are you wet enough?'

Wiggins looked up. The owner of the voice shouted from the driver's seat of a motor car parked on the other side of the road. 'Sure, you look it.'

'I ain't sure,' Wiggins grunted.

'Well get in then,' the young man shouted. 'Quick.'

Wiggins glanced up and down the road. Fine, misty rain filled the air, hanging there rather than falling. He turned just as the great prison door shut behind him.

'Are you coming, or what?' the driver said at last. 'I won't bite.' Wiggins then recognised him as the younger man who'd been in the street brawl a week earlier. His memory of the fight was a bit hazy, but he remembered his voice – shouting at the older man to flee.

Wiggins sauntered across the road and got in the front of the car beside him.

'My name's Fitz.' The driver grinned. 'In case you couldn't remember, you know, what with all the fighting and the fellas hitting you about the head and all.'

'Wiggins.'

'And how was the Joy?'

'What?'

Fitz gestured at the prison as the car pulled away. 'His Majesty's Prison Mountjoy.'

'It's a prison. Is it always raining here?'

'Ach, this isn't rain! This is a fine spring day, so it is.'

Wiggins looked out of the window as the motor picked up speed. Grey houses sped past. In the gaps, the grey sky met the grey streets and the mizzling air hung heavy with the threat of storms to come.

'Where are we going?'

'To the OC, of course,' Fitz said. 'The fella you saved last week, the boss, the big man. Mr O'Connell himself.'

'Why?'

'Ach, I'm just the help.'

Wiggins grunted again. He closed his eyes and felt the rattle of the car as it bounced across the cobbles. In that moment the week before, when he realised he'd been trussed up and was about to be thrown in the river, he'd shouted 'Help!' as loud as he could. No reason to play dead if you were dead anyway.

'Help!'

It startled the men carrying him, and he fell to the ground. 'Hurry,' one of them hissed as they half hauled, half dragged him across the slimy quay.

'What's going on here?' A sharp, upper-class English accent punched the darkness. 'Stop there, at once!' A lantern bobbed and flickered out of the night.

Wiggins dropped to the ground again. The three men stood up, as if to attention. He angled his eyes and saw an officer – in a uniform he didn't recognise – striding towards them. He held a lantern in front of him like a weapon. He wore a captain's cap, a different military fig altogether from the police. Wiggins hadn't been in town long enough to differentiate the insignia, but the man had authority. He also had a revolver.

'This is a Dublin Met matter, sir.'

'What was that? What did you say?'

'The RIC have no jurisdiction here.'

'Jurisdiction? This isn't the bloody law courts, it's Dublin.'

Wiggins started to whistle, a dry, reedy noise, but a song that might just save his life.

The young officer who'd been arguing the point of administration (or for Wiggins's life, if you looked at it in a different way) broke off. 'What's that? Is it the—'

'March of the Gunners, sir,' Wiggins managed to croak.

'You're army?'

'You're English?' one of the coppers said, surprised.

Wiggins ignored him and focused all his attention on the captain. He kept his wheezing voice as steady as he could. 'Once. Gunner Wiggins, as was. I fought the Boer.'

'Shite,' muttered the copper.

'What are you doing here, man?' The officer peered at Wiggins. 'Are you involved?'

'He assaulted a policeman, sir,' the copper broke in. 'A vagrant – a violent threat.'

Wiggins gasped. 'One too many is all, sir.'

By this time the officer had been joined by three subordinates, also dressed in quasi-military kit. The policemen around Wiggins had stepped back now, as if he was stinking. Or almost dead.

The officer sighed. 'Put him in the Mountjoy for a week and be done with it. I don't want him on the street looking like that.'

'But, sir . . .' The large policeman looked down at Wiggins, already defeated.

'We'll take it from here, Constable. We have a van.'

Wiggins put his head back on the stone flag and grinned.

'You're a lucky man, so you are.'

'What was that?' Wiggins opened his eyes and looked at Fitz, who steered the car down a side road.

'Talk about the luck of the Irish.'

'Why do you say lucky?'

'Wasn't it you thrown off the big boat?'

'*Titanic*. What of it?'

Fitz gaped at him. 'Don't you know?'

'I've been in shtuk, ain't I? They put me in the hole.'

Fitz whistled to himself. 'It's all gone, down to the deep. The whole ship, gone.' Fitz prattled on, relating the biggest news story since for ever. The *Titanic* had sunk, downed by an iceberg, hundreds dead.

Wiggins shook his head and thought of John Coffey, off the

ship in Ireland; he thought of the rat-faced American, too, and wondered whether he'd met a condign end. 'How did you know?' Wiggins said at last.

'It was in the papers, of course.'

'No, about me. How did you know I was on it?'

'Ach, the OC knows everything. Have you got the clock on you, have you?'

'You mean the time?' Wiggins fiddled in his pocket, surprised to find the watch the old Doctor had given him, bullet-scarred and ancient, had survived.

Fitz went on. 'Mine has gone, so it has, a lovely little thing it was, a woman's watch they say, but I didn't mind. Ah, here you are.' Fitz gestured towards a right-hand turn.

The motor car – a gleaming, polished, leathered Daimler – slowed, and they turned onto a small gravel road. There were a number of low dwellings stretching down one side, dwarfed by the huge chimneys of a factory behind. A two-storey terrace filled the other side of the dirty street. Fitz killed the brakes. The car squealed. 'It's a pig,' he muttered.

It was the only car on the street. Wiggins got out. At the corner stood a pub – another pub – but it looked closed. Wiggins guessed they were somewhere nearby where he'd been drinking the week or so before, near Francis Street. He didn't have a good sense of the city yet, but they'd crossed the river in the car back from the Mountjoy. Fitz got out and nodded at the pub.

Wiggins looked again. Even in his short time in Dublin, he'd noticed the pubs, the pubs everywhere, like a golden, booze-soaked heaven. Yet they always seemed closed. Dark windows, day and night, sealed doors, dirty little secrets or remembrances of drunkenness long ago. A secret the whole city knew. He glanced back at Fitz.

'On you go.' The boy smiled, showing one big bucktooth on top and a crooked bottom set. A scrap of a boy, eighteen or nineteen at most, not above five foot three, but his smile never-theless reassured Wiggins. True warmth was always welcome, especially in the rain. 'The OC'll be in the back. And don't mind

Mr H. He'll hate you, but he hates everyone, so you won't be lonely.'

'Mr H?'

'You'll see.'

Blackened wood panels lined the walls, and three silent men sat in a line at the bar. They each had one hand resting on their glass, intent on nothing but the booze. A pint and a short in front of them, at ten in the morning, Wiggins noted on the big clock. They looked like mourners at their own funerals. He paused, then caught the barman's eye. The man gave him the once-over, then cocked his head at a door to the back. Wiggins squared his shoulders and pushed through it without knocking.

A burst of laughter met him as he entered. The snug was low-ceilinged, small and warm. A fire crackled in the hearth. Four men sat on stools, legs wide apart. A fifth stood, holding court, the fire at his back. As soon as he saw Wiggins, the man, undoubtedly O'Connell, stopped. He was as well turned out now as when Wiggins had saved him on the street: immaculately pressed white shirt (spotless), a tweed waistcoat that almost shimmered in the light, brogues. His hair, now visible without the hat, was swept back high from his forehead in a filigree wave of soft, dark blonde. A full barnet for his age, Wiggins thought, and he was proud of it.

'Is it you now?' O'Connell asked, raising his well-trimmed eyebrows. 'My knight in shining armour.'

A stool clattered to the floor. Hannigan – the man from Rooney's pub, Wiggins realised instantly – leapt up from his seat and pushed his face close. 'Him?' Hannigan glanced back at O'Connell. 'He's the fella?' He stared, incredulous.

O'Connell nodded back, half confirmation, half question.

'He's a fucking spy!' Hannigan roared. 'He was in Rooney's the other day. He knew me. And he's fucking English. I'm telling you. He *knew*.' Hannigan took a breath, but kept his dark eyes on Wiggins. He shot a hand through his hair, which was black and lank on the top and badly shaved around the sides and back.

'What did he know?' O'Connell said, interested.

Hannigan faltered. 'He knew things about me, is all . . . what I used to do.'

'That so?' O'Connell tipped his head and smiled, as if faintly amused. But Wiggins saw his hands tense and release. He was a man working hard at bonhomie, but a hard man all the same.

Wiggins grinned. 'You mean the shit-shovelling?' Hannigan stepped forward in anger, but O'Connell stilled him. Wiggins went on. 'I ain't never met you in me life, 'cept down that boozer the other day. But yous wear your past like a bloody target, hanging round your shoulders it is, waiting to be poked.' Wiggins stepped forward and poked Hannigan in the chest as he said this.

Someone gasped, Hannigan seethed, but O'Connell waited for more, and Wiggins obliged.

'The shoes, turned in just so. The cut of his back, stooped, the bent knees. That's the labouring tell. You can't smell for toffee neither. At Rooney's you didn't even blink an eye when they changed that stinking barrel. But most of all, it's your hands, it's always the hands. Look at 'em.' Wiggins gestured for Hannigan to hold them up and, stunned into submission, he did so. 'Them nails are cut to the quick, so they are, but cut, mind – not bitten. Filed close, too. But your hands are as rough as old boots – yeah, yeah, I know how many men you've banjaxed wiv 'em, you've got fighter's hands, don't give a stuff who knows it. So, yous don't care about your hands being hurt. But what you do give a stuff about is how clean they are. There ain't no shit under your fingernails . . .' Wiggins paused, then added, '. . . any more.'

Hannigan's rock-face features reddened as Wiggins told his story, and his eyes spoke of deep, dark murder, mixed with shame. But Wiggins went on relentless and spoke beyond him, directly to the OC. 'Shit shoveller, see. It ain't hard, once you know how to look. I don't know what you call them here. Back where I come from we used to call them night-soil men, scraping the crap off the street at all hours.'

For a moment, Wiggins expected Hannigan to explode. But behind him, by the fire, O'Connell had listened to Wiggins with increasing glee. He barked out a laugh before Hannigan could move. 'He's got you there, Vincent, so he has.' He laughed again and brought a whiskey to his lips. 'How he knows is a mystery, but didn't I find you shovelling shit off the streets of Belfast myself? You were knee-deep in the stuff, so you were.'

Wiggins released a breath. He was all chest and chin and confidence on the outside, but these weren't people to get on the wrong side of, he knew that. But he also knew that if you didn't have the chest and chin and confidence, you would get on the wrong side of them.

'I don't trust him still,' Hannigan muttered.

O'Connell flung his half-empty glass into the fire. It shattered and flared into the silence. 'Should I trust you, Vincent, should I?' he bellowed. 'Here's the man, standing here, who pulled me out of a beating, out of a killing for all we know. Where were *you*?'

Hannigan kept his head down.

'And who the fuck was it? Eh? Eh?'

O'Connell looked around at his speechless men. He shot a hand threw his hair and laughed, smiling at Wiggins. 'You see what I have to deal with, Mr Higgins.'

'Wiggins.'

'Right you are. Almost Irish there, too. I've known many a Higgins. A rough clan.' He chuckled again. 'Sit down, Vincent. Jaysus. You're not the mutt, are you?'

Hannigan glowered at Wiggins as he sat, put in his place. None of his men seemed surprised by O'Connell's outburst, nor by the shattering speed with which he turned off the anger. For now he stood, grinning once more, faintly amused, urbane, almost detached. He pinned Wiggins with his eyes. 'Now me,' he said.

'You sure?'

O'Connell nodded and held his hands out wide.

As before, his clothes were exemplary – bespoke suit, bespoke shirt, creases in all the right places, nothing out of place. Given the mud and the mist and the rain, it was truly remarkable how clean his clothes were – not even a spot on the cuffs or the trouser legs, the usual tell. O'Connell's brogues fairly shone in the light of the fire. A triangle of yellow silk poked from his top pocket, unmarked. Only the moustache was a tell, newly waxed, for the first time. Otherwise, Wiggins could draw only the usual conclusions from how he held himself, his walk, the set of his shoulders.

'You're ex-army,' Wiggins said. 'But not for long. In the Horse. Saw time in Africa, too – the Zulus, at a guess. Farm boy once, city man now. You're rich, and careful, and your ma or da drank till they died of it. Oh, and you're not a man who cares what other people think of you – except today.'

O'Connell squinted, unsure. A silence swelled amongst the other men. Even the fire seemed to stop crackling.

'I'm flattered,' Wiggins said at last. 'But I'm taken.'

O'Connell gaped at that, and then exploded in laughter. 'Jaysus, you're a fly man, so you are. But you're wrong about my father. I never knew the man, God rot his soul. I would be asking how you do those tricks, but then where would the magic be in that? Eh, Vincent, where would the magic be?' He looked down at his hangdog number two. 'Did you not hear that, Vincent? Your man here can beat up a gang of thugs with his bare hands, and then rip you a new arsehole with his brain. Ach, don't sulk.'

He shot his cuffs and gestured to one of his men to hand him his tweed jacket. 'I said, don't sulk.' The jovial edge had left his voice. 'There's work to be done, and yous all know what it is. Englishman, walk with me.'

They left the pub through a side door. O'Connell set off almost at a trot. Wiggins kept half a pace behind him. The rain had stopped, as if ordered by O'Connell himself. A shaft of watery sunshine glinted off the wet cobbles.

O'Connell barked a series of questions out of the corner of his mouth. 'Why, man? You stepped in there like a boxer. I know boxers, I've got a gym full of them. You'd have pasted half the boys in there. Did you fight?'

'Never for a prize.'

'Nah, I guess not. You've got the looks still. Jaysus, so you have.' He skirted a corner and hurried on. 'But why did you fight for me?'

Wiggins ignored the lightness in O'Connell's tone. This was the crux. 'I was drunk.'

'Ach, not so drunk that you'd fight a battalion.'

'What do you want me to say? That I wish I hadn't? True.' Wiggins waited, but O'Connell wanted more. 'All my life I've been up against bullies. It don't sit well, coppers or otherwise.'

O'Connell half nodded, and cut through the traffic. Wiggins hurried to keep up. A tram clattered past. They were on a larger, wider road now, with finely dressed people walking by and busy shops. O'Connell glanced back at Wiggins, unsatisfied.

'I was angry, if you want the truth,' Wiggins said. 'I was pissed up, I was broke, and I'd just lost my ticket to another life. It ain't every week you get tossed from the biggest boat in the world.'

'That saved you from the locker, though.'

'I didn't know that then, did I?'

The older man cocked his head, but walked on, at least partially content.

'Who were they, anyway?' Wiggins said, after a moment. 'Who'd attack *you*?'

O'Connell's eyes flashed with anger. 'I don't know who, or why. And that's not how I like to run my business.' It was evident that O'Connell had informants everywhere and thus such a lack of information was what annoyed him most. He seemed less bothered by the threat of violence than he did by not knowing the reasons behind it.

'Why New York?' he said.

'Why not?'

'Evasion. I don't like that, sure I don't. Where do you pray? In the chapel or the manse?'

'I pray when I'm in trouble.'

O'Connell halted and looked at him askance. 'You without God, man?'

'I think He's without me.'

The older man thought for a moment, then nodded. 'Perhaps that's just as well, in this city of all places.' He set off again, and Wiggins followed. 'And you won't mind working Sundays.'

'Who said anything about work?'

'Sure, you wouldn't have got in the motor with Fitz if you didn't need a job.'

'Maybe he forced me.'

'Ha! Fitz isn't brawn. I'm not sure if he's much of a brain either, for that matter, but there you are.' They walked on for a moment in silence. O'Connell strode along the pavement like he owned all Ireland, and he barely acknowledged anyone as he passed. They made their way into an altogether smarter part of town. Fine red-brick buildings, well-to-do gents looking up at the sky warily.

They came upon a parade of shops, hotels and a plush café. O'Connell stopped. For the first time, he looked a little unsure. 'Tell me again, why were you so angry that you'd fight another man's fight and take a beating too? And why are you wanting to go to New York?'

Wiggins looked him straight in the eye. 'I told you, I was all bent out of shape cos of missing out on New York. And . . .' He hesitated, picking his words carefully. 'New York is where she is – or was, anyway. I ain't see her two year since, I ain't lived those years neither, not proper like. I almost had it, the chance to start it all again, and then it was gone. That's the truth of it.'

O'Connell examined his face minutely as he told this story. Then he nodded. 'You're to meet Fitz at noon, at the Pillar.'

'What is it you do?'

'Ach, don't be coy. You're wanting to New York, right?'

'Right.'

'I'll pay you – more than any man in Dublin, probably. It won't be much, but you'll get there. Now, is this straight?' He put his hand up to the pin at his throat. Wiggins squinted, nodded. O'Connell grinned suddenly. 'Noon, the Pillar.' And then he went inside.

Wiggins scanned the café window. A woman sat alone at a

table. Dark red hair fanned across her back. She wore electric blue.

The Pillar turned out to be a Nelson's Column. It stood in the middle of a grand thoroughfare that Wiggins guessed was the centre of the city. Large, busy shops lined the double-width street. Single doorways led to upstairs offices with names like *Murphy Maritime Insurance* or *Doyle's Dentistry – Make your smile gleam again!* stencilled in white letters on the glass windows.

Trams rattled past in every direction, for the Pillar stood at a crossroads. Wiggins waited in a recessed doorway and kept an eye on the central column. He wasn't so green as to wait there in full view. This was the only place he'd been to in Dublin that could stand up to the Smoke, not that anywhere could, really. If you were going to be in a city, why not be in the greatest city in the world – London?

But he wasn't in London, and he wasn't in New York either. He wondered if he'd ever get there and, if he did, what he would do. Find Bela? Kill her? Profess a deathless love? He tried to bring her face to mind, to conjure up feelings, to remind himself why he was meant to be in New York in the first place. He even formed the words on his lips: 'She is my love, my life. Is it for love? I ain't sure. But then, would it be love if you was sure? Ain't that the point?' He intoned these words under his breath as he glanced up Sackville Street towards the river.

Fitz hurried along the pavement. Wiggins caught sight of him as he dodged past a huge policeman, gurning at a couple of kids as he did so. The boy might not be brawn, but he carried an air of goodwill, a warmth and generosity of spirit that mocked his stunted frame. Wiggins couldn't help himself. He grinned. Still, he let the boy stew for a few minutes all the same.

'Jaysus, you scared the shite right out of my arse.'

'You'll have to wait for Hannigan if you want it cleaned up.' Wiggins pulled his hand back from Fitz's shoulder.

The young Irishman laughed. 'Watch that now, Mr H can get

angry. But you came up on me awful sly. Here at the prick and all. I never saw you.'

'I'm here now, ain't I? As per your boss's instructions.'

'Aye. The OC said you'd come. He knows everything, so he does.'

Not quite, thought Wiggins. O'Connell didn't know who attacked him. He didn't know why. And, Wiggins guessed, there was a lot about the woman in the electric-blue dress that he didn't know either.

'Are you ready to go?' Fitz said, pulling a long woollen scarf tight around his neck.

'Go where?'

'Why, up the long ladder and down the short rope, to hell with King Billy and long live the Pope.'

Fitz didn't in fact take him up a long ladder, nor down a short rope. He took him along the wet and shining streets, past the rattling trams, the sandwich boards, through the large Hanover Square, past a van marked THE WAR ON CONSUMPTION and out into the Dublin slums. Fitz kept up a bubbling stream of chatter all the while, a commentary on the town, the people, the bosses and whatnot.

It wasn't until they reached their destination, though, that Wiggins finally understood what he was there for. They turned into a grand street some way north of the Pillar. A large and beautiful terrace of Georgian houses was ranged down one side. But instead of the carriages and motor cars, servants and masters, gleaming windowpanes, polished doorknobs and scrubbed-clean steps that the terrace's grandeur suggested, there was an evident squalor. The street lamps were cracked and broken. Rubbish collected in the gutters. Many of the windowpanes were half-mooned and filthy.

As Fitz and Wiggins approached, a gang of children ran away from them, barefoot children, trousers torn at the knee; tiny children, half the size they would be in the richer streets. 'Swaddlers, swaddlers!' they shouted as they ran. 'Gown out of it.'

Wiggins glanced at Fitz.

'They think you're a Protestant,' he said, grinning. 'A bloody swaddler.'

'Why?'

'We're here to collect the rent, course.'

And so they did. The great houses, where once old nobility must have roistered, now contained hordes of grimy children and hollow-cheeked mothers, two families to a room. Each building was packed to the rafters with folk and Fitz took Wiggins into every one of the houses in the terrace, bar one. 'That's the nuns, doing the laundry, so it is – we only goes there once a month.'

It took a long time, for Fitz was slight and sweet and he heard every tale of woe as if for the first time. They went from floor to floor, house to house, knocking for pale, exhausted women or angry, red-faced men. Wiggins began to understand the reason O'Connell had sent him along. He was muscle. The poor tenants took one look at him, heard his London accent, saw the hang of his shoulders, and knew their stories wouldn't fly for ever.

After they left Henrietta Street they moved on to another street, and a third, each time the same routine. All through the afternoon and into the evening they went on – collecting the OC's dues. Ragged children their filthy sentinels wherever they went, broken brickwork, mouldy walls, choking blocked chimneys, and people, people, people, as poor as dirt. For Wiggins it was nothing new, but it sickened him still in this, a British city.

The clouded sky had turned from blue-black to night by the time Fitz turned a sharp corner and pushed into yet another secret, apparently closed pub. 'This is us,' Fitz said.

'Us?'

'Mulligan's. Ya day's done here. The OC telephones at eight, like clockwork. Yous get a sandwich.'

'And a pint?'

'Sure. Whatever you want. As long as it's black.'

Wiggins took a stool at the bar. This was a nicer boozer altogether than Rooney's or any of the others he'd been to in the city. The air was thick with conversation and clink, and the drink didn't feel like medicine here. He settled into his pint. He'd been a debt collector once, back in the Smoke, until Vernon Kell had recruited him for the Secret Service. He picked at the corner of his roast-beef slice. He wasn't sure what was worse – spying on people for the Empire, or terrorising them into handing over what they owed. It came to this again, it always came to this – he'd never be free of such choices, the moves you needed to make to survive. He thought again about New York, his trip, and began to form the words when—

'You're in.'

He looked up at Fitz, who stood grinning at him from behind the bar. 'The OC says you're to bunk with me,' he went on. 'I told him you'd do.'

'What's the pay?'

'Ach, I'm just the help.'

And so it went. Wiggins became Fitz's fist, connected to him day and night, ready to flatten a recalcitrant payer at the word. Fitz took him all over the city, and not just slum houses. They went to gambling dens, to hidden bars serving vile home-stilled liquor ('It's called a shebeen, you numps') and an endless number of brothels. ('Kip houses, though not much kipping takes place, I'm thinking. Ha.') O'Connell's empire spread across the underside of Dublin's map. As he and Fitz jogged and jagged across the city from one hell pit to the next, Wiggins began to understand Fitz's own power. For he had no notebook, made no record, but he knew the exact amount owed at each place. He might not have had the brawn, but he had a mind for numbers, for all his crooked grin and jolly songs. Every so often they would drop into a bank branch to deposit the cash. Different banks, in different parts of the city. Wiggins would stand back, by the door, now not only Fitz's sword but his shield too, a guard for the money as much as for the man.

It wasn't only collection. Some nights, Wiggins and Fitz would stand the door at late-night gambling sessions, Fitz's eyes bright with information and jest while Wiggins glowered. No one took on the house on those nights. O'Connell had promised Wiggins

he would make passage to New York in two months and so
earning dishonest money was the plan, to get back to 'My love,
my life,' as he told Fitz more than once. Fitz would look at him
warily and say, 'You're hot for your hole, so you are,' and laugh.

The only problem was Vincent Hannigan. He seemed to
glower from every corner, his presence hanging over the city
like a thick mist. He was clearly the OC's number two and he
had nothing but enmity and suspicion for Wiggins. He would
drop in to Mulligan's in the evening and stare over his pint at
them, barking incomprehensible questions to Fitz in a deliber-
ately thickened accent so Wiggins couldn't follow. Or else he'd
turn up on their rounds, hands thrust deep into his coat pockets,
head nodding grimly. He never said a word to Wiggins. He
didn't need to.

'Why's he such a bastard?' Wiggins asked as he and Fitz crossed
the corner of St Stephen's Green on a misty, mild, mizzling night.

'Hannigan?' Fitz grinned. 'Surely not.'

Wiggins had been with him about three weeks and felt easy
enough in Fitz's company to press the point. 'He's a bastard,
Fitz. You know it.'

'Ach, we're all bastards every now and then, are we not? At
least, my ma and da were never married.'

They'd been ordered to attend another gambling night. Every
evening at eight o'clock, the OC would telephone Fitz at
Mulligan's, or had Hannigan do it, and Fitz had to report back
the day's news. Wiggins didn't care to think what would happen
if Fitz weren't there to take the call. Afterwards, Fitz would sit
back down in the pub beside Wiggins and down another pint of
porter. Once or twice, they'd been ordered on to some job or
other taking place later in the evening. Tonight was one of those
nights.

'Here we are,' Fitz said, pointing. Wiggins recognised a large
terraced house with double doors and a fan of yellow light above
the entrance. It was one of the OC's swankier brothels. He and
Fitz had stopped in there the week before. It was by far the
smartest place Wiggins had visited with Fitz, with gilded portraits

on the walls, electric chandeliers and Persian rugs. 'The big spenders are in, so they say,' Fitz went on as they tapped down the stairs into the basement area, which led to the kitchen. Not the gleaming, polished front door for them. They were definitely trade.

'The big spenders?' Wiggins said. 'And what do they want us for – grizzled arse?'

'Jaysus, you old men have perverted minds, I tell you, perverted. We're for the hell.'

The 'hell' turned out to be a large gaming room on the ground floor. They walked through the servants' hall, up the backstairs and then down a narrow passage to a doorway with a heavy velvet curtain over it. Fitz peeped through, then gestured for Wiggins to take a look.

O'Connell obviously moved in more of the circles of hell than Wiggins had credited. The men wore dinner jackets, the whores – if that's what the women were – looked smart and almost demure, and the gaming tables were doing a roaring trade. Great gusts of cigar smoke hung over the card players. Wiggins spotted games of loo, faro, roulette and even dice.

'Yous are not dressed properly,' Hannigan hissed from behind them. Wiggins turned. Hannigan scowled at them in the poorly lit passageway. He had on a ragged dinner jacket. His eyes never left Wiggins.

'O'Connell said to be here, Mr H.'

'Well, find him then. Leave this one here.'

Fitz skittered off into the shadows. Hannigan stepped so close to him that Wiggins could smell the vanilla and lime of his pomade, the acrid tang of his fags, even the double gulp of whiskey he must have taken minutes before.

'I don't like the English.'

'That's a shame. Half the folk out there are English by the sounds of it, and most of the people that run this country an' all. What does that make you?'

'I don't like you.'

'You're making me cry.'

'That's for later, when the boss fella gets tired of his English bulldog.'

Wiggins chewed, and glanced back into the gaming room. 'Is that a cosh in your pocket, or are you enjoying this more than you should?'

Hannigan's face paled in fury. The sinews in his neck tightened. But then he forced a grin. 'Funny. You'll be laughing too, when I tell the OC how you got out of prison.'

'I came out the front gate.'

'Aye, but why? That's what's wondering me. You've got Castle written all over you, so you have. And it don't pay to be Castle, not around here.'

Hannigan let the words linger. Wiggins hadn't been in Ireland long, but he knew what the Castle meant. It meant Dublin Castle, the seat of British power, the government, the powers that be, the oppressor. It meant British, and British meant English, and the English were the enemy, at least to a man like Hannigan. It was the worst thing Hannigan could say to him, or think of him, for that matter. He thought he was a spy.

'Vincent!' O'Connell called from down the corridor.

Hannigan turned, straightened. 'Sir.'

'What are you doing? You look like yous about to propose to the man.'

Hannigan stepped back from Wiggins. 'I was just passing the time of day. Wondering why our man here is so fly at getting out of the Joy, you know.'

'Fly enough to answer that, I'm sure.' O'Connell nodded to Wiggins. 'But more importantly, do you have the information?'

As before, O'Connell – dressed to the nines in evening dress, like the punters – had a breezy, urbane air, but there was no mistaking the intent. The silence after the question was a silence that demanded to be filled.

Hannigan shifted, glaring at Wiggins like he should answer. In that moment, and it was only a moment, Wiggins felt a pang of compassion for him. He'd been on the end of that expectation, not so much scrabbling for answers but having to do what someone else told you, no matter what; always having to bow the head, scrape the heel, yes sir, no sir, otherwise it'd be the poorhouse or the grave. It was ever the lot of the likes of Hannigan, and him.

O'Connell's problem was this: he didn't know who had attacked him and Fitz out on the Coombe. Almost a month later, he still had no clue and none of his informants had shed any light on the attack. Fitz had told Wiggins all about it, but this was the first time Wiggins had seen O'Connell since the day he recruited him. For all his unruffled air, the lack of information was clearly a thorn.

'Gogarty and Malone swear it wasn't DMP,' Hannigan said. 'Lynch's men are blind it wasn't them either, but I'm not so sure.'

'Ach, Lynch is just a culchie chancer.'

'He's a Protestant,' Hannigan said.

'So the fuck what?' O'Connell barked.

'I'm just—'

'Are we caring about that now, are we? No, we are not. Lynch doesn't have the balls, anyway. But it's vexing, so it is.'

Hannigan said nothing. Fitz had appeared behind O'Connell, but he too kept quiet. Applause and cheers suddenly burst from the other side of the curtain. Someone had won big.

The noise sparked O'Connell out of his reverie. 'Is she in yet?' he asked. Hannigan nodded. 'Grand. And all's well on the floor? There's some money in tonight, boys – pots.'

'Aye,' Hannigan said. 'All's well.'

'I wouldn't say that,' Wiggins said, quietly.

'No one asked you.'

'Wheesht, Vincent.' O'Connell turned to Wiggins. 'What's this?'

For answer, Wiggins drew O'Connell to the curtain and whispered into his ear. 'Young bloke at the far table, with the cowlick and the knock-off dinner jacket? He's working with the old geezer by the door.'

'The one with the pipe?'

'That's how he signals. They won't take you for much. But they'll take you all the same.'

'Jaysus, you're right.'

'And down here, on the loo table. The dealer's on the take.'

'But that's Mooney!' O'Connell hissed.

'Well, Mooney takes money. Watch careful like.' The two men, Wiggins easy, unstudied, O'Connell eyes bulging, looked over at the card table. There were about eight players tossing chips down at every hand, and a middle-aged dealer who collected the money and called the game. As he did so one more time, he flicked a chip under his cuff so fast, yet so lazily too, casual and quick, that even those staring directly at him might miss the trick. Wiggins hadn't and now neither had O'Connell.

O'Connell swore under his breath. Wiggins's gaze wandered across the room. A woman had entered through the main doors. He noticed her first because of her walk – confident, careless, quite unlike the other women in the place (who were, admittedly, paid to be there). She was no prostitute, that's for sure. Her hair was tied in a loose bun of deep auburn. Stray tendrils hung about her face, and she wore an expression of amused indifference. She'd draped a bright blue shawl across her shoulders.

'Do it quiet, see-ho?' O'Connell was issuing instructions to Hannigan behind Wiggins. 'Mooney's not to work here again.'

'But Mooney's been with us for years,' Hannigan said.

'Get him out!' O'Connell glared, then pointed at Wiggins. 'And I want *him* on the floor.'

'He's just for the bounce,' Hannigan complained.

Wiggins only half heard this argument. He continued to gaze at the red-headed woman. She was about his age, with large eyes that danced with curiosity, and she swung her free arm around like a schoolgirl. In her other hand she held a book. She looked like a painting.

'You go on the door,' O'Connell barked finally. 'Wiggins takes the floor.'

'He isn't dressed smart enough.'

'And you aren't smart enough, see-ho? Give him your jacket. And tomorrow yous'll sit down with him and go through the investigation. We need to find out who the hell it was.'

Hannigan scowled but began to pull off his dinner jacket all the same. O'Connell peered at Wiggins. 'You hear that, man?'

Wiggins's attention had been snared once more by the redhead. She was staring across the room at him, his face just visible through the crack in the curtain. Her lips parted slightly, her eyes widened. 'Is that another con you've found, or what?' O'Connell pushed in beside him.

Wiggins half turned his head and said carefully, 'You want me to find out who mugged you?'

'Yes.'

Wiggins finally broke eye contact with the woman and looked at O'Connell. 'Does that mean I get paid more?'

'What was it like, in the hell? Was it rich?'

Wiggins pulled a blanket to his chin. He'd gone back with Fitz in the early hours to the room they now shared in the Liberties. Fitz had turned off the gas lamp and now spoke through the darkness from his bed. It was cold but dry, unlike the rest of Dublin, as far as Wiggins could see. He pushed his boots off and curled into the wall. It was a small room, but it was luxury compared to some of the other joints he'd already seen.

'Money, that's all them lot care about,' Wiggins muttered.

'Sure, the eejits.' Fitz laughed.

Wiggins turned to face him across the dead-black room. ''Ere, who was the woman in the blue shawl? Tall redhead, didn't stay long.'

'Aha,' Fitz said. 'She take your fancy?'

'Nah,' Wiggins said. 'Just curious like.' In fact, Wiggins had spent at least twenty minutes looking at her earlier in the evening, before she'd eventually left without playing a game of anything. She'd read her book, looked around her and almost laughed when the OC went over to talk with her. Wiggins's eyes kept coming back to her, the high colour in her cheeks, her flashing eyes, the full red hair. And now she'd lodged in his head.

'Good job,' Fitz said across the dark room. 'That's Margaret Lansdown-Smith. Molly to her familiars, I'm thinking, by way of telling all us poor folk she's one of the people, you know? She comes and she goes from London, and the OC lolls out his tongue, so he does, and yaps around when she's due back in town, like she's the only redhead he ever did see.'

'Why is it a good job?' Wiggins asked. 'That I don't fancy her.'

'Oh, you don't, do you?'

'I told you, I'm for America, when I can get the scratch.'

Fitz began to sing a soft, plaintive song – an Irish lullaby perhaps. Wiggins flopped off his elbow and back into bed. He closed his eyes. 'I'm not here to chase skirt,' he said softly into the darkness. 'I'm here so I can get there, to . . . you know . . . my Bela.'

4

'There's nothing here,' Fitz said. 'Except a whole load of shite.'

'Scene of the crime. That's what the old . . . man used to say,' Wiggins replied. 'Study the scene of the crime.'

'Your oul' man a copper?'

'No, I didn't mean . . . It doesn't matter,' Wiggins said, and waved the question away. Sherlock Holmes. Not his old man exactly, but an old man, probably the only old man he'd had as a child. Not that running the Irregulars was much like a family. They were a gang of street kids, and they'd worked for Holmes whenever the detective needed them, for whatever he was happy to pay them. Still, Wiggins had liked the old man all the same, even if he were the boss.

Wiggins looked absently up and down the street. He and Fitz were on a long, gently arcing road called Coombe Street, at the exact corner where O'Connell had been attacked. Mr Holmes had told him as a kid that the single most important element of investigating any crime was the examination of the scene. The Irregulars hadn't been allowed near crime scenes as such, but Wiggins had watched and listened, and had picked up scraps of knowledge and built them into a deducing scheme all of his own. Holmes would always be the master, but he didn't know what it was like to be down here, on the street, in the gutter. That he didn't know.

Maybe this was the same with all men and their fathers, those that had them. They didn't know what it was like to be their sons, and never would. Maybe Mr Holmes wasn't such a bad stand-in. At least he wasn't a drunk, like Fitz's old man, like his own mother neither.

Wiggins spat, and looked to his right. Coombe Street bent away in a long row of shops, watery morning light flashing in the plate-glass windows. A smaller, felt-ash road led away to his left, the cobbles breaking up into gravel and mud as it tapered down towards Newmarket.

'The OC always walk this way?'

'Clockwork, once a week, just after the strike of noon, as the fairy once said. He likes the Coombe, so he does, but only once a week, just after the strike of noon. He walks all over Dublin, but whatever else, he'll be here on a Wednesday.'

'With you?'

'Mostly.'

'Why here? Why at that time?'

'That's a harder one to know. Some say his oul' fella died out here, hit by a horse. But then some say it was his ma dropped dead in the middle of the road. But I'm not sure either of that's true, since I'm thinking his family weren't even from Dublin, you know. But he likes the Coombe, sure he does.'

'And who knows that?'

'Ach, everybody near enough. You'd only have to watch him for a week to work out he's a man of his habits.'

Wiggins nodded. He and Fitz had walked down to the scene first thing in the morning. He'd woken up spry and energised – whether from the fact he'd been given something interesting to do, or because the redhead had given him something interesting to think about, he didn't want to dwell.

Fitz's room sat above a tiny hardware shop just south of the river. Up a tight staircase, it at least had a sash window that opened onto the back. To the south stood the huge whiskey distillery, Powers. Each morning, Wiggins pulled up the sash and breathed in the faintest tinge of sharp alcohol vapour caught in the air. Off to the west, sprawled the even bigger Guinness factories and storehouses. You smelled them when you went out the front door – a yeasty, slightly sickly blast, depending on the wind. All in all, it wasn't a bad spot, if you didn't mind the fungus that clung to the brickwork.

Fitz had complained all the way down from the room, but in the same half-amused bantering tone that he said everything. 'Yous the OC's detective now? What do they call it – a sleuth?'

A crocodile of chattering schoolchildren swam past. 'Hardly,' Wiggins said. 'All we know is that five very large geezers – with iron chins, judging by the cuts on my knuckles – jumped you and the OC with vicious intent.'

'Is that what it was?' Fitz chuckled and pulled at his coat. 'And there was me thinking it was a lover's embrace.'

Wiggins looked at Fitz carefully for a moment. The boy was clever. Fitz knew about the money: he knew who owed what; he knew where the money was coming from (and how much); he knew the business like no one apart from the OC himself. And he knew much more than he'd ever let on. It suddenly occurred to Wiggins that O'Connell had more than one motive for putting him with Fitz. Protecting the money, of course, but maybe it was the OC who needed protection from Fitz? Maybe Wiggins was there as much to *watch* Fitz as to *watch out* for him. Certainly, they'd not spent an hour apart ever since the OC had ordered them together.

'What do you think?' Wiggins asked him after a moment.

'Ach, I'm just—'

'—the help, I know. Why don't you help me?'

Fitz grinned. 'What can I be telling you?'

'Who're the enemies? Another gang?'

'Sure, this isn't New York.'

'Politics? Is the OC into that?'

Fitz shifted slightly, and looked along the road. 'This is Dublin. What are you on about the politics for?'

'Motive.'

'Everything in this town is politics.' Fitz paused. When he didn't smile he looked older and wiser. He shook his head, but slowly, almost softly, yielding. 'You want the penny tour? All right, I'll give you it once, you hear? The OC's not the only fella you saved a beating out here on the Coombe, is he?' Fitz adjusted his hat and beckoned Wiggins a little way into the side road, out of earshot from the main street. 'The OC's a big man in Dublin, sure enough. But he's not the only big man.'

'Lynch?'

'Aye, you're catching up, Englishman. But I can't see him playing this kind of game.'

'Does he run Dublin, or does the OC?'

'Sure, the Castle runs Dublin, right. The Britishers. Your mob.'

'I'm London.'

Fitz shook his head. 'There's not that many in Dublin that likes the Castle. But some do, and they's rich and they's powerful. The businesses, the bosses, they's all Castle. The rest of us are just trying to make enough for dinner. Ach, you'll get trouble every now and then. The unions, Larkin's mob, they'll fight for higher wages, shut down the docks, whatever, but that's not really the OC's business, or Lynch's for that matter. Folk will still want drink, they'll still want a bed and they'll still want women.' Fitz laughed without humour.

'What about Home Rule? Ain't we giving you Ireland back soon anyway?'

'Home Rule? Hark at yous – up in the Parliament, are you?'

Wiggins frowned. 'I just thought . . .'

Fitz opened his arms and began to sing.

> *Edward Carson had a cat,*
> *It sat upon the fender.*
> *And every time it caught a rat,*
> *It shouted, 'No Surrender!'*

Fitz held up his fist in mock declaration.

'What you on about?' Wiggins said.

'Ach, I'm just teasing. We might get Home Rule down here in Dublin right enough, and some would be happy with that. But up in the north, Ulster, Belfast, man, they'll not be happy. Edward Carson is more British than you are, Wiggo, and he'll die fighting for it too. Home Rule is Rome Rule, so they say.'

'Fighting for it?' Wiggins asked. 'Is there an army up there or what?'

'And how would I know that? A good jackeen like me – what would I be wanting with the northern men?' Fitz smiled again. 'But no, thank the big fella in the sky, they don't have an army up there. Nor do we have one down here. I don't know if you've noticed, but the only army in Ireland is the British Army – aren't there hundreds of barracks in Dublin alone? The only army in Ireland is yours.'

'It sounds like you need someone to keep the peace.'

'No chance.' He shrugged. 'They're not fighting yet because no one but the British has any guns. You can't be an army without arms now, can you?'

Wiggins shook his head. 'Christ, what a country.'

'Ah, but at least now you're admitting it *is* a country.'

'The OC's not into the politics then, is that what you're saying?'

Fitz looked sharp at the question. 'Well, there's your new lady friend . . .'

'Fitz.'

'Ach, she's a bit of all right, sure she is. Margaret Lansdown-Smith – Molly to her familiars. She's always talking the politics, so she is. She says Ireland should be its own nation once again, that she should be free.'

'She don't look like no rebel. Where I come from you get them in factories, on the streets, in the docks. She's a posh sort, ain't she?'

'She's posh all right, an Anglo. A Protestant too, with a horse. Ha. But that's Ireland, see? Most of us just don't want to be poor. These dreamy rich folk are droning on about the fresh winds of independence, even if the rest of us are only dreaming about our own home not smelling of shite. Jaysus, not above one in ten of them can even speak the language, despite what Pearse says. Ach, she likes the politics, sure she does.'

Fitz suddenly turned his face away, unsure. Wiggins saw a faint blush on the boy's smooth cheek. It was clear Fitz had talked more than he wanted to about Molly. Clear, too, that he was sweet on the woman – she *was* good-looking, and she was the boss's woman. It touched Wiggins unexpectedly, Fitz's shy reticence, the innocence of it, this scrappy youth with the crooked grin and the mind of numbers, that even talking about a woman made him awkward.

'And the OC's interested in all that?'

Fitz relaxed, back on safer ground. 'But sure, the OC's interested in money mostly. Business, he calls it. What's good for business is good for the OC. Now, are we coming away? Or are you going to spend the rest of the morning scratching your arse like the last drunk copper in Dublin?'

Wiggins grinned. He hadn't known Fitz more than a month, but the lad lifted his spirits like an old friend, almost as if it didn't matter what they said as long as they were talking, being *seen*. People like him and Fitz spent much of their lives wearing invisible coats, walking the richer streets at the heels of their masters, never even registering as individuals separate from their supposed tasks. Butler, batman, sweep, soldier, beggar, valet. It was part of their station in life; they *were* their jobs in the eyes of other people.

But then, when someone did see you for who you were – not for what you did or what you could do – it felt like a shaft of warm sunshine breaking through the clouds. Wiggins looked at Fitz again, his crooked grin, his bones and bounce, counting all the OC's money in his head, while back down a shit-streaked alleyway of slum Dublin his mother and her pickled husband shared a room with Fitz's three siblings, counting the cold, wet, hungry days until Fitz came round with a coin or two.

Wiggins had visited the family's room with Fitz the week before and wished he hadn't. The old man stank and glared, boozed, and wore his overcoat indoors, while Fitz's ma and little sisters made matchboxes on the room's only table.

'You sure the old man didn't pawn your watch?' Wiggins had asked after they left.

'Ach, that little thing? Nah – it wouldn't be worth owt to anyone but me, you know.'

Now, as Fitz waited impatiently to get going up the Coombe, Wiggins said, 'You found your watch?'

'I have to ask the punters, don't I?' Fitz replied. 'Here, gis your money. And by the way, gis the time and all, you know. I feel like I'm asking too much.'

'Here, take mine.' Wiggins pulled out his own pocket watch from the Doctor, complete with Peter the Painter's bullet mark.

'No, no, you're grand. Now, are we coming?'

'I've got to stay. The OC told me to investigate – he wants me to find the fellas that attacked yous.'

'Murphy's at lunch, then?'

Wiggins shook his head again. 'I've got to report to fucking Hannigan.'

Fitz whistled. 'Right enough. Mulligan's at eight?'

'Mulligan's.'

Fitz mock saluted, then turned on his heel elaborately, the drunken soldier as music-hall act.

'Here, Fitz,' Wiggins asked suddenly. 'Why that watch mean so much to you?'

'Ach, it's nothing,' he said without turning around. And then, 'The old man gave it to me before . . . you know, the booze.' And with that he was gone, shambling off into the morning bustle of the Coombe. Wiggins waited until he'd disappeared and then set off in the other direction.

He didn't take a second glance at the scene. As a rule, he didn't mind lying to people for a good cause. But there was something about young Fitz that made such deception uncomfortable. He reminded Wiggins of his fellow Irregulars, twenty-odd years ago back on the streets of London. The only way he and Sal and the others had survived their childhood was by relying on each other, with absolute trust and fierce honesty. Being on your own, and that poor, was like going to war every day of your life, and the only way to go to war was with a comrade. He knew real war, too, what with Bill and the Boer and the big fat flies crawling over the bodies that lay beside them, and the big hollow bellies of the guns without no billy to fire, and the shrieks and cries of once brave men left to die in the dirt. Poor Bill.

But they weren't at war. Yet. And lying to Fitz kept him safer than telling the truth. It began to rain, almost like a whisper. He pulled his belt tight around his mackintosh and strode north towards the river, to the scene where the coppers had almost thrown him into the Liffey. This was the first time since he'd been out of prison that he'd had a moment to himself, and he wasn't wasting it on the wild goose chase that was searching for O'Connell's attackers. He wanted to know who had almost killed *him*, and why. They'd failed, thanks to the RIC captain, but that didn't mean they wouldn't try again. It didn't do having people out to kill you without having a dicky bird as to why.

It'd been devil-dark and he'd been almost unconscious, but he tried to remember back to the night he'd been careened across the quay. He knew that the Dublin Metropolitan Police had broken up the fight with O'Connell's attackers, but Wiggins had no idea why they'd then tried to dump him in the river. He scouted the quay where he'd been rescued, then traced the logical steps back as best he could, replaying the episode in his mind. He'd found out that the DMP's headquarters were some way north of the river, probably too far to carry a man of his size and weight through the streets without attracting comment, and certainly they'd have had to cross the river to get him to this point – something he was sure they did not do.

He walked the alleyways and streets south of the river for three hours, and each time, when the limits of his memory ran out, his mind extrapolated to the same destination, the place he must have been taken from that night, the seat of British power, the evil outpost of Empire at the heart of the city: Dublin Castle.

'I don't trust you.'

'Does that mean I have to buy my own drink?' Wiggins said.

Hannigan sat at a shadowy table tucked away at the back of

Mulligan's. He nodded Wiggins into the seat opposite and said, 'Put your hands on the table where I can see them.'

'I ain't armed,' Wiggins grinned. 'I don't like guns.'

'Yous can't hurt me,' Hannigan rasped. 'But yous have the look of a thief. A dirty, pickpocketing thief.'

Wiggins shook his head, but placed his long, slender hands on the table. 'Before you carry on with all your pleasantries, "You're a dead man" and all that witty stuff you like, just remember that the OC sent me here because you've failed. You've no leads.'

'I'm not the polis,' Hannigan snapped. He squeezed his hands out, and looked out into the pub for a moment. 'But no, I have no leads. Lynch makes the most sense, but theys swear blind it wasn't them. And even he doesn't make any sense, not really.'

'Where is Lynch?'

Hannigan hesitated. Then he pulled a cosh from his pocket and put it on the table. He began to stroke it absently, like an old family cat about to die. 'You wanting to New York? That true?'

Wiggins said nothing.

'I don't trust you, see? I'll pay your way out of here, if you leave us alone. I'll pay the billet to New York.'

Wiggins considered for a moment. 'You'll pay me to leave Dublin?'

'It's the only offer yous are ever gonna get out of me.'

'That's interesting that is, cos there was me thinking you was just an angry ha'penny thug, and then you go and say that. I might be thinking, what a fine fellow Vincent Hannigan is after all, full of the milk of human kindness. But then I'm also thinking, hold on half a mo, why? Is it because Mr Hannigan finally found his heart? Or is it – I'm only musing here, like – is it because he's got something to hide?'

Hannigan slammed his hand on the table. 'Who the fuck *are* you?'

Heads turned at the bar and the conversational hubbub died for a moment. Hannigan glared around, then pushed his face closer to Wiggins. 'I would never cross the OC, ever. And if you say that again, I'll pluck out your eyes and feed them to the eagles myself,' he hissed.

Wiggins grinned. 'So what are the rozzers saying, about this attack? Surely the OC has 'em on wages?'

Hannigan shrugged. 'Ach, you can buy anyone in the DMP. No one gets enough money in this town. You can buy half the RIC too, 'cept the officers, who've already been bought off by the Britishers.'

'Hold on, this *is* Britain.'

'It's not called the Royal Irish Constabulary for nothing. This is Ireland.'

Wiggins gestured at the barman for a drink. 'So, it weren't the coppers.'

'No.'

'So tell me where to find Lynch, and I'll get on with it.'

Hannigan chewed for a moment. 'He owns a hotel, up near Rutland Square. He keeps the bar company, then takes a woman up the stairs. You'll find him there most nights, I reckon.'

'He a serious rival?'

'Every rival's serious in this business. But no, he's young and he's foolish. He's blundered around like he knows everything, and he can't see the danger of being too smart and too clever. You get me?'

Wiggins grinned again. 'I get ya. And what about the lorry?'

'What lorry?'

'They scarpered on the back of a lorry,' Wiggins said carefully. 'I couldn't see the side, but it was a closed one, like a baker's van or something. They jumped in the back.' Wiggins made sure to describe the van incorrectly.

'Jaysus. I'll ask one of the boys to check Lynch's stock. What'll you do?'

'Investigate.'

Hannigan scowled, then reached for his coat. He got up, pulled it tight. 'You're to meet the OC tonight at seven thirty, outside the Abbey.'

'He's taking holy orders?'

'No, you're taking orders. It's a theatre, and you're to watch the car while he's at the play.'

'What about Fitz?'

'What about Fitz?' Hannigan turned back smartly and frowned. He seemed almost upset by the question, unnerved.

Wiggins put his hands up in mock surrender. 'I'll be there,' he said. 'I'm sure Fitz can fend for himself.'

'Clear off, Rashers! We were here first.'

'I've got every right.'

'I'll banjax you if you don't get off now!'

Wiggins stepped past the warring musicians. An old tramp with a penny whistle – Rashers – sloped off while a younger man holding a huge harp continued to play. The street glared with gas as Wiggins picked his way along the bulging theatre queue. Wiggins knew the OC wouldn't have to wait for his tickets.

The theatre – the Abbey – was lit up in the early-evening wane. It was a jolly little theatre on a corner, with coloured light bursting through its stained-glass windows. People jostled and chatted as they waited for the ticket queue to move. The harp music warbled up the street, as if following Wiggins as he went. He stepped aside from a beggar and approached the door.

'Here ya are,' O'Connell called out from the scrum. 'My man.'

'Evening, sir.'

'Ach, less of that nonsense.'

O'Connell looked even smarter than usual. Wiggins couldn't even see any lint on his serge suit, which hung on his shoulders with such lightness that it could have been hand-stitched by a flight of angels up in the clouds of heaven. His brogues shone; his green-blue tie glinted like a promise.

'There's the motor.' He gestured across the road to the Daimler. 'Keep an eye, will you. I might need you to drive Miss Lansdown-Smith home later. There's some business I have to attend to.'

'Of course.'

'Any news?'

Wiggins glanced behind O'Connell into the lobby of the theatre. The ticket queue started to move. 'We can't rule out Lynch.'

O'Connell opened his mouth to respond, then checked over Wiggins's shoulder. 'Molly,' he called out.

Wiggins turned to see the redhead from the gambling hell. She strode towards them, tall, angular, sure-footed. She was enveloped by a lush shawl and wore a hat pinned to the side of her head almost as an afterthought. A rippling electric-blue dress swayed around her legs. O'Connell took her by the hand.

'This is one of my new ones – Wiggins.'

Molly looked at him. 'What *are* you wearing?' she said.

Wiggins stepped back a moment, surprised. Her accent was pure posh, Hampstead, not a hint of the Irish lilt he'd expected. Fitz had called her an Anglo, but he didn't think she'd actually be English. She sounded more English than he did. He glanced down at himself. He'd taken to wearing a cheap mackintosh, belted around the middle. Dublin was so wet that he could see no other way to keep dry. Underneath, he wore breeches, and leggings wrapped around his ankles. Just visible under the coat was a long-sleeved, thick cotton shirt that he'd picked up in one of O'Connell's boxing gyms. It was light and easy to move in, just the thing if you ever needed to fight. But looking at himself at that moment, in a theatre queue full of the bright and the beautiful, of fine clothes, carefully brushed suits, feathers and silk, he had to admit she had a point.

'Molly, please,' the OC said.

She grinned. 'I'm sorry. It's just, you look so unusual.' Her green eyes flashed wide for a moment, and Wiggins felt the heat in his face. She was a looker, no question. No wonder Fitz got tongue-tied just thinking about her.

Inside, a bell rang. 'That's us,' O'Connell said, taking Molly by the elbow.

She glanced back at Wiggins. 'I really *am* sorry. It's not important. Clothes, I mean, they're not important.' And then the two of them were gone, swallowed by the lobby.

Wiggins got in the car and waited. Rain intermittently peppered the windscreen. As eight o'clock neared, Wiggins checked his pocket watch, got out of the car and entered the lobby of the theatre. It was all quiet apart from the muffled sounds of the play coming through the double doors in front of him. A ticket clerk fussed behind a long wooden bar.

'Excuse me, miss,' Wiggins said quietly. 'May I use the blower?'

'What's that when it's at home?'

'The telephone.' He pointed to the contraption bolted to the wall. 'It's for Mr O'Connell.'

She had a severe bun at the back of her head, and a prim collar. But her eyes were kind. 'On you go then, but be quiet. And quick.'

'Mulligan's,' a barman shouted into the receiver. 'What you want?'

'Fitz,' Wiggins hissed. 'For the OC.'

'He's not been in.'

'You sure? It's gone eight.'

'Sure I'm sure. He's not been in all day, and haven't I been here myself?'

I don't fucking know, thought Wiggins. He returned to the motor and waited for Molly and the OC to appear. He closed his eyes and slipped into a dreamless sleep. Suddenly, he heard the cries and laughter of the crowd and opened his eyes. The side doors of the Abbey had sprung open and the front lobby was filled with people. More people streamed out of the side door.

He got out of the car and crossed over towards the crowds. They saw each other straight away. Molly stood at the kerb, staring at him, with the OC beside her, unaware. Wiggins said nothing. He stopped and waited. Finally, the OC looked the right way. 'Ah, Wiggins, good man.'

'How was the play?' Wiggins muttered, unsure.

'Macauley!' the OC hollered over his shoulder. 'Macauley! I'll be back in a mo.' He patted Molly's arm and left.

Molly pulled her shawl tighter in an absent-minded way, and

angled her body slightly away from Wiggins. 'Are you an enthu-
siast of the theatre, Mr Wiggins?' she said at last, surprising him.

Wiggins shuffled slightly, and shrugged. 'Last time I was in a
music hall, someone tried to kill me.'

Molly laughed, surprising him again. 'A music hall, I wish!
There wasn't even a joke in this one, let alone a song.' The harp
player had started again, and the haunting tones echoed towards
them while the crowd dispersed. The air was thick with cigarette
smoke and chatter and the gentle, prickling moisture of a falling
mist. 'It was called *The Man Who Missed the Tide*. That's your
story, isn't it? You were on the *Titanic*?' She stepped a little closer
to him as she spoke, perhaps jostled out of the way.

A clasp at her neck caught the light, and Wiggins shifted back
a step. 'What was it about?' he asked helplessly, fighting an
uncontrollable urge to talk. He went on. 'Was it political? Fitz
said you liked the politics.'

'Did he? Well, the play was awful. It was a tedious domestic
tale that showed the worst of Ireland. That men and women can't
love freely, it's so—'

'There you are!' O'Connell interrupted, waving. Wiggins
instinctively stepped back again, this time into the gutter. It put
him a few inches below O'Connell and even Molly, who stood
only an inch shorter than him on the level.

'You're all right then?' O'Connell said. Molly flashed him a
smile, and glanced back at Wiggins. 'Good-oh, good-oh. Listen.
I've got a bit of business to get to.'

'You want me to drive you?' Wiggins said.

'No, no, you take Moll— Miss Lansdown-Smith home, would
you? I'll just be talking.' He turned back to Molly, gazing at her
so hard and longingly that Wiggins had to look away. 'Will you
be all right, my love? This thing, it can't wait.'

'Mr Wiggins can take me home, my dear.'

'Right you are, I'll be off then,' O'Connell said. 'Wiggins, I'll
see you at Mulligan's, tomorrow at nine sharp, see-ho?'

'Yes, sir,' he said, then added, 'Er, did you give Fitz the night
off?'

'I certainly did not. Now get yous in the car and get her back to Blessington Street.' He pushed his hand up into the air, then drew it quickly across his body in a kind of salute-cum-wave that acted more as a dismissal than anything else.

Wiggins expected Molly to get in the back of the car, but before he could bend to open the door she got in the passenger seat herself. It was darker on this side of the road and he could no longer see her face. The compartment felt warmer now, despite the rattling draught as they pulled away.

Molly lit a sweet-smelling cigarette and blew into the night. 'Take me to the north end of Grafton Street, will you.'

'Not home?'

'You're quick, aren't you? Don't worry, you can leave the car – I'll drive it back later.'

'You can drive?'

'That's our little secret.' She inhaled again, then pointed across his chest to the turn she wanted to take. As she did so, he smelled a waft of her scent. A very faint, flowery smell, crossed with tobacco and soap. She pulled back and wrapped her large shawl about her once more.

'You always wear blue,' he said at last.

'It matches my eyes.'

'You're eyes are green.'

She let out a soft noise, part chuckle, part purr. 'My own brother couldn't tell you that. Ah, here we are. Just put the motor in here, will you.'

They got out into a side street. A close terrace, poorly lit, with a row of buildings that crowded the road. There was no one else to be seen. The lamps from Grafton Street cast long shadows. Molly pointed to one of the houses. The downstairs windows shone yellow in the mist. 'Thanks for the lift,' she said.

'You'll be all right?'

'You can see me to the door, if you like. Don't worry, Mr Wiggins, this is an entirely innocent meeting. I would never, ever play unfair with Patrick.'

The heat rose in Wiggins's face again. 'I didn't mean . . .'

She laughed lightly as they reached the door of the softly lit house. Molly banged the knocker repeatedly. Wiggins noticed the power in her arms. She was no posh sap used to high-society drawing rooms, that was for sure. Those arms had lifted more than just a tea cup or a parasol on a hot day.

'Politics, is it?' Wiggins ventured, finally. 'I don't know why I keep saying that.'

She turned to him sharply. 'You're a bit of a surprise, Mr Wiggins. I might even say—' The door opened before she could say more.

'Molly,' a man said, casting a suspicious glance at Wiggins. He was tall, skinny, with sunken cheeks and a thick black moustache that clung to his top lip like moss. His cheeks were weather-beaten and slightly browned, although he was elegantly dressed. A gentleman for sure, but one who sailed, Wiggins realised, when he saw the man's hand go to his chin. The man angled his square shoulders away from Wiggins. He clearly didn't like opening his door to strangers.

'Good evening, Civ,' Molly said. 'Oh, don't mind him, he's just the help.' She shot a smile at Wiggins as she said this, as if to make a joke. Then she went inside, past the man. Civ looked at Wiggins for a moment longer, glanced up and down the street, nodded, then closed the door.

Wiggins pulled his mackintosh close and began to walk back to Fitz's. On the way, he realised he was ravenous and stopped at a late-night café for a plate of peas. The meeting with Molly had unsettled him. She was hard to read. Not hard to look at, of course. He tried not to picture her with her clothes off – what had she said? *'They're not important.'* But her accent, her dress, put her in a whole different class from him. The OC obviously adored her, but who was the other man, Civ? And why wasn't Fitz at Mulligan's? He hadn't pushed it with the OC, didn't want to get the boy in trouble, but something felt off.

He finished his peas hurriedly and went home, over Grafton Bridge and out to their little room. It was late now and down the poor side streets it felt like a country night, surrounded by a forest of bricks. He noted without much enthusiasm how close their room was to the Guinness quay, all that beer, all those barrels, splish-sploshing about yards from his front door.

When he got to the door that opened directly onto Fitz's staircase, he felt for his tells – two small shards split from a packing case. The pieces of wood were on the floor. Wiggins pocketed them with a sense of relief. Fitz had returned. He must have known that the OC was going to the theatre, that for once in his life he didn't have to be at Mulligan's at eight.

Wiggins crept up the stairs, soft-footed, not wishing to wake his young friend. As he ascended, however, he saw a thin crease of light around the door frame. Then someone dropped something. He put his hand to the doorknob, pushed in and called out, 'Fitz, you lazy bastard, the OC'll—'

CRASH! The door slammed into his face. Wiggins stumbled and rushed back in. A dark figure threw a gas lantern into the middle of the room in a great burst of fire. Wiggins watched as the squat figure rattled the sash. He leapt across the room and caught the man by his collar as he slipped halfway out of the window.

The man squirmed and turned his face upwards. The whites of his eye flashed in the glare of the fire, the only thing clear in his heavily bearded face, a tight woollen hat wrapped around his ears. 'Who the fuck are you?' Wiggins roared.

He felt the fire at his heels and turned, distracted. The man squirmed clear.

Discarded clothes and an old newspaper flared up; flames danced about the room. Wiggins battered them out with Fitz's heavy blanket, then swung back to the window ledge. He looked out into the night. The small backyard behind the shop lay dark, unseen, but the bearded man had obviously dropped down and then climbed the wall at the far end. Wiggins saw his woollen hat flash in and out of the street lamps at the end of the entryway off to his right. He was heading southwards.

Wiggins didn't hesitate. He swung wide out of the window

and leapt onto the yard wall that adjoined the next building. He ran along the high wall and vaulted straight into the alleyway at speed.

As he reached the street, he could just make out the bearded man labouring south, his bulky form popping in and out of the pools of light. Wiggins's boots skittered and slithered on the slick cobbles as he crossed the road in pursuit. Where the fuck was Fitz?

The bearded man hared down a long, wide road, lit every fifty yards or so by street lamps. If only he could keep him in sight, Wiggins backed himself to catch the man, who was carrying too much weight.

A high wall bounded the street on the right and Wiggins gained on him as they ran in its lee. He was slowing. The man must have made a mistake, Wiggins reasoned.

Then he disappeared. Wiggins gasped in surprise and ran on. When he'd reached the spot, he realised the bearded man had ducked into an alcove and through a small wooden door recessed into the great wall. It was locked shut.

He breathed in, heavy and fast, glanced quickly down the empty street, then threw himself at the door. He burst through at the second attempt. How could the man have had a key? Who tries to steal from people who have nothing? And where was Fitz?

Wiggins looked across a big brewery yard that was lit by lamps at each corner, burning brightly. A range of lower buildings lined the far yard, and Wiggins spotted a door ajar. He raced towards it, rage building in his heart. Who the fuck was he?

He ran through the door into an unlit space. It was coffin-dark, but Wiggins felt the size of the room, or heard it, more like, in the echoes and the silence. And then he heard his prey.

The floor was covered in what felt like hard little beads that cracked, skittered and crackled as they were crushed underfoot. And someone was walking away from him, through the darkness. 'Who are you?' Wiggins shouted. The words echoed into the darkness, but the man kept walking.

Wiggins walked on, crushing the beads – were they wheat or barley? – under his feet, feeling for stone columns, arms outstretched in the darkness, with only the sound of the bearded man's stumbles to guide him. 'Stand and fight, you fucking coward,' he shouted. The smell was intense, stale, sickly almost. 'Who are you?' Wiggins shouted again. 'What do you want?'

Wiggins shifted left and tried to feel for something in the dark. A creaking sound broke in on them, and suddenly the bearded man appeared in a wedge of pale light on one of the walls, at an open door. Wiggins roared and stumbled onwards.

The door opened out into another yard, a huge one this time, lit with street lamps dotted here and there. It was the coopers' yard, and Wiggins hesitated, awed. Thousands of large beer barrels were spread out across the yard, in various formations. Not only spread, but stacked in three huge pyramids, like shrines to Egyptian gods, the gods of Beer. The pyramids stretched up into the darkness, out of reach.

At the far side of the yard, running through the vast barrel stacks, he saw the bearded man. There were other people about too, coopers and watchmen. Someone shouted, 'Hey, who are yous? Out of there.'

But Wiggins was running now, running fast. The bearded man approached a gate at the far corner, limping now. Wiggins knew he might lose him if he got to the gate – there could be a motor, anything. His own breathing grew louder, the shouts of the men muffled. The bearded man turned at the corner of the furthest stack. It stretched way up into the air, ten, fifteen barrels high, racked like a pyramid. The man halted, looked back at Wiggins, then picked up a discarded shovel.

'*Nooo!*' a voice echoed out across the yard.

More shouting . . . A man running towards the stack.

'Watch it!'

'*No*, man! Jaysus!'

The bearded man bent double, straining with the shovel, levering out one of the bottom barrels. Wiggins skidded to a halt at the other end of the stack. As he did so, the man sprung the bottom barrel free – and the stack came crashing down in a thunderous roar.

Rolling, splitting, bumping, crashing, splintering – the barrels cascaded and collapsed, filling the yard, the air, even his nostrils with the smell. The bearded man rushed to the far gates and disappeared. Wiggins could only look on, immobile – unable to cross the sea of broken wood, beer and confusion.

5

'So, the boy's finally found his balls, has he? Ha ha. I've been telling him to take one of the girls for months. That little Becky up at the Talbot would have done him. It doesn't do not to know, you know, the feel of a woman. Most of the men of Dublin, since for ever, had their first feel of a woman at a kip house. It's not called strumpet city for nothing.'

The OC went quiet for a moment, not embarrassed exactly, but suddenly slightly uncomfortable with his own words, as if he was thinking about sex with someone specific. Wiggins wondered, not for the first time, whether the OC had yet to sleep with Molly. He assumed he had, but they seemed like a mismatched couple. And whenever the OC spoke of her – and to her, the night before, outside the Abbey – he had a quiver of nervousness about him, an almost pathetic need to please, hidden as best as a powerful man could. O'Connell was a man who never wanted to show anyone he needed anything – *needing* was weakness – and yet he needed Molly, needed something from her, and Wiggins felt it. He felt, too, that the OC didn't know of the man Molly had met last night, the 'Civ', or what their meeting might mean. Wiggins didn't think theirs was a romance exactly, but it was secret. Thinking of Molly confused his own mind, not least because he knew Fitz was sweet on her, as he could imagine any man being. But there was no joy to be had there, or if there was, it was too dangerous to contemplate.

Instead, he examined O'Connell and said nothing. Fitz hadn't returned to the room on the previous night. Wiggins had managed to slip away into the darkness before anyone at the Guinness Brewery could ask any awkward questions. He had too many of his own still unanswered, mind. Nothing appeared to be missing from the room, other than Fitz himself, so what had the bearded man been after? Was he trying to steal something from Wiggins or Fitz? And did it have anything to do with the DMP men who'd tried to kill him? He still had no answers, and no Fitz.

'You ain't anxious, like, about Fitz?' Wiggins said at last.

'What? Ach, like I say, he's probably got his end away. He didn't come home one night, is all. But it's nice of you to care, so it is – for a fighting man you've got a soft heart.'

Wiggins shrugged. He hadn't told O'Connell about the telephone call last night, that Fitz hadn't been at Mulligan's at 8 p.m. as ordered. He didn't want to get his young friend in trouble with the boss. He hadn't told him about the break-in, either.

O'Connell stood at the bar with a glass of milk and a cup of black tea. He sipped from one, then the other, but never mixed them. 'Why ruin both of God's greatest gifts by mixing? Aren't they most perfect apart?'

He placed the milk down carefully, and went on. 'Are you a ladies' man, Mr Wiggins? You're a hard man to read.'

'Not really my cup of tea.' Wiggins nodded at the bar. 'It don't end well when we mix.'

O'Connell frowned. 'But I thought it was a woman waiting for you in New York? Or was she escaping?'

'Zackly,' Wiggins said, and inwardly chided himself for his misstep. 'Bela's my love, my life. And she's there, and I'm here, which is the problem.'

'Don't worry,' O'Connell said slyly. 'You'll get there soon enough, and then you can ease away that frustration I see building up inside you, eh? Eh? Unless you want a kip with little Becky yourself? Ha!' He grinned.

O'Connell had twenty or so years on Wiggins – probably the same age as Wiggins's father, whoever that was. His mother had died when he was seven and she'd never told him who it was. He hoped that at least she'd known. The OC bantered with the barman, his white cuffs shining brightly as he pointed and laughed. Was that what fathers were like, asking you if you liked the ladies? Joking about your younger brother getting his end away at a brothel?

Wiggins surprised himself with the thought. *Younger brother* – he meant Fitz. He'd only known the lad a month, but Wiggins doubted he'd lose the hollow feeling in the pit of his stomach until Fitz turned up. Maybe O'Connell was right, maybe he'd taken the night off to make a man of himself. Wiggins smiled. Better to get it done with one of the girls than spend the next year mooning over the unobtainable, mooning over Molly.

'. . . she wants you,' O'Connell said, finishing a sentence.

'What?'

'Miss Lansdown-Smith has turned her ankle. She needs you to drive her today. She wants the car.'

'Can't she . . .' Wiggins trailed off.

O'Connell looked sharply at him, then pushed his empty cup back towards the barman. 'You'll do as she says, you hear?'

'I hear.'

'Ireland must be a nation unto herself – you do understand what I'm saying?'

Wiggins grunted.

'Oh, I don't suppose you care. Gosh, you're probably one of those army veterans who fought for the Empire and can't believe anyone would wish it ill.'

'Well, I did . . .'

'Bother. I'm sorry,' Molly went on. 'You probably don't give two hoots about Irish independence, but to me it is simply the most important thing. This country can never truly be a country, fulfil her potential, while she is held back by the British, ruled by the British. Ireland must be herself once more.'

'Right.'

'I know I'm right. The British Government knows we are right, the—'

'I meant, is it a right here?' Wiggins took one hand off the wheel and motioned.

Molly glanced at him across the front seat of the motor car and nodded. 'Gosh, yes. I'm sorry, what a fool I am.' Her cheeks reddened a touch. Wiggins didn't mind.

He'd driven the motor down to an address in Brighton Square. Molly had seen him from the window and had come striding out of the beautiful Georgian townhouse before he'd even got out of the car. She wore a narrow, high-waisted blue linen dress and what Wiggins would call swagger shoes. Scraps of rubbish danced and jiggled in the blustery winds as she'd picked her way across the road towards him, shrugging on a long alpaca overcoat as she did so. As on the night before, she'd got in the front of the car rather than the back. She wasn't limping.

Now, twenty minutes of Irish republican politics later, they were nearing their first stop, a flat on Mount Street. Molly directed him to the place and he pulled up. She sat for a moment without moving.

'Sorry,' she said, pushing her hair out of her eyes. 'Ranting and raving like a damn lunatic. But it does get me hot under the collar.'

'Ain't the country gonna get Home Rule soon anyways? It was in the papers.'

'Home Rule! This country will never be free until it is free.'

Wiggins didn't know what to say to that. Molly went on. 'Does it shock you, a woman speaking like this?'

'What, like a Kensington mama?'

She hesitated, then burst out laughing. 'You mean my accent?'

'Well, you don't sound very Irish to me, ma'am. All due respect. You sound like a lady. An *English* lady.'

'You see, that's the trouble. My Irishness has been crushed by years of oppression. But I am taking lessons in the language, yes I am.'

Molly opened the car door herself before he could get round to it. She strode off into the block of flats, shouting over her shoulder that he must wait.

Wiggins got back into the car. He thought of Constance Kell – she certainly wasn't shy of talking politics, and so, no, he wasn't shocked by Molly and her ranting. Her relationship with the OC did still surprise him, though, certainly from her perspective. It was easy enough to see why O'Connell liked her; why Fitz liked her, too – any man might, if they could put up with those searching green eyes that saw too much, and said too much, and all. But then, in his experience, the men who thought women talked too much were men who were scared of what they might say.

He wanted to ask her more about Irish nationalism, whether it was really true that the country was in desperate need of independence. From what he'd seen of Dublin, it was certainly in need, but then so were London and Glasgow and Leeds and Manchester. When he'd toured the country a year before for Kell's spy-catching exercise, you couldn't ignore the poverty. The poor were always in need and always would be, regardless of who was in charge. It wasn't as if the British Government was any more hostile to the Irish poor than to the English poor, at least from what he could see. Then again, Molly wasn't poor (she wasn't very Irish either, as far as he could tell), yet it was the likes of her and not Fitz's family who seemed to be agitating.

'Here,' Molly yelled from the doorway of the building. 'Could you help? Could you?'

Wiggins carried back two heavy boxes of papers and stowed them in the motor car. Molly watched him until he'd finished, then disappeared inside. A moment later, she returned with another woman on her arm. She was dressed like Molly, but in addition wore pink stockings and swung a cigarette-holder around wildly.

'Don't mind Wiggins,' Molly said to her friend as they got into the back of the car together. 'He's an incurable romantic too.'

'How wonderful, darling,' the woman said. 'Are you a Kerry man?'

Molly laughed as Wiggins drove off. 'No, no, Connie, he's not a romantic for Ireland. I think it's for a woman. You were going to New York for a woman, Wiggins?'

Wiggins grunted. 'Something like that.'

'What's her name?' Molly asked with glee.

He hesitated, hoping for the moment to pass. But Molly clearly expected an answer. 'Bela,' he said at last.

Molly turned to her companion. 'He was thrown off the *Titanic*, Connie, at Queenstown! Can you believe it?'

'How marvellous!' Connie exclaimed. 'Could we use him, do you think? There must be a story here. What did you say your name was, man?'

Wiggins glanced back. Connie sounded as English as Molly, although if anything even posher. She was kitted out like a theatrical version of an English aristocrat and she had the voice and manner to match.

'Don't worry about my name, ma'am. Just tell me where you need to go.'

Molly directed him to the Inghinidhe rooms in a tall building in the centre of town. 'Can you bring up those boxes,' she said as Connie flounced through the doors and began climbing the stairs. Wiggins struggled to the foot of the stairs and waited for Molly to go past. 'You go first,' she said, smiling. 'It's six flights up.'

'All we're interested in,' she went on as Wiggins strained, 'is Ireland becoming herself, completely. She should no longer labour under the yoke of British imperial rule.'

'No more labouring?' Wiggins grunted under the weight of the papers.

Molly had a head of steam now. 'But it's much simpler than that. It's the very struggle for existence.' As opposed to the struggle up the stairs, Wiggins did not say. 'Ireland must be free from London, from Britain, free to make her own way in peace and love and happiness. And yes, we may have to fight for it. But it's worth fighting for. Freedom is everything.'

Wiggins strained up the stairs under his load. He thought of pulling the heavy artillery up the hill at Ladysmith, him and Bill with their shoulders to the wheel when the poor nags died of hunger; the sickening *thwupp* of a big shell landing nearby; the heat, the stench of death; Knightly's liver bleeding out on the dry earth; the sight of what bullets actually do. He hated guns, always had. And he hated it even more when people talked of 'fighting', of a cause worth fighting for, a country, a border. He'd yet to meet a man or woman who actually *had* fought sound so happy to talk of fighting. They wouldn't feel the same with a bullet in their belly; they wouldn't even feel the same if they'd *seen* a bullet in a belly. But that was the curse of the world – the only thing that cured bloodlust was blood, and by then it was too late.

Molly pressed up close behind him as he rose up the stairs. He could smell her. Sweat prickled the small of his back. He was glad he'd managed to grab a bathe first thing that morning at Tara Street, a neat little bathhouse Fitz had shown him.

'And what about the workers?' he grunted again. 'Will they be free too?'

'But of course! Ireland will be free and prosperous, but only if we shrug off the imperial yoke. The only thing we Irish lack is guns. A nation is only truly a nation if she's armed. We can't fight with our bare hands.'

Wiggins finally reached the top landing, where he put down the boxes with a heavy crash.

'Not yet,' Molly said breezily. 'In here.' She pushed past him towards a glass-paned door. As she did so, her hand gently kissed his upper arm, unacknowledged. She opened the door without knocking. 'I've got the copies of *Bean na hÉireann*,' she bellowed.

Wiggins crabbed in behind her. The room was an office of sorts, with three desks rammed in any old how, and a glass partition through to another set of the same. Overstuffed bookshelves lined two walls, with stray paper everywhere. A bald man sat at one of the desks reading from a sheaf of papers and smoking. He looked up as Wiggins came in, and gestured to the one corner of free floor space. 'Over there. Thanks a million,' he said, and continued reading.

Molly's pink-stockinged friend Connie was nowhere to be seen. Molly stood by the far desk, waving a cigarette at the person who sat by the window, opposite the bald man. The smoker was actually a woman dressed as a man. She wore a tailcoat, pinstriped trousers and a white shirt and collar. She was younger than Molly, but as she poked a cigar in the air, Wiggins guessed she held some kind of seniority.

'Tell him he can squeal for the monkeys,' she said.

Molly laughed, then glanced back at Wiggins. 'I'll see you back at the motor car.' She said this lightly enough, but Wiggins knew when he was being dismissed. He doffed his hat to the company in mock salute, then left.

He hesitated on the landing and listened. 'Is the Civ here?' Molly said loudly.

'Not here,' the bald man said. Wiggins heard a hand on the door, and went down the stairs hurriedly.

Molly came down a few minutes later. She was alone. 'I'm starving,' she said. 'Drive.'

She talked once more about Ireland and the cause, at turns prattling, at turns passionate. 'You're not political?' she asked suddenly, as the motor crossed the Liffey on one of the wide, flat, elegant bridges that Wiggins admired.

'Not if I can help it,' he said reluctantly.

'Everything is politics.'

And I'm driving the car, he thought. The day wore on like this. She would indicate a place to stop – Hugh Lane's modern art gallery on Harcourt Street, the Café Cairo on Grafton Street, private houses – and leave him in the car. In between, she talked politics mostly, but occasionally she tried to draw him out on his romantic interest in New York. He would not be drawn beyond Bela's name and his repeated declarations of love for her.

At lunchtime, she made him park opposite the vegetarian restaurant on Westland Row. 'I'll be an hour and a half.'

'What, in there?'

She laughed. 'You do have to chew rather a lot.'

'Shouldn't be a problem.'

She shot him a glance at that, but let herself out of the car and strode across the road, her long coat-tails flapping in the breeze.

He watched her go into the restaurant. A moment later, the man she'd met the night before, the 'Civ', came walking down the street and followed her in. He walked with the air of someone used to being in charge. Army once, Wiggins knew, but not army now. English by the cut of his clothes and his accent (though that was no tell in Dublin, he'd discovered). Still, the two of them weren't carrying on like lovers, not that he could see. It didn't take much of a skip in his mind to think of Molly in a clinch, but the Civ seemed above all that somehow, uninterested in her. He let the thought rest and decided to go for a drink.

Wiggins found a big red-brick pub on the corner. He ordered a half-and-half – ignoring the barman's disgusted 'Ah, that's a waste of both, man' – and asked for the telephone. He rang for Fitz at Mulligan's, but there was still no sign. If he was getting his end away, it was taking an awfully long time.

He wondered again about the murderous men of the DMP and why they'd tried to kill him, and whether that had anything to do with the worrying absence of Fitz. Dublin was still a mystery to him. 'You wanting a bread and cheese with that?' the barman said, pointing with unconcealed disgust at Wiggins's drink.

Wiggins looked at the pint pot in front of him. 'What do you think?'

He wasn't in the mood for small talk. He couldn't shake the hollow feeling in his stomach. Fitz hadn't shown up at Mulligan's for lunch. It was the only place with a telephone where Wiggins knew to reach him. Listening to Molly all day had distracted him a little, but now he was on his own his fears for the young man welled once more.

Molly still mystified him too. He'd known political women – God knows, Constance Kell had almost caused a riot at the King's funeral, protesting for the vote – but something didn't

quite sit right when it came to Molly. She had all the enthusiasm of a convert, someone fresh to the game, ready to push
it to the hilt, but it didn't always sound true. She wasn't poor,
that was for sure, so why would she be rebelling? Wiggins had
known revolutionaries too, but the ones he knew had been shit
poor. Peter the Painter, Yakov – they hadn't even had the money
to pay the rent, not unless they stole it. And where they came
from, their people were even poorer than here. They had
nothing, but where they grew up they'd had less than nothing.
Peter and Yakov didn't have hearts, either, he remembered, and
would sooner have sent you to the grave than argue a point
too hard.

Yakov turned his mind sour. Peter the Painter may have got
the coffin he deserved, but Yakov had escaped the noose. Not
only that, he'd even escaped prison. The year before, in the trial
following the Siege of Sidney Street, most of the Latvian gang
had walked, thanks to the incompetence of the police. Yakov had
gone back to Russia, despite twice having tried to kill him. Wiggins
signalled for another pint. He tried again to frame his story. Bela.
She had blood on her hands, he was almost certain, yet he was
meant to be chasing her halfway across the world. Was that the
kind of man he was meant to be? Was that the kind of man he
was?

'Mooning over your sweetheart, I see.'

Wiggins swivelled. Molly stood before him, bold as brass in
the public bar, the only woman in the place, alone. 'Oh, don't
look so scared – I know Kennedy fine. Finish your drink and
let's get on. I need cigarettes.'

'But—'

'My lunch partner didn't turn up in the end.'

They exited the pub together and walked towards the car.
Wiggins noted the lie, but didn't rise to it. 'I wasn't mooning,'
he said instead, 'I was just . . .'

'There's nothing wrong with mooning,' she said, and opened
the car door. 'Connie was very touched. I knew you were a
romantic.'

They drove north before she again directed him to park. 'Wait here,' she said. Wiggins watched as she walked along the street some way – she obviously didn't particularly want to be seen in the Daimler. But he could just make out the paper shop she went into. It had all the news posters up outside, and five or six young men loafing and smoking on the street. The lettering above the door was in Irish.

After an hour, she came back with a jaunty swagger. 'Your leg's better,' Wiggins said as she leaned into the car.

'Oh, that. Sometimes I need to tell a little white lie to get what I want.'

'Did you get what you want?'

She opened her eyes – her green eyes – wide. 'I'm not sure.' Then she thrust a piece of paper at him. 'Take the motor back to this address, and then you can go.'

'You're staying in the paper shop?'

She smiled. She was still leaning through the passenger window. Wiggins tried not to look at her chest. 'It's more than a paper shop. But no, I won't be staying here. I'm leaving town for a few days.'

'Anywhere nice?' Wiggins asked, and looked out of the windscreen, down the long, windswept road. A tram rattled across the junction up ahead, *Fatima: The Turkish Blend* emblazoned on the side.

'It's not what you think,' she said.

'I ain't paid to think.'

She turned away then, but he called her back. 'Oh, miss . . .'

'Molly.'

'Miss – do you have any idea who mugged off the boss?'

'Me?' she said, surprised. 'Why would I know?' And with that, she turned away, back down the street, into the wind and the grey afternoon.

Wiggins didn't drive straight to the address she'd given him. He knew the way; it was one of the OC's houses. Instead, he consulted the map in the glovebox and turned northwards to Dromgoole's

Hotel, supposed lair of the criminal leader, Lynch. Hannigan had by turns been dismissive and fearful of Lynch's gang, but Wiggins wanted to see for himself. He knew Lynch had nothing to do with the first attack on the OC, but Wiggins had learned as a child on the streets of London – even before he'd met Holmes – that information was never wasted. The more you knew, the more powerful you were. And right then, he knew almost sod all.

He parked up the motor around the corner and decided to walk past. Immediately, he realised he wasn't dressed to go inside without causing remark. The hotel was double-fronted, with six gleaming windows across the façade. A highly polished door stood open, across a tiled entry, the words *Dromgoole's* pieced into the tiling with a beautiful swish. This was no rank old boozer, not like the places where he met Hannigan and the OC. Maybe Lynch's operation wasn't as down at heel as the OC seemed to think.

Rather than passing by the front door a second time, Wiggins ducked around the corner and walked along the mews lane that ran behind the four-storey terrace. These were the entrances for the servants and tradesmen, where all the work of the house was actually done. And Dromgoole's looked grand enough even from behind, with six wide windows on each floor amid the blackened brickwork.

The weather had turned once more and the late-afternoon sun pierced the clouds here and there, reflecting off wind-whipped puddles. The air was fresher here, away from the river and the breweries and stills; fresher than the docks too, with the traffic and the foundries.

As he sauntered closer, Wiggins made out four or five men standing about joking and smoking cigarettes around the back of Dromgoole's. They were young, as out of place around the front of the hotel as Wiggins. Wiggins stepped into a doorway, out of sight, and watched for a moment.

A young maid with a wash bucket came out of the back door. She tried to skip past the men, but one of them plucked at her skirts as she went past. A great laugh went up. Wiggins couldn't make out the words, but he could make out the meaning. The maid had to go to the drain and bend down with the bucket. Another great cry went up from the lads and one of them – big, fluid, dangerous – swaggered out to the maid as she bent. He wore his shirtsleeves rolled up over strong, leathery arms. Even from a distance, Wiggins noted the long, straight, livid scar on his wrist, inches long, like a brand. The man placed his hands on her hips and thrust his crotch up against her. She tried to pull away, but he held her tight, laughing.

'There ya go, doll, something for the priest! Hey, boys, what do you reckon, the Pillar's—'

The words choked in his mouth as Wiggins slammed a fist into the side of his neck. The big guy stumbled back, holding his throat. Wiggins strode towards the other, shocked men. A smaller man bundled forwards. Wiggins met his nose with a straight right. He swung his boot into the side of the next man's leg, crumpling him to the ground.

It was all over in seconds. Wiggins grunted at the maid, 'Back inside, love.' Then he surveyed the damage he'd done. The first man gripped his neck, still gasping for air. The second man knelt on one knee, holding a bloodied hand to his nose, while the third lay screaming and clutching at his buckled leg.

Two other lads hung back at the door, wary, watchful, scared.

'I don't want no trouble,' Wiggins said.

'What do you mean, you mad bastard? Yous broke my fucking nose.'

'Then keep your hands to yourself. She can't be more than sixteen.'

He swept his eyes over the men, now craven in his presence. They glowered at him. The large man rubbed his throat, then held up his hands in surrender. He had a strangely flat palm on his left hand that caught the light, as if the skin had been sanded and polished clean, with no ridges or lines. He ducked his head low and edged towards the back door along with his mates. Wiggins thrust his hands into the pockets of his mac and made no move to leave.

The man with the broken nose finally got up and swiped his cap away. Blood splattered his pink, freshly shaved face. 'Yous are messing with the wrong lads, so you are, mister.' Despite these defiant words, he too retreated to the back door, limping. 'Why's don't you fuck off,' he said once he'd reached relative safety.

Wiggins walked slowly towards the door. 'Like I said, the OC don't want no trouble.' He let that sink in. He could see the boys knew who the OC was. The shock was written on their faces.

At that moment, a ripple of noise came from inside the hotel and then, pushing through the cowering yobs, a tall, muscular man strode out in front. His men stepped aside and almost bowed their heads. He wore no hat, leaving an unruly mop of red-brown hair to flop around as he walked. His bulky arms sausaged out of a heavy tweed waistcoat that strained against his chest. His flat, broad face was spattered with freckles and not a hint of kindness.

'You the boss man?' Wiggins said. 'Lynch.'

'I didn't know O'Connell was sleeping with the English, so I didn't. And him a Catholic too.' He thrust his hands into the pockets of his waistcoat, playing the big man, the squire, for his men, although his eyes betrayed the nervousness that they could not see. 'You're the latest one to fall for his charms, are you now? You sure you're happy with his Roman ways?'

'Where's Fitz?' Wiggins rasped.

'Like I keep saying to your man Hannigan, we didn't take a swipe at the old man O'Connell. Why would we? He'll be dead soon, so.'

'Where's Fitz?' Wiggins repeated.

A faint look of puzzlement wrinkled Lynch's face. 'That's not my business.'

Suddenly, a commotion started from behind Lynch. He looked round and out strode one of the young lads with a hunting rifle at his shoulder, trained on Wiggins.

Lynch grinned. 'So, as a gesture of goodwill, I'll *tell* you to fuck off. I won't *make* you fuck off – that's the goodwill, you see?' He nodded back at the boy with the gun. 'To be honest, I wouldn't want him setting that thing off. He'll kill you, sure as, but he might pepper my arse in the process. So, fuck off.'

Wiggins looked from Lynch to the gun and back again. And then he strode off without a backward glance.

'Where the bloody hell is he?' O'Connell shouted down the telephone line at eight o'clock that night. There was no sign of Fitz at Mulligan's, and no one had seen him, which left Wiggins to field the OC's telephone call.

'I ain't seen him. I told you.'

'His hole doesn't take all day, does it? There's a boy up there at the Talbot kip houses sniffing around. There's money sitting up in them too. It'll be chaos. They don't know how to keep it.'

'I can get it.'

'Just get me Fitz. Tomorrow, you come round here – see-ho – and if he hasn't got his cock out of that woman by then, I'll chop it off, so I will.'

Wiggins handed the telephone back to the barman and left immediately. He knew by now that Fitz wasn't snuggled up with a woman. He was too neat, too conscientious, too damn sharp for that. He hurried back to their room, but Fitz hadn't returned. And no one else had been there. He rifled through Fitz's things and found a torch.

It was dark by this time, and the air felt wet and cool. He pushed on to Fitz's family. They lived a mile or so away, down an alley so thin that even on a bright day you couldn't see the sky. The flickering beam of the torch fell on dark doorways and wide, scared eyes as he pushed deeper into the lane.

There was no one waiting at the entrance to Fitz's family's tenement, so Wiggins clambered up the stairs alone and knocked on their door.

'Who's there!' Fitz's mother cried.

'It's Wiggins.'

'Who?' She opened the door.

He shone the torch into the room. They had a small lamp burning on the table amidst the detritus of the box-making. Fitz's dad lay sprawled on the only bed, his chest rising and falling to the rhythm of snores so monstrous they made the bedframe jangle. The smallest sister lay asleep, camp-style, in the corner, while Fitz's twin sisters – maybe eleven or twelve – sat at the table and looked up at him, wide-eyed.

'I'm Wiggins, we met once before.'

'So we did. How are ya?' Fitz's ma said absently.

'I'm looking for Fitz.'

'Sure, he hasn't been here today,' she said, and shooed one of the twins off her chair. 'Are you wanting a drink?'

'No, ta,' he replied. This was a family who had almost nothing. 'When did you last see him?'

'Yesterday morning. He dropped by, you know, as he does sometimes . . .' She trailed off. Wiggins knew Fitz gave them money, but his mother was too ashamed to say.

'Did he say anything?'

'You know Fitz, he came into this world with a joke.'

'Did he leave anything with you? A book or something?'

She shook her head and smiled. 'What would I be wanting with a book? Are you all right, son? You can lie down here if you like?'

'Don't worry, Mrs F. I better get back.'

'If I see Fitz before you do, I'll tell him to – well, I don't know what I would tell him, do you?'

'Tell him to take care.'

Wiggins had already reached the hallway at the bottom of the stairs when he heard a faint sound skittering down towards him through the darkness. It was one of the twins.

He waited while she reached him, all shy and jumpy in a white pinafore. She dashed the hair from her face. 'Last time he came, Fitz told me not to worry about money.'

'And?'

'But that's funny. It's funny, isn't it? I mean, we *always* worry about money. Ma does anyways, and me and Maggie too. The ould man just worries about drink, and wee Kathleen worries about me ma.'

'Didn't Fitz always bring you money?'

'Yeah, course, but a shilling or something. The way he said it this time . . . "Don't worry about money." I mean, come on. Who *doesn't* worry about money?'

Wiggins heard shouting from the streets outside. He'd got back from Fitz's ma's the night before and had fallen asleep hanging over the window sill. He awoke, looking out at the Powers distillery, breathing in the whiskey fug. Fitz had not returned.

Now, with the chilly dawn light flooding the room, he felt a tight knot of dread in his stomach. He scrambled into his boots and down the stairs. On the street, a shopkeeper stood in her doorway; three children ran past towards the sounds of an uproar on the quays. He ran after them. The knot in his stomach tightened.

Out by the Guinness wharf a crowd had gathered, with more running to join them. Wiggins pounded towards the hubbub. People were shouting. An older woman in a black headscarf stumbled away, saying, 'Oh God, oh God. Oh God.' Wiggins could barely breathe with anxiety. With dread. A leathery man slewed past him holding his mouth, and then Wiggins was in the crowd, a giant horseshoe around some event. 'Where's the polis?' someone shouted.

'Sure, it's the ambulance you need.'

'Polis!'

Wiggins pushed his way to the front. His boots slithering on the wet cobbles, his heart pounding. A huge barrel cart stood by the water, loading onto a barge interrupted. As he burst through the outer ring of the crowd, he saw a small group of men, four or five, circling around something by the end of the cart.

In front of them, a split barrel on its side, its contents (black porter, always the black porter of Guinness) spilling across the stones, wet and sticky. A young Atlas of a man, stripped to the waist, wailed, 'The weight was off, the weight was off. I've never dropped a barrel.' Wiggins thrust himself forward, into this inner circle, then lurched away, appalled.

For inside the broken barrel, half in, half out, lay the remains of a body, washed grey, twisted and bent.

Fitz's body.

6

'How in the name of Jaysus did you know I'd be here?' O'Connell asked, astonished.

Wiggins stood by, breathing hard. He'd run all the way to the hammam on St Stephen's Green. He'd pushed past O'Connell's bodyguard – a tall, slow-witted man called Toner – and burst into the first-class suite up the stairs. The OC had been lying on a high bed in one of the curtained cubicles that surrounded a large, steaming bath. Now he pushed himself up on his elbows, naked to the waist. 'And where the hell is Toner?'

At this, Toner appeared by Wiggins's shoulder. Wiggins ignored him, caught his breath and said, 'Fitz is dead.'

'And I've got monkeys flying out of my arse.'

'Murdered,' Wiggins said. 'I've just seen his body.'

The OC leapt from the bed as if prodded by the devil's pitchfork, a white towel pinned round his waist. As he stood up, he demanded the details. Grey-black hair rolled from his shoulders, down his back and chest and along his upper arms. Like an ape almost, Wiggins thought suddenly, his mind still scrambled by what he'd seen on the quay, by the horror of it, and by the multiplying unanswered questions in his mind. He tried to shove them away, just as he tried to forget the image of Fitz's mangled corpse, as he told O'Connell what he knew.

O'Connell nodded, then stepped out of the cubicle and bawled at one of the uniformed assistants, 'Clear the floor, now!'

'But—'

The OC glared and within minutes, Wiggins, Toner and the OC had the large bathing chamber to themselves. O'Connell bellowed for the long-line telephone and turned to Toner. 'Get Hannigan here – get them all here, Mahoney, O'Shea, every man jack of them, now.' Toner lumbered off.

'Was he tortured?' O'Connell asked Wiggins.

'It weren't no picnic.' He'd managed to get close enough to the body to confirm it was Fitz, and to see what clothes he had on – the same as the day before last, the day he'd last seen him on the Coombe. The boy's body was diminished, small, like the child he'd only stopped being a couple of years earlier. Death did that to people; it made them so much smaller, like nothing more than the clothes they were in. He didn't believe in God, or the spirit, or even heaven and hell, but you couldn't look on a dead body without feeling the actual loss, as if something phys- ical had been taken away, as if the soul itself was real and weighty and somehow located in the body. He felt that loss in his stomach – the deep, hollow sensation he'd begun to feel when Fitz had gone missing had solidified and filled him, like a sickness.

The OC had grasped a telephone by this time – brought over to him by the steward using a long, winding line – and was making a series of terse calls. Wiggins kept a discreet distance, though the subject of the conversations was clear enough. Cash money, and where it was. Every now and then he would put the speaking horn back in its cradle and direct a question at Wiggins.

'You didn't see him yesterday, you say?'

'I was with Mo— Miss Lansdown-Smith,' Wiggins replied. 'And when he didn't come back, I believed you – I thought he was with one of the girls, like.'

And later, after another hurried phone call: 'And the day before?'

'He left me down the Coombe, 'bout ten. I told you yesterday.'

Soon after, O'Connell's men began filtering into the large chamber. They looked ill at ease, a little scared. Toner had obvi- ously spread the word. The OC directed each of them to seats or benches or the side of the steaming tub. He paced up and down, still mostly undressed. It was an odd sight for a man so clipped, so groomed and precise in his dress. He looked such an animal without his shirt.

'Should we talk to the coppers?' Wiggins said after a while.

O'Connell stopped pacing and stared at him. 'You joking? Fitz is a slum kid. Was. They won't give a pisspot's worth of beer for the boy.'

'But the barrel, the quay? Won't it be in the papers?'

'Ach, it won't get anywhere near the press. Man dies in barrel of porter? Sure, Guinness will never let that story go beyond the quay. Aren't they the biggest gang in Dublin?' He waved his hand in dismissal.

Wiggins leaned against the side of the huge tub and waited. He needed to find out what the OC planned to do, what he thought the motive had even been. Wiggins had his own ideas, but he'd yet to pull together the whole picture – partly because he didn't want to face up to the fact that he might have been to blame, partly because his mind was in confusion, jumping this way and that, and then collapsing into unformed suspicions and despair. A ghost of a thought flitted in and out, a tiny whisper almost washed away by the wave that filled his heart with grief. Grief for a poor young boy crushed and beaten and killed.

But whatever else he felt – these doubts, this grief, this whirl of uncertainty – he knew with cold, hard certainty that he would not rest until he'd got his hands on Fitz's killer. This murder would never go unpunished.

The doors to the hammam crashed open at the far end. Hannigan strode in, hatless, red-faced, fist clenched. 'English fucking bastard,' he cried as he leapt at Wiggins. He wrestled him to his knees.

Wiggins chose not to react immediately. Hannigan forced his head into the steaming bath, crying, 'Murderer!' Over and over, he plunged his head into the water, crying out all manner of curses. Wiggins let the water rush in his ears.

Then he relaxed. Warm water, the muffling of the violent language. It was strangely comforting to have his head fully submerged in the hot mineral waters of the tub, like the last lullaby before sleep, a sleep he so desperately needed. He thought of pulling Hannigan in with him, of fighting, but the water was so warm, so—

'Control yourself, Vincent. Jaysus,' O'Connell cried as Wiggins was hauled out of the tub by the OC's men. Two of them had dragged Hannigan back and he now stood, breathing hard and glaring.

Wiggins gulped in air, suddenly indecently happy to be alive, to feel the rush of oxygen. It never failed to surprise him, this urge to stay alive even in the deepest of deep shite. Since for ever, deep within him, he'd had the urge to live – though never anything much to live for.

Hannigan's blood was still up. He pointed. 'He's a killer. Look at him, he didn't even try to fight – he's as guilty as sin. I'm telling you, I know.'

'Don't be so stupid,' O'Connell hissed. He handed Wiggins a towel. 'How would he have cooped up the body and all? And why? Are you telling me that? Why would he want the boy dead?'

As he dried his head, Wiggins kept his eyes on Hannigan. The man was distressed. His leathery, impervious skin had coloured around his cheeks, his eyes reddened too, slightly. He was obviously trying to control his agitation, but Wiggins could see the signs, the quivering of his left hand. Hannigan's emotions were running hot. He was at sea.

'I may be stupid, but I'm not blind. As soon as he turned up, yous was attacked and now and now . . .' Hannigan couldn't say the words. He turned back to Wiggins. 'You're fucking Castle, I knows you're fucking Castle. You're just a spying fucking British bastard is what you are.'

'And what would the British want with Fitz?' O'Connell roared. Hearing the name quietened everyone in the room. *Fitz.* Hannigan dropped his head. Wiggins looked away. Toner and the rest shrank back. O'Connell breathed out slowly. He still wore the towel at his waist and nothing else. He looked at each of his men in turn, until their eyes met his. First Toner, then around the others, finally resting on Hannigan. 'Vincent,' he said. 'Are you here?'

Hannigan straightened, made eye contact and nodded.

'What's with Lynch? Did you find anything?'

Hannigan shook his head. 'He's not been in our business, as far as I can tell.'

'And you?' O'Connell said to Wiggins.

'He's up to something, sure as, but this? I don't know,' Wiggins said. 'He knew who Fitz was, I know that much.'

'And how do you know that?'

'We had a little disagreement,' Wiggins said. O'Connell looked at him from beneath a pinched brow.

'Shall we torch Dromgoole's, boss?' Toner said. 'Me and the lads. Send the bastard a message.'

O'Connell nodded absently. 'Wait on that. It's war, all right, but take a look-see first. You and you, up to his kip houses and the boozers. See what his men have been doing. Ask around. And no need to be quiet, see-ho? This will not stand. Well, on yous go. Back at Mulligan's at five.' The men hurried out, leaving Hannigan, O'Connell and Wiggins alone.

Hannigan had regained some self-control but he couldn't disguise the murder in his eyes as he stared levelly at Wiggins. The colour had gone from his face, but his intent had not.

O'Connell glanced between the two of them, rubbing his hands on the towel around his middle. 'Vincent, this is important, you hear? I know, well . . . I know the boy meant—'

'He meant nothing to me,' Hannigan snapped. 'It's what *he* means.' He pointed at Wiggins. 'This man's a snake, I'm telling you, he's Castle. We've got a name for his type back in Derry.'

O'Connell laid his hand on Hannigan's shoulder. 'Wheesht, man, come away.' He led Hannigan behind one of the curtains – out of Wiggins's earshot.

As they mumbled to each other, Wiggins tried to collect his thoughts. He needed a drink. Fitz, dead. The knot in his stomach hadn't gone. If anything, it was growing inside him, like a cancer.

He thought of Fitz's family, up the alleyway to hell; he thought of his own part in it. Was he to blame? Should he have found him earlier? Should he be in Dublin at all?

'You,' the OC called, bringing Wiggins out of his reverie. The OC stood by the blood-red velvet curtain, buttoning his shirt. 'Here now.' Hannigan strode to the doors, glancing at Wiggins. 'On you go, Vincent, do as I say, you hear? Mulligan's, at five.' Hannigan lifted his hand in acknowledgement and left.

O'Connell swiped on his braces. As he continued getting dressed, he glanced up every now and then at Wiggins – the rich master engaging with the valet. Wiggins had played the servant often enough; he didn't mind standing there now, indulging O'Connell. He was too shocked and stunned to do anything else.

O'Connell gestured to the ornate tiling. 'The Turks,' he said. 'Richest empire in the world, once. The Ottomans. They know how to keep clean. There used to be a bath on Lincoln Place, like a mosque. You ever been? To the land of the Muhammadan?'

Wiggins shook his head.

'I have. Clean people. Like a bath, unlike the bastard Irish.'

'You're Irish, ain't you?'

'You got me. Don't drink, though, the Muhammadan. Could never stay in a place that didn't serve a drink.' He'd completed his dress. He took his felt hat off the peg, smoothed its rim. 'Vincent thinks you're a wrong 'un. He's probably right, but I don't think you killed Fitz. That I do know.'

'Who did then?' Wiggins asked. Ever since he'd come into the baths, Wiggins had been trying to draw a bead on O'Connell, to chart his emotional state and what that might mean. He'd gone through the shock, the anger and now the anxiety. The OC was a cool head, but Wiggins knew he was rattled too – and it wasn't just because he'd lost a man. He'd lost something more. Wiggins went on. 'What's gonna happen to the business? Fitz weren't just a boy, were he?'

O'Connell looked carefully at Wiggins, unsurprised at the insight. 'That's my business. And I'm dealing with it. Vincent and the lads, we'll sort it. It's an attack on my business, all right, but I'll repel it. What I want you to do is follow Fitz.'

'He's dead.'

'Follow him backwards. It seems you were one of the last of us to see him alive. Find out who killed him. Something tells me you'll be a good man for that.'

'But what about—'

'I told you.' O'Connell shot his cuffs, edges folded like white knives. 'The polis won't give a damn. Sure, Vincent will find out what he can from his snouts in the DMP, but they'll bury it faster than they'll bury Fitz. You're the polis now.'

~~~

Brave mariners no longer pulled lifeless bodies from the North Atlantic, some frozen, some drowned, but all once aboard the great *Titanic*. The press stories drifted on from tragedy to blame. The German Reichstag voted to expand the navy, and Captain Vernon Kell stretched his net of information nationwide. He tapped his fingers on his desk and read of suspicious publicans and nosy tourists, of German-speaking academics with their hackles up. He even thought of Wiggins every now and then. The House of Commons forced through the Parliament Act, which meant that the first People's Budget could pass. It also made Home Rule for Ireland – so long stymied by the Tories in the House of Lords – all but inevitable. And Dublin's crime world became gripped by conflict. Dromgoole's Hotel was burned out, Mulligan's torched, guards stood at kip houses and wary hooligans worried who might be next, and whether to fight them off with a cosh or a knife.

~~~

Wiggins rode the Sandymount tram back into central Dublin. During the week since Fitz's death, he'd been to banks, brothels, shebeens, slums. He'd consoled tearful whores, nervous tenants, red-faced, sweating hooch merchants. He did the same walk he'd done with Fitz, he took their money, collected the tick and reported back to O'Connell each day. He visited Fitz's family whenever he could, and dropped them a shilling too. The search to find his killer had gone cold. But O'Connell didn't care about that; O'Connell cared about something else entirely.

The tram jagged and squealed. Wiggins stood downstairs by the back door, facing a woman with puckered lips and too much rouge. A boy with a brown paper parcel on his lap rustled and fidgeted. The tram clattered over the Liffey and onto the wide and windy expanse of Sackville Street. 'All change, all change,' the conductor cried as the Pillar rose up before them. 'And for the love of mercy, stop fondling that parcel. It couldn't like you any more if you tried.'

The tram lines jangled, the conductors cried out their routes and people jostled and bumped their way about. It was midmorning and Dublin was as busy as parts of London even, Wiggins thought, though not quite the mad scrum that you'd get at Waterloo or down Piccadilly Circus. He scanned the boards, as if searching for his destination, then paused to look at his watch. Then he set off down the road towards Clerys, the large department store he'd noticed on the way up.

As soon as he was inside and on the shop floor, Wiggins sped up. He swiped a felt hat from a display and slipped through a rack of coats. It took him less than a minute to change his coat into a dark green one with a wide collar – again, unnoticed by a young sales assistant who was gossiping to his colleague about the absolute state of the mutton stew at O'Grady's, it was so bad they had the polis in, so they did, and excuse me, sir, do you mind, this is the gentlemen's outfitters here and tradesmen's supplies is in the basement, although by the way that is a nice coat, and what was I saying, the gristle . . . Wiggins glided on towards the large exit at the far side of the shop.

Out on the street, he ducked across the wide road, through the criss-crossing trams, and slunk into the shadow of an office doorway, *Pioneer Teeth Institute Ltd* picked out in white letters on the wall. Wiggins ran his tongue around his own mouth as he waited. Always had nice pearlers. Two minutes later, the man who'd been following him since Wiggins had left Fitz's room that morning came out of Clerys. He swivelled his head left and right, searching the crowd.

Wiggins watched all this and waited. The short, clean-shaven man wore a greatcoat that almost brushed the pavement as he walked. He eventually gave up his search and turned north. Wiggins – now the hunter, not the prey – followed.

The short man darted through the crowds, but Wiggins was by far the better tail. With his new hat and coat, he went unobserved. After a few minutes, Shorty turned off the main street and entered a bustling restaurant already gearing up for early lunch. Wiggins entered too, and melted into a space at the counter. Shorty marched straight to the telephone, paid his penny and made a call. Wiggins ordered cheese and a roll, with a cup of tea. He watched while Shorty grew redder and redder as he spoke and then listened on the phone, his shoulders getting tighter and tighter. It didn't take Sherlock Holmes to know this was a bollocking in progress. Finally, Shorty put down the phone and hurried out.

Wiggins got up and went over. 'Do you mind?' he said to the man at the counter as he pointed at the telephone.

'Sure, you and your money are welcome.'

Wiggins put down a coin and picked up the horn. 'Exchange. This line just dropped. Can you reconnect it?'

'One moment, please.'

Wiggins waited. After a moment, a voice he knew came on the line. 'And what do you want this time?' Wiggins did not reply.

Later that day, Royal Irish Constabulary Captain Roderick Masters whistled as he left Dublin Castle by a side exit. He walked past the guardhouse on Exchange Place without stopping and approached his natty little motor car. He did this every other lunchtime, alone, for he didn't like to use a driver. The reason he didn't like to use a driver, Wiggins knew, was because he drove to a rather high-class kip house out towards Dalkey, owned and run by O'Connell. It was a nice brothel, in a good area a little way out of the city, away from prying eyes, but it wasn't the sort of place to take a driver. Captain Masters, Wiggins also knew, was the same young officer who'd saved him from being thrown in the Liffey on his first day in Dublin.

Masters, still whistling, started the motor and got behind the wheel.

'Don't flood the engine,' Wiggins said from the back seat.

Masters started in surprise. He grasped the back of his head. 'Don't shoot,' he cried.

'I'm not armed.'

Masters scrabbled at his waistband, then twisted round and levelled a revolver at Wiggins. 'One move and you're dead.'

Wiggins shook his head gently. 'You don't need no gun.'

'The only thing keeping a lid on this bloody country is that the army have guns and the people don't. Now, what the hell do you want?'

'I thought you was police, not army?'

'And I still have the gun.'

Wiggins nodded in acknowledgement. 'Why did the police try to dump me in the river?'

'Not an earthly,' he said, then sighed. 'Look, it was the DMP, not us. They were all over you, but I haven't got a clue why. I was just doing my job. I don't know why you need to go on about it. We saved you.'

'Who killed Fitz?'

'I have got no idea what you're talking about, man.' Masters pinched the bridge of his nose in irritation. He'd started to wear a moustache, but it was so sandy and sparse that the effect was to make him look younger and more callow – precisely because it was obvious he was trying to appear older. He moved his gloved hand along his top lip and fixed his eyes on Wiggins once more. 'You should get out of the bally car.'

Wiggins held his look. 'Fitz was the body in the barrel.'

'Oh, *that*,' Masters said. 'That's a matter for the DMP. The word is it's a local dispute between criminals. One less thug to worry about. Why, did you know the man? Do you have any information?'

'I don't spy for you, Captain.'

'Then get the hell out of my car.'

Wiggins stood outside a pub with no name. It was the same bar Fitz had driven him to when he'd first got out of prison, just near Francis Street. He remembered Fitz's face that day, gently nudging him on, into the belly of the whale, but with a grand smile and a kind word.

The barman looked up as he entered, and nodded gravely. Wiggins continued on to the back room where he'd found O'Connell in such high spirits less than two months earlier. Now, even before he got to the heavy curtain that separated the snug from the bar, he heard O'Connell in a very different mood.

'When have I not been good for it before?' he hollered. 'Jaysus, Macauley, you owe me.' Wiggins pulled back the curtain and went in.

O'Connell glared as Wiggins entered. He was on the telephone by the wall, bellowing into the horn. The snug was empty apart from that, with no fire in the grate. He jammed the receiver back into its cradle and turned to Wiggins. 'What have you found?'

Wiggins opened his arms out in a kind of shrug.

O'Connell picked up a small glass and threw it at him. He ducked and it smashed against the wall behind him. 'What kind of fucking answer is that? You know, maybe Vincent's right, maybe you are a fucking rat. Were you in on it with Fitz, were you? Did you put the wee bastard up to it, did you?' He grasped a poker from the grate and strode towards him. 'Do you have my fucking money?' he cried, weapon at the ready.

Wiggins stared at him levelly. 'If I was up to that, if I had all your money, why would I still be here? I can ghost out of Ireland in a second, and you wouldn't hear a dicky.'

O'Connell calmed his breathing, then threw the poker aside, his temper seeming to subside as fast as it had risen. 'Then tell me, what have you found?' he said.

'You're right. Cops buried the Fitz case. RIC think it's local criminals, not their bag. DMP don't give a toss.'

Wiggins had found out more than this. He'd found out that Fitz had been taking money from the OC for a while, skimming it from rents, the brothels and the bars. He'd found out that, far from spending it, Fitz had been trying to redistribute it among those who most deserved it – hence the soft words to his sisters, hence the fact that all the rents, all the payments, had gradually been going down without the OC realising it, until now.

What Wiggins didn't yet know was how Fitz had planned to escape. You didn't slip away from a man like O'Connell, let alone Hannigan, without a plan. He'd been loath to tell the OC any of this, for he couldn't help but think Fitz had had his reasons, but the conversation Wiggins had just heard – combined with what he'd heard at the bathhouse the week before – convinced him that O'Connell now knew about the missing money. And what better way to keep a man happy than to tell him something he knows, but which he doesn't know that you know he knows?

'Fitz was stealing,' Wiggins said. 'I don't know how much, or for how long, but he was skimming off every chop.'

'I know that,' O'Connell snapped. 'But do you know where it is?'

'Not yet.'

'And have you found his books?'

'No.'

'Jaysus.' O'Connell ran his hands through his hair, then plucked a cigarette from a box on the mantelpiece. He offered one to Wiggins, who refused. Wiggins watched him closely as he drew the smoke in, then funnelled it through his nostrils.

'As to who killed him,' Wiggins said slowly, 'it looks like you've got the biggest motive.'

O'Connell stared at him, outraged. He raised the cigarette as if to throw it like a dart, when Hannigan flew through the curtain. O'Connell checked himself. 'I'll deal with you later,' he said to Wiggins. 'Vincent, what news?'

'Lynch put a man into one of the hells last night. We ran him to ground out by the Joy. He won't be dealing cards in a hurry.'

'The staff?'

'We got some new boys in from Kerry. Don't worry, we can pay them on the turnover. I reckon we can take a look at Vicetown. These boys'll do anything for a drink and a kip. And what has his nibs, Mr Scotland fucking Yard here, found out?' Hannigan turned to Wiggins, his leathery face stretched into a sneer.

'I don't know if I found it out, like, but I can tell you smashing up pubs and brothels and scaring women cos they're owned by another fella never made anyone money. Never made you a man neither.'

Hannigan reacted, setting his fists to fight, but Wiggins shook his head sadly. 'And what I want to know from you – or anyone else – is why Lynch would kill Fitz, if you think it really is Lynch? How does he gain?'

'He doesn't,' said O'Connell dryly. 'Fitz could have been working for the bastard, all the harm he was doing me.'

'What about *him*!' Hannigan jabbed a finger at Wiggins. 'Here's the rat, standing right in front of you. He even speaks with a London accent – a sewer rat.'

'Wheesht. I'll not have fighting in here, see-ho?' O'Connell stared him down, then lit another cigarette. 'Now, Vincent, I know you don't like the English—'

'Nobody likes the English.'

'But now's not the time for getting overexcited. We've discussed this before, haven't we, for sure?'

Hannigan nodded. Something passed between the OC and him, something Wiggins couldn't really guess at – but he didn't like it all the same. Personal history ran as deeply as any of the stuff in the books, and these two held a bond he could never hope to break. But he didn't need to break it, he just needed to—

'Patrick! Patrick O'Connell!' A loud English voice broke in upon them, echoing through from the bar. 'I demand to see Patrick O'Connell.' It was a woman's voice. Wiggins was familiar with it, and so was the OC.

The OC hurried to the curtain. 'Molly? What are you about? Come in here, now, out of the public bar.'

'Patrick!' she cried, and strode towards them. Her hair hung about her face, badly pinned, the edge of her skirt was wet and muddy and she had to catch her breath before she spoke. Her cheeks were pink with exertion, her eyes aflame. She looked magnificent. 'Is it true? Your note, you said—'

'We may have to delay, my dear, I'm sorry. Now then, a drink perhaps . . . ?'

'But we can't – the bill's going through, we must be ready,' she implored. 'You promised us, Patrick. You promised me.'

O'Connell opened his arm out to the room, trying to usher her inside, behind the curtain and away from the bar. 'It's not that simple, my dear. Fitz . . .' he whispered. Wiggins stood by the curtain, but noted the drop in the OC's shoulders, his whole body in an attitude of defence.

'What did Fitz say?' Molly faltered, then looked around, almost embarrassed.

'Well, not very much, seeing as he's all bone and dead now, eh? But no, it's not that,' he said. 'Come away in here, Molly.' He looked daggers at both Wiggins and Vincent, as if they were to blame. 'Get out of it, you two. Can't you see the lady's upset?' He pushed her gently into the room and then gestured Wiggins out, with Hannigan following on behind. 'Find it, Wiggins. You understand? Find that money.' He was turning to go back behind the curtain when he said, almost lightly, as an afterthought, 'Oh, and Vincent has a wee job for you later. Now piss off.'

Wiggins looked back over his shoulder, but Molly had moved out of view. 'Outside,' Hannigan hissed in his ear.

They stood on the street, in the same place Fitz had parked the car all those weeks ago. Hannigan seemed to sense it too, for he looked down at the empty space where the motor had been. Then he looked up at Wiggins and put a hand on his chest. He held it there, palm first, gently, warm. It shivered Wiggins something awful.

'We need you,' Hannigan said. 'A heavy mob, up at one of Lynch's bars.'

'You need *me*?'

'Aye. The boss says you can fight. I think you're a weasel. But that's as he said. I'm short-staffed.'

Wiggins took Hannigan's hand and slowly removed it from his chest. 'At least you admit it.'

'Oh, I'll admit I need you, but not how the boss means it.' He glanced up and down the street. 'I need you because you know what happened to Fitz and you know where the money is. I'll get it out of you one way or another.'

'With your heavy mob?'

Hannigan snorted and began walking away up the street. He raised one hand in a fist and called back without looking, 'Be at the corner of Rutland and Summer Street, ten tonight.'

There was no escape. When orders came out of Hannigan's mouth, they came from the OC. And if Wiggins didn't turn up, then the OC would ditch him for sure – and if he was ditched, then he'd be back where he started, with a couple of shillings more in his pocket but a murder unsolved, blood on his hands perhaps, and the cause not advanced one inch. He wouldn't let Fitz's murder count for nothing.

After a couple of uneasy pints, Wiggins made his way on foot to the rendezvous. On the way he passed a show in a large hall on one of the big Dublin roads. It was crowded by the doorway, with folk straining for a look, but his curiosity got the better of him. He pushed inside, squeezing between those standing at the back of the audience. It was more of a public meeting than a show, though, and packed benches lined the hall all the way to the stage at the far end. Posters dotted the walls, advertising 'Classes in the Irish Language'. A number of men (men, always men) sat in a silent row at the back of the stage while another man addressed the crowd. Sure enough, the speaker used a tongue Wiggins guessed to be Irish, though what was happening was clearly no 'class'. Although Wiggins had to admit to himself that the last time he'd been in anything resembling a classroom was at the age of seven, and they'd learned nothing there except how to avoid the blows of the sadistic master. No formal teaching ever took place.

The man on the stage wasn't teaching either. He was speechifying, to an intensely interested audience. His passion grew. His fist waved. His finger jabbed. Every now and then, he broke into English, either to embellish the point or to translate it, Wiggins wasn't sure. He was about Wiggins's age, with a pale, clean-shaven face, a square head and a long nose. He wore a shabby suit, but he commanded the stage and the room with the power of his oration. He knew crowds, and he knew how to move them.

'I know what my work as an Irish nationalist is, and would have you know yours and buckle to it!' he cried in English, then lapsed once more into Irish. From the phrases he could make out, Wiggins realised this speech could have been delivered by Molly. She and the woman, Connie, could be this man's disciples. 'We are the voice of an idea,' his English broke out again, 'which is older than any empire and will outlast every empire!' The crowd – for it was a crowd, not a 'class' – roared.

Between the snatches of English and Irish, Wiggins got the point. Here was someone wanting to rid his country of the British Empire, to take it as their own. Wiggins thought of the Dublin he'd got to know, Fitz's Dublin, so poor that half the folk didn't even have the space to put a pot to piss in. He thought of the London he knew, too – not Kell's London, the London of Whitehall and Hampstead and Kensington, but his London, of the East End, Soho, down Lambeth and the rest. They lived in different countries, his people and Kell's; it wasn't only the Irish who were treated as foreigners in their own country.

'It's a terrible responsibility to cast on a man,' the speaker burst out in English once more. 'That of bidding the cannon speak and the grapeshot pour.' Wiggins glanced around. This was sedition, certainly dangerous talk. Not one of the massed men there batted an eye. Women neither.

'What's the fella's name?' Wiggins asked a man standing next to him.

The man looked at him oddly. 'That's Pearse, of course.'

Wiggins realised he'd made a mistake. A bum note on the piano. The man shifted uncomfortably and glanced around him, perturbed. He turned his gaze back on Wiggins for a moment. 'You English?' he said.

Wiggins nodded slightly, and looked back at the stage. The man instinctively followed his look, and Wiggins melted into the crowd.

He left the hall and walked quickly north. He realised he was going to be late for the rendezvous with Hannigan. It was another mistake. Those pints had put him off his game. Being late put him at a disadvantage. He'd learned it as an Irregular on the streets: whenever you're meeting anyone, anywhere, always turn up early to see the lie of the land, but appear late to the person you're meeting. It's the safest way, the only way.

This night, though, Wiggins was approaching blind, unprepared. He saw a tight knot of men on Rutland Street. They stood on the cusp of light cast by the street lamp. A dark point on a darkening night. It had taken a long time for the May sun to set, its red fronds disappearing after yet another cloudburst. Wiggins strode towards the men, Hannigan visible at their head, muttering. Six men in all. Even Wiggins didn't like those odds.

Hannigan saw him coming and stepped back from the group, almost in a welcoming gesture. 'Here's the man,' he said, grinning. 'Meet the lads. Toner, you know.'

Hannigan presented Wiggins to each of them. He had to lean in to shake their hands. As he did so for the third time, he heard a rustle behind him.

Hannigan roared, 'Now!' Wiggins avoided the first blow, and the second skimmed off his left shoulder. He crunched his elbow into someone's nose and took out another with his left boot. A man yelped in pain. Then a cosh caught him on the side of the head, someone got him in a headlock and his vision clouded.

As he passed out, Wiggins heard Hannigan's muffled shout. 'I'll kill the fucking bastard. I'll kill him.'

Wiggins dreamed. He dreamed of Bill, poor dead Bill. He dreamed about his boss, Captain Vernon Kell – *You do as I say, I pay you for Empire, for Country, for King*. He dreamed of Constance Kell, too, of Jax and Sal – of little Sal, back home on the streets of Paddington, boys screaming out in the night, *Come on, Wiggo, scarper, scarper, he's dead*. He dreamed of the woman with half a face, of Bela, falling into a deep black hole, falling into her face, her mind, drowning, drowning – d—

WHOOSH!

'Ahhh!' Wiggins gasped in surprise.

Whoosh!

Another bucket of cold water, full in his face, he realised with a surge of fear. His head and chest were soaked and his dreams were over.

As he opened his eyes, another blast of cold water met his face.

'He's alive,' a dark shape shouted, then left the room.

Wiggins's head pounded. He tried to lift his hand, but his arms were tied to the back of the chair. His legs were bound. He looked about him, squeezing his eyes tight to focus and to deal with the pain behind his left ear.

He sat in the centre of an unfurnished room. A single electric light bulb swung from the ceiling. The only window was shuttered, the floorboards were bare. The walls were bare too, apart from dirty smears here and there and one large, sinister stain that bled onto the floor. There was no furniture, save for an ornate wooden coatless coat stand. Wiggins guessed he was in the front room of one of the neat terraced houses north of the city; he guessed it was gone midnight too, judging by the silence. All he could hear was the fizzing of the bulb, and his own heart pounding in his ears.

After a moment, the door banged open and Hannigan swaggered in, with the huge lump Toner by his side. Hannigan, in his shirtsleeves, moved towards him without saying a word and then punched him flush in the face.

Wiggins's jaw sang with pain. He closed his eyes, set his shoulders. 'Ah, I needed that,' he said, and looked back at Hannigan. 'Ta.'

'Why did you kill Fitz?' Hannigan spat out the words. He wore a makeshift white bandage across his nose. Wiggins had to smile – it must have been Hannigan's nose that Wiggins had elbowed in the fight.

'Couldn't happen to a nicer bloke,' he said, still thinking of Hannigan's crushed nose.

Hannigan stared, then shifted his head slightly. Toner stepped forward and slammed a heavy fist into Wiggins's chest. It left him struggling to breathe.

'I'll wait for you to catch your breath,' Hannigan said. 'I wouldn't want you to miss the fun. Take off his shirt!'

Wiggins spluttered and gasped. Toner pulled his coat down around his arms, then ripped his shirt open to the waist.

'You a spy? Working for the Castle, are you?' Hannigan rasped, repeating again the accusation he'd spat at Wiggins almost every week for a month.

'I ain't working for the Castle,' Wiggins said truthfully. 'I keep telling you.'

'Is that so?' Hannigan pulled a cigarette from his top pocket and lit it thoughtfully. Then he stepped forward and put his other hand on Wiggins's bare chest, around the heart. He held it there, like a lover might.

'You should know,' Wiggins said carefully. 'You've had me followed for days.'

Hannigan's face hardened. He dragged heavily on the cigarette, tapped off the ash, then plunged the bright orange tip into Wiggins's chest.

Wiggins roared. Hannigan grinned, pulled back the smoke, then tossed it aside. 'Mahoney said he lost you in the Monster House. No one loses a tail like that lest they've been taught. Now, why are you here?'

Wiggins gripped the sides of the chair seat with his strapped hands. His muscles shook as the pain dissipated through his chest. 'That's done wonders for my hangover,' he gasped.

Hannigan nodded at Toner, who punched him in the face once more. 'What was that you said?' He lit another cigarette.

Wiggins tasted the blood in his mouth, the iron as familiar as death. 'I'm only working my way to New York, you know that.' He tried to catch his breath again. 'Ask O'Connell.'

Hannigan casually tapped the lit cigarette into his chest once more, lightly this time. 'Now, now,' he said as Wiggins screamed. 'Don't take the boss's name in vain. I'm going to ask you again. And if you lie to me this time, Jaysus alive, I'll find a gun from somewhere and blow your fucking kneecaps off, you understand?'

Wiggins cried out again. He writhed. He spat. And then he nodded.

'Good. You're getting the idea. Now, see. The OC may think the sun shines out of your arse, but I don't. So, what are you doing in Dublin?'

Wiggins tried to focus. His head was pounding, his chest felt on fire, the burnt-flesh smell caught in his nose. He spat more blood and rolled the words around his mouth, what he needed to say. 'I'm going to New York. My love, my life,' he mumbled at last. 'Her name's Bela. She had my best friend killed. She tried to get me killed. She played me for a fool. But she's still my love.' The closer to the truth he got, the hollower it sounded and so he gave up speaking. He closed his eyes, waited for the blow, waited for the cigarette, waited and waited. For he knew he'd cough up the truth eventually, then that would be the end. Everyone always coughed it up in the end, and Hannigan would kill him for sure. It was only a matter of time, but he had no other card to play. His head swam with pain. He was bound tight. The giant Toner glared at him, ready to punch once more. It might be a long night, a long last night. But he wasn't going to give it up easily. He'd been fighting all his life, on the streets, in the army, and he'd fight to the end. Fighting was what he did, what he'd always done. It's what they called living where he came from, and he'd live until he drew his last breath.

'Get me the pliers,' Hannigan said after a moment. 'I don't have a gun on me, so your kneecaps are staying where they are. But we can't have everything, so. I'll just have to pull your nails out one by one. You'll give up the money by then, and Fitz, and the—'

Wiggins heard a shout and more voices, and the sound of the front door opening. He looked up just as the door swung open and O'Connell appeared. He wore a spotless white suit and straw boater. In that bare room, under the buzzing of the single bulb, against the scarred and ripped and stained wallpaper, with the bloodied Hannigan by his side, and the sweating, hairy-knuckled Toner watching on, O'Connell looked like a unicorn. Magical, pristine, unreal. He stared at Wiggins. 'What the hell have you done to him?'

'He killed Fitz,' Hannigan said. 'He's Castle, too, I reckon.'

'Did he say that?'

'He will.'

O'Connell paused, then gestured at Toner. 'Untie the man, Toner. And get the fella a towel, see-ho.'

'But—' Hannigan stepped forward.

The OC put up his hand. 'Enough, Vincent, you hear? Enough!' He softened, dropped his hand back down. 'I know what the boy meant to you, but this ends now. Your man didn't kill him, sure he didn't.'

'What about the money?' Hannigan glared at Wiggins as Toner undid his bonds. 'He's a thief if nothing else.'

'Ach, and why would he still be here if he took the money? You said so yourself, this fella could melt into a desert, so he could. If he was rich, he wouldn't be sitting here taking tea with you now, would he?'

The fire still blazed in Hannigan, but it was behind his eyes. Wiggins saw the fight go out of him. He would never cross the OC. Something had passed between them, silent as smoke signals, but clear enough just the same. Master and servant. Hannigan put his head down silently, his shoulders slumped. 'Go on now,' the OC said. 'And get yourself to the sawbones – that nose looks awful bent.'

'What about him?' Hannigan said.

'He's coming with me,' O'Connell replied.

Wiggins, unbound, tried to stagger to his feet. 'Where to?' he gasped.

O'Connell turned to face him. 'New York.'

7

'Deal me in, boys.' A tall man approached the table and pulled up a chair. 'I feel lucky.' He handed his comically small derby to a follower, sat down and rubbed his hands together. It was stifling hot, so he wasn't rubbing them to keep warm. It was the action of a man sitting down to a feast.

Wiggins felt the hairs on his neck rise. The atmosphere of the table changed. The other poker players sat up straight, or shifted in their chairs, or checked their dollar bills, glancing twitchily at the clock. The tall man looked closely at everyone around the table in turn, his big, much-broken nose pointing at each player like an accusation. 'Let us make it five-card stud,' he said, and grinned. Nobody demurred.

The dealer nodded slightly. 'Mr Zelig,' he said. 'Five-card stud, gentlemen.'

Wiggins had been standing back from the table, behind O'Connell, who sat in the game. The OC nodded along to the change of rules. Wiggins couldn't see his face, but the twitches and sharp movements of his boss showed his anxiety. It was not the best state of mind in which to play cards.

They were in Segal's International Café, a large bar on Second Avenue, deep in the Lower East Side of Manhattan. The card table was one of three at the back of the joint, while up front men and women drank and danced and generally caroused. An enthusiastic band belted out a succession of upbeat tunes, fast and furious and unlike anything Wiggins had heard back in London. Heavy on the piano, with banjos, the ragged tempo jumped, and the dancers jumped too. There were even a couple of pool tables with painted signs hanging above: *1 cent a cue*.

Chalk dust filled the air, along with the smell of cheap bourbon, spilt beer and the smoke of countless cigarettes. Despite the gaiety and frivolity of the front of house, the card tables at the back were serious business.

Wiggins had spent most of the evening sipping a weak and frothy beer and studying the back of the OC's neck as he played. He'd also spent most of the evening wondering whether the OC was indeed responsible for Fitz's death. He could find no alternative suspect – except Hannigan, but Hannigan wouldn't have wiped his own arse without O'Connell's say-so – and yet too much didn't quite fit. Even if he did find evidence that they'd had Fitz killed, Wiggins wasn't quite sure what he could do about it. Justice wasn't a straight die.

To his credit, O'Connell *had* rescued him from Hannigan's grip back in Dublin and almost certainly saved his life. He owed him that debt if nothing else, although part of Wiggins – the cynical, sceptical part that had kept him alive his whole life – thought that O'Connell had been in on the whole set-up. Either way, he'd saved his life on the night itself.

'Help the man here, Toner, you hear?' That night, O'Connell had even put his own arm out to help Wiggins across the pavement and into the car. 'And get Vincent to the doctor, now. Sure, you've broken his nose, so you have.'

O'Connell had placed Wiggins carefully in the back seat of the Daimler and then got in beside him. Wiggins tried to breathe, tried to remember clearly the stories he had to tell. Why he was in Dublin and what he wanted. The OC always had to know what anyone wanted, and until he could find it out he would always be uneasy. Wiggins clung to that, and clung to the life raft the OC had offered him in those two words: New York.

One of the OC's men was at the wheel. He started the car and O'Connell waited for a moment. 'You're wanting to go to New York, aren't you, son?' he said.

Wiggins slumped beside him, bleeding and aching, and nodded his exhausted assent. 'Something like that,' he said quietly. 'To my love.'

O'Connell examined his sleeves in the light, dusting them as he spoke. 'You look after me, see-ho, and put me on the boat back in one piece, and I'll settle on you well enough, you'll find your lady love, and happy ever after.'

Wiggins, his body singing with pain from the burns, the punches and the deep, dark terror, whispered back, 'Why do you trust *me*? Ain't you got an hundred fellas who'd jump at the chance?'

'You're the best fighter I've ever seen, you're sharper than a room of Trinity dons, and most of all you're not Irish.'

'But why—'

'New York is a vipers' nest, a nest full of more Irish than the southern counties combined. If I took an Irishman, like as not he'd be related to half the Whyos in town. And could I trust a man to kill his own blood, if needed?'

'You're the boss.'

'Boss!' A waiter approached the card table and hissed at the big man, Zelig. Wiggins watched carefully, as he'd been doing the whole game.

'Not now,' Zelig said, without taking his eyes off the table. The waiter scuttled away. Zelig lifted his gaze to the OC. Another player took the opportunity to slip away, avoiding Zelig's eye. Only three players remained, and it was clear to Wiggins that Zelig had eyes only for the OC – the new guy in town. Wiggins leaned down to say something in his ear, but O'Connell waved him away, intent on the play.

Wiggins's mind drifted back to his own situation. After that initial confessional in the back of the car as they drove away from Hannigan and his pliers, the OC had become tight-lipped. He wasn't prepared to share his reasons for going to America, nor his plans for once they got there. Wiggins could guess well enough, however, and so it had proved. The OC needed cash. The OC had clearly lost money when Fitz had died (that Fitz had stolen), and he needed more. And America was the place for money.

New York, though, wasn't the ripe peach the OC had expected.

'Big Tim'll see me right,' he kept saying when they arrived. Big Tim Sullivan had indeed arranged for the OC to have a room in one of his hotels, the Metropole on 43rd and Broadway, but in the three weeks they'd been there, he had still refused to meet with O'Connell in person. Each day, the OC, with Wiggins at his side, trooped down to the Occidental Hotel on the Bowery – owned by Sullivan and where he lived, too – and waited for an audience that never came. Instead, O'Connell fretted and fidgeted and swapped telegrams with Hannigan in Dublin about 'the business'.

After the third day at the Occidental, Wiggins had asked, 'Who is this, anyway?'

'He's a Kerry man, or was. Big Tim Sullivan ran this town. When I was here in the nineties, he controlled downtown.'

'What do you mean "controlled"?'

O'Connell considered for a moment. 'New York was a gang town. Still is, as far as I can see. The Whyos, the Black Hand gang, the Irish, the Italians, the Jews, the Polacks. There's even a crowd called the Hudson Dusters now, by God. But it's not just these so-called criminals – the police are the biggest gang in New York, then you've got the judges, the councillors, the governor and the senators. It's a machine, a well-oiled machine, if you get my meaning.' He rubbed his finger and thumb together. 'Everyone's trying to make sure they get their cut of the pie. Big Tim controlled that machine downtown – the politics – which meant the coppers and the judges and the criminals, too. Aye, Big Tim'll see us right.'

'If he'll see us at all.'

Still the call didn't come. By their third week in New York, the OC's drinks had got larger. He spent more time in the bars that littered downtown Manhattan, and had now become embroiled in the gambling games going on in the stuss houses that seemed to line every street and alley in the city. Wiggins traipsed after him each evening, watching as the spruce, pristine big wheel of underbelly Dublin sweated and crinkled and diminished in front of his eyes.

And now, in Segal's International Café, with the big man Zelig hovering over the table, O'Connell seemed smaller than ever. Beads of sweat on the back of his neck glistened in the light as they played on.

Wiggins had guessed the reason why O'Connell was putting himself through the drawn-out humiliation, and why he was starting to become unhinged. She had reddish hair, green eyes and a way of moving that made even holy men blink. She'd been there the night Hannigan had tortured him, back at one of the OC's houses in Blessington Street. Molly.

The OC had helped him into the drawing room there, after cajoling him out of the car and up the steps – no easy feat after what Hannigan and Toner had done to him.

'What have they done,' Molly cried. She helped him to the purple chaise longue. 'He's half dead.'

'Vincent's enthusiasm got the better of him, so it did. But what can you expect from a Derry man?' O'Connell said.

She shot him an evil glance and turned her attention to the patient. Wiggins closed his eyes and listened as she tutted and gasped. He felt a flannel pressed against his brow. His muscles loosened and his breath slowed. Her hands kissed his cheek again, and he could smell her lemon-drop breath. Despite the searing pain, and the exhaustion as he passed out, he thought he was glad the OC was there, that he wasn't left alone with this dangerous woman.

Molly ended up coming with them to America. By design or on the spur of the moment, Wiggins didn't know. She and O'Connell took adjoining cabins above decks, while Wiggins slummed it in third. He didn't mind, the slow trip over gave him a chance to recover. He spent most of the journey in bed, tended to by a small boy who would bring him food and water in return for the odd penny. The bruises on his face began to pale. His cracked rib hurt only when he laughed. Though it was only the children, the wild children running the corridors and saloons of third class, that made him laugh. And the livid, open burns on his chest began to scar.

A nervous energy rippled through the corridors of the ship, especially at night, for it sailed the same route as the *Titanic*. But for most of the journey, Wiggins was too sore and too tired to care too much about his own fateful escape.

He spoke with Molly again only once, when they found themselves alone together at the rail. People had crowded towards the front of the ship when New York City first came into view. Wiggins, despite his studied cynicism and world-weary mien, felt a surge of excitement. He pushed forward like the rest in the stiff summer breeze.

'Is she there, do you think?' Molly said in his ear, surprising him. 'Your Bela? Your love?'

He swivelled towards her. She wore a long blue scarf that flapped and jerked in the wind. Her high cheeks reddened; her mouth turned up slightly, almost as if in mockery, but not quite. He thought about that adjoining cabin, and about her and the OC.

'I have no idea,' he said truthfully, and turned back to gaze at the far-off city.

'Is she why you're working for Patrick?'

Wiggins hesitated, momentarily disappointed. Something about Molly had made him think she was different. All her talk of Irish independence and of standing up to the Empire had carried some weight with him. It wasn't often you heard toffs prepared to take on the world, to overturn the way things were. But, just like everyone else in her class, she assumed that Wiggins had much choice in who he worked for or what he did for money. Kell was the same. It was as if they thought that people actually wanted to be chimney sweeps or powder monkeys or street sweepers. He shrugged away her question.

She placed a hand next to his on the rail. Wiggins didn't look at her. Instead, he counted eight tiny red cotton diamonds that were stitched into the beaten blue leather glove. She gripped the rail hard, no flimsy woman here. His hand went instinctively to the healing cut above his eye. The OC had told him that Molly would be catching a train to Boston as soon as they arrived.

Wiggins knew he'd probably never get a chance to talk to her alone again.

He moved his gaze from her hands back out to sea. 'You know who killed Fitz?'

'Who?' she said. 'Oh, Patrick's boy, the body in the barrel? I don't know. Awful, utterly awful.'

He caught her eye for a moment. 'He was sweet on you, you know?'

She shook her head slightly. Just then the horn let out an ear-splitting blast. The passengers at the rail cheered, and the men waved their hats. Molly looked back at the great funnels.

'Sweet,' she said at last. 'Such an innocent word.' She turned to go, then paused. 'Patrick's doing something very important. Look after him, won't you?'

'Look after him,' she'd said, *look after him*. Molly's words on the ship came back to him as he looked over the game. He moved close behind the OC's chair at the poker table. Zelig dominated the game now, as if none of the other players felt comfortable taking money off him. There were only two players left, other than Zelig and the OC.

O'Connell wasn't a bad poker player, but Wiggins had realised the game wasn't straight. Never, ever gamble against the owner of the house. He'd tried to get O'Connell to leave once already, but seeing the size of the pot, he leaned down again to whisper in his ear.

'Get away from me, you old woman,' the OC shot back angrily. 'It's the big boys here.' He reached for his glass quickly, but ended up tipping it over part of the table.

'Hey watch it, Mick,' Zelig said.

'The name's Paddy,' O'Connell scowled. 'Deal the cards, see-ho.'

Zelig grinned, and gestured to the waiter to fill everyone's glasses. 'Easy, Pops, these are on me.'

Wiggins shifted closer to O'Connell and stood by his shoulder. For all his easy words, Zelig exuded power and impatience. Something was coming.

Another hand was played, the notes piled up, the OC's head swayed slightly, a glass smashed at the bar, distracting him. He got up. 'I need a piss,' he muttered, holding a hand halfway towards Wiggins as if to ask for help.

'Hey, old man,' Zelig said. 'Where is your dollar?'

'I'm pissing.'

'But this is my pot, and you are a dollar light.' Zelig stood up and began sweeping the money in the centre of the table towards him. The OC stumbled. The other players scraped back their chairs.

'Hold it there, mate.' Wiggins thrust his hand onto Zelig's, pinning the money to the table. 'That ain't your pot.'

An audible gasp went around the table. 'Says who?' Zelig said.

Wiggins stared at him and didn't let go. Zelig glanced towards the bar and shifted his chin in a clear signal. In that moment of hesitation, Wiggins cracked Zelig's fingers back. The huge man let out a great yowl as Wiggins swept up the notes. He grabbed O'Connell by the shoulder. 'Come on.'

Zelig clattered over the table, roaring. He aimed a haymaker at Wiggins with his good hand. Wiggins swayed back, then drove his palm into Zelig's chin.

The OC stared, mouth agape. Wiggins pushed him towards the door, but again Zelig came spluttering back. Wiggins feinted right, then caught him flush with a straight left. He followed with a stamp on his knee and a right hook as Zelig crumbled to the floor. In his peripheral vision, he could see men hustling towards them from the bar, angry shouts, a dicey spot.

He ripped a pool cue from the wall and smashed it into Zelig's back and head repeatedly. He didn't like knocking a man out, but they weren't going to get out alive if the big man stayed up.

The cue snapped in his hands and he tossed it towards the bar and roared at the OC to run.

Uproar and chaos. The band ground to a halt, all but the lone, faltering piano. Women screamed. Men swivelled and bristled. And through it all, Wiggins hustled the OC out onto the street.

As he got there, he heard an outraged cry: 'There, there! Get that fuckhead Englishman. Leave the old guy. I want the Englishman. Go go go!'

The Second Avenue streetcar groaned and rattled as it left the nearby stop going north. Wiggins half pushed, half carried the OC alongside. In a final act of strength, Wiggins pitched him onto the back platform as it picked up speed, and clung on himself. In a second, he hauled the OC and then himself out of view just in time.

As it sped up Second Avenue, Wiggins looked over the lip of the conductor's seat. Three of Zelig's heavies burst out of the café, followed by the man himself. They looked around, clearly without a motor car and without any idea where Wiggins had gone.

All this time, the conductor hadn't batted an eyelid, and neither had any of the other passengers. The conductor waited until Wiggins had pushed the OC into a seat and then swung towards them.

Wiggins held up one of the dollar bills from the poker game and slumped back. No one said a word.

O'Connell had recovered a little by the time they got off at 43rd Street, enough that he could walk unaided. Wiggins helped him to the sidewalk, and they turned their sights back to his hotel – which stood a few blocks away, just off Times Square. The streets alternated between darkness and light, rich and poor, loud and quiet, empty and full. Out ahead of them, the lights of Times Square grew stronger and more brilliant, an electrified wonder of the world glimpsed along a straight road, funnelling up into the night sky above them.

Wiggins lifted his head and looked up. Off to his left, high up on one of the fire escapes that zigzagged down the front of the buildings, he saw a large man standing in only his underpants. And then he saw the rest. Men, women and children lying on mattresses, fanning their faces, sleeping, living outside. Over the last three days, New York had become a furnace. Wiggins had experienced heat on the veldt, out in South Africa, but nothing like this all-encompassing, dripping sweat. What made it worse

– incredible, almost – was that everyone dressed the same, in heavy suits, wide felt hats, waistcoats, long skirts, as if they were living in a normal northern city and not an oven. The only concession to the heat was this night-time display, this inside-out living, as people clung to the tenements like seabirds scrabbling for purchase.

'I'm sorry about that, back there,' O'Connell said at last. 'I lost my edge for a moment.' He shuffled some more. Wiggins put his hand to his nose. Every now and then they passed a sewage vent and in the heat the smell was unbearable. O'Connell didn't seem to notice. 'So I'm guessing you know why we're here, in America,' he added.

'Money?'

'But you don't know the why of the why, clever clogs, do you? Do you?' O'Connell repeated.

Wiggins shook his head. 'I know what you tell me.'

'That's right, by God it is!' O'Connell barked angrily. After a while, he sighed and went on. 'I'm sorry. That's the drink talking, so it is. I'm feeling a little melancholic, see-ho? You've found your lady love, have you? No, of course you haven't. You've been holding my hand. I'm sorry, so I am. Love is a bastard to find, and even when you've found it, you can't know if you've ever got hold of it. I don't like not knowing, Wiggins, you see? I was the oldest of twelve. Think of that, the oldest of twelve. And I never knew which of them would grow up to be my brother or sister. Three did. They've gone now, too, but I hated not knowing. I've always hated it.' He heaved another breath, and looked ahead.

'Is Big Tim going to come through?'

'Ach, maybe Big Tim's not what he was – not since Little Tim passed over. But he's still my way in. He'll still see me right. He knows I'm Dublin, and that means something.'

They were almost at the hotel now, with the gleaming city of light that was Times Square only just beyond.

'Vincent is telling me things about Fitz over the wires,' O'Connell went on. 'I'll get to the bottom of his death, with your help or without it. You understand?' O'Connell's voice had regained its hard edge. He bent his head towards Wiggins until the younger man grunted an assent.

Wiggins couldn't read his face in profile, couldn't quite decide whether or not O'Connell meant these words as a threat. Whatever else this was, though, it was an assertion of power. 'Is that why we're here?' he asked, as artlessly as possible.

O'Connell laughed suddenly, breaking the tension in a second, flipping his mood. They'd come to a halt outside the Hotel Metropole. Wiggins had digs in a flophouse over the other side of Broadway, while O'Connell was put up in the hotel as a guest of Big Tim. The OC placed his hands on Wiggins's shoulder and looked him in the face. His eyes were glassy and slightly awry, but there was still affection in his manner. Like an older man who'd known him since he was a child, and could smile fondly at such simple-mindedness. 'Wiggins, boy, we're here for a woman.'

It was gone two in the morning by the time Wiggins found himself the other side of Times Square. He'd avoided the drunks and the panhandlers, the bawling cops, the streetwalkers, the women, and the bars open to the street, with the same ragged music spilling out into the electric night; now he walked east along 48th Street the other side of Eighth. It wasn't far to his flophouse and he felt the weariness in his bones that comes after exertion, but also after relaxation. He didn't have to look out for the OC until the morning, he didn't have to look out for anyone.

Up ahead of him, he saw a gaggle of poor children bunched around a game of some sort. They crouched down on the sidewalk, as awake and alive as if it had been two in the afternoon. It was hot enough, for sure.

Beyond them, a large figure suddenly appeared, striding towards the kids with intent. He was massive, with his shoulders, gut and upper body forming one enormous slab. A monolith, topped by a bullet-shaped head, small and violent atop the bulk. 'Get outta here,' he cried at the children as he swung wild blows at their heads. 'Go on. It's out of bounds!'

A wail went up as the man-mountain kicked the dice they'd been using into the gutter and connected with a small child who'd slipped to the ground in his attempt at escape.

'Easy on.' Wiggins came up and reached out a hand to the big man's arm. 'He's only a nipper.'

The man swivelled. His eyes flashed dark. 'Who the hell are you?'

Wiggins hesitated. He was exhausted, physically beaten, and this man rippled with violence and anger and must have had three weight divisions on him if he had an ounce. 'Look, I don't want no trouble. It's just they's only small.'

'They're vermin.' The man spat, then glared suspiciously at Wiggins. 'I don't know you. You English?'

'London.' By this time, the children had all run off and the remains of their dice game lay scattered in the street. Wiggins went on. 'They's gone now anyways, no harm done.' He patted the big man on the chest in a friendly way.

The big man, momentarily distracted by the escaping children, now glared back at Wiggins. He was downlit by the street lamps, a face of shadows and menace. He put his hand up. Wiggins edged backwards, his arms now out wide, placatory.

A motor-car door slammed across the street and the big man turned to see who was there. Then he looked back at Wiggins, hatred in his eyes. 'This is a warning, mister,' he called. 'I don't like men who get in the way of my business. And I don't like your face. Stay out of this precinct, you hear.'

It wasn't until Wiggins had made it back to his room in the flophouse, a slither of an attic space up six flights of a stinking, broiling, dirty, overstuffed, loud, drunken, drug-addled, extortion racket of a flophouse, that he slumped down on the bedroll and pulled from his waistband the two items he'd dipped from the large man's breast pocket moments earlier.

Wiggins didn't enjoy thieving as a rule, but the big man who liked hitting children deserved a lesson, and Wiggins had been too tired to deliver a physical one. He looked at the items.

One was a letter inside an envelope addressed to a John J. Donohue.

The other item was a polished brass badge in the form of a fat, six-pointed star. Underneath the star, attached and also in brass, was the number 35. Just above this, in small, squashed letters, was the word *Lieutenant*.

Written in even smaller writing, etched in a circle around the inside of the star, were the words *City of New York Police*.

8

Wiggins dreamed deeply once more. This time he dreamed of London, of the smell, of the river, of the old Blockmakers on Sunday. He dreamed of Bela, he dreamed of Molly too, with pleasure and shame. The OC screaming in his face, *Your lady love, your lady love, ain't it grand?* Bela's face, then gone, back to the old Covent Garden, rotting onions crushed in the gutter, back, back, *get the little bastard.* A copper's whistle blowing, blowing again, *whee, whee*—

WHEEE!

Wiggins woke with a start, sweating. *Whee, whee!* The air was thick with the sound of whistles coming up from the street. He heard a great crack as a door downstairs burst open. Shouts and screams echoed through the building.

He thrust open his door and glanced down the stairs. A man stood on the landing in cotton shorts and nothing else, shaking his head. Down the stairwell, half-dressed people shouted and complained. At the bottom, just as Wiggins looked over, two gigantic policemen came into view. 'This is a raid! Nobody move,' one cried, and held his club up high.

Wiggins skipped back into his room and hurried to the window. On the street below, more policemen stormed the front door. An open van stood on the road. And beside it, directing operations, the man-mountain from the night before – this time in uniform, but his physicality nevertheless unmistakable. Just as Wiggins looked out of the window, the man glanced up. His dark eyes widened and he pointed his enormous finger. 'There!' he cried.

Wiggins ducked back out of sight. He could hear the cops beating their way up the stairs towards him. 'Get outta here!'

someone shouted angrily. 'I haven't even had coffee.' Wiggins pulled on his boots, filled his pockets and then, without a second thought, he clambered through the window.

As he did so, he heard the police lieutenant cry out once more, but this time Wiggins didn't hesitate. He didn't look down either. On tiptoe, he swung across onto the rickety iron fire escape that zigzagged down to street level.

'Top floor, top flop,' the lieutenant cried. 'You're going down, Englishman.'

Wiggins did not go down. He balanced on top of the handrail and stretched for the roof. He leapt. His fingers caught, just. With his cracked rib complaining, he hauled himself onto the flat roof of the tenement, the policeman's angry shouts ringing out from below. 'I told you,' Wiggins shouted at him. 'I ain't English, I'm London.' And then he ran off.

He slid to a halt over the far side of the building. Strung between the back of the tenement and the next one – on the other block – were hundreds of pieces of laundry. They hung on lines between the two buildings, over the yards below. Like bunting at the old Queen's big event, flags flapping, red, white and blue, and green and white, and white, white, white, like the flags in South Africa, the white of surrender. But Wiggins would not surrender.

Before he could persuade himself otherwise, he jumped. He missed the first line but caught the second under his armpits. It snapped at one end and he swung down, swaying, ripping sheets as he fell into the next line, and then another and a third, slowing each time in the madcap tumble. A big sheet ripped.

'Hey, that's my best shirt,' someone hollered.

For one second, he thought he was a goner. A line snapped in the middle, but his arm caught at the last moment onto a stronger cable. He swung down the last ten feet and dropped to the floor.

'Sorry, guv,' he shouted up to the windows above, sparing a thought for the stranger's ripped shirt.

He set off at a run to the far tenement building, fighting his way through the fallen bed sheets as he did so and into the open back entrance of the ground floor. A charwoman stared at him open-mouthed as he barrelled past. In the distance, he could still hear the whistles of the policemen. Despite the ruined washing, he knew no one would lift a finger to help the cops. This was Hell's Kitchen, that wasn't how they did things here.

Wiggins came out onto 47th Street and turned towards Broadway. A streetcar rattled north up Eighth Avenue and he just had the energy to run and jump its sideboard. The conductor yelled at him. 'No jay riders!'

Wiggins grinned. 'What's the fare?'

He got off at Columbus Circle. He'd escaped the police, he was sure, but he took no chances. He got on another streetcar, then changed again until, an hour or so later, he was walking back down Broadway north of Times Square and considering what to do. There was no way he'd be spotted on this street. Broadway was a river of humanity at most times of day, and certainly at ten in the morning. He couldn't go back to the flophouse, that was sure. The angry policeman was certainly after his badge, and possibly the letter too. He wondered whether he could go back to the Metropole and O'Connell. There was nothing left in the flophouse to connect him to the OC, so there was no reason to suppose that the cops would find him there. On the other hand, he didn't know how they'd found him in the flophouse in the first place.

His mind began to wander. Ever since he'd arrived in New York, he couldn't rid his thoughts of Bela. Each night since he'd arrived, Bela had infiltrated his dreams in one way or another. That lie he'd spun in Dublin, first to Fitz, then to the OC and finally to Molly. Was it really a lie? Outside the Occidental, past the Bowery, was the area called the Lower East Side, and he and the OC had walked through parts of it a couple of times. It reminded Wiggins of the East End and the people reminded him of Peter the Painter, Yakov and Bela. Not only their clothes and their looks, but even the languages he heard spoken on the streets. If she was in New York, she would be there, he knew, or if not there a route to her could be found among its people. Did he really want to find her? Was that the truth?

And what if it wasn't true? Did that mean he could sleep with Molly without guilt, for he couldn't deny that she, too, was stalking his ever-more vivid dreams. Each day he saw the OC diminished, part of him – a deep, dark part of him – became excited at the thought of taking her in his arms, forgetting all that was due and all that might happen, and letting the cards fall as they may. But maybe Molly was an impossible play.

Undecided in heart and mind, he turned into a bustling diner just north of Times Square. He squeezed into a booth opposite a man hidden by the two folds of a daily newspaper.

'Whaddayawant?' The waitress slapped down a knife and fork.

'Steak and eggs.'

'Drink?'

Wiggins hesitated.

'The java here is passable.' The man opposite drew down his paper and nodded at his coffee cup. 'If passable is the step above dishwater, but below actual drinking water.'

Wiggins nodded at the cup, and the waitress sped off. He surveyed his table companion. He was about his own age, with a strong chin and a petulant mouth, slightly turned down. He wore the stiff collar and pressed cuffs of someone due in an office at some point. But his eyes danced with curiosity and a rare kindness.

'My,' the man said. 'You look on me as if I am an exhibit in the Metropolitan Museum of Art. I do not think anyone has looked at me with this much attention since I was first introduced to my ever-loving mother. What do you make of me?'

'You sure?' Wiggins said.

The man nodded.

'Newspaperman. Reporter, writer, whatever you call it here. Sport maybe, not the hard stuff. Ain't from round here.'

'But I am from Manhattan,' the man interjected.

'Really?'

'Manhattan, Kansas.' The man smiled.

Wiggins went on, encouraged. 'You're recently married, you like a drink, but . . .' Wiggins paused '. . . you ain't touched one in a while. 'Cept the old java here.'

The man stared back, smiling still, but it had set at this last revelation. He shifted in his seat and pushed his newspaper to one side. 'It would appear you know everything about me that you need to know to make a bet, other than my name. Are you a magician? A mind-reader?'

'What's your name?' Wiggins asked, grinning.

'My name is—'

'Baseball!' A voice rang out across the diner. It belonged to a very smartly dressed man in a white linen suit, tie and a straw boater. He gestured at the man opposite Wiggins. 'Save me a seat, I'll be with you directly.'

The newspaperman shrugged. 'My last secret gone,' he said. 'Baseball is my name, and my trade too, by way of the written word. And what brings a soul such as yourself to my table? I do not possess your godlike powers. I guess – you are an Englishman?'

'London,' Wiggins said automatically. Just then, his steak and eggs appeared. Baseball gestured for another cup of coffee. It wasn't in Wiggins's nature to confide in people. Where he came from – the streets – knowledge was power, and you never gave it away without a price. But he was a blind man in Manhattan, he'd just escaped the cops and he needed to know where he stood. He needed knowledge himself, and the best way of acquiring it was by sharing his own. Baseball had the kind of face that you could confide in too – open, trusting, but smart. He wouldn't miss a word, and wouldn't punish you for a wrong one. He had the look of a man who'd been listening to people's stories all his life.

Wiggins finished his first mouthful, then fished out the lieutenant's badge and put it on the table. 'I took this off someone last night,' he said. 'Teach him a lesson, like. Turns out he's a body who wants it back.'

Baseball looked down at the badge. 'This is a rare object. I take it the body to whom it belongs is still alive.'

'Alive, big and very angry.' Wiggins told him what had happened the night before, and his subsequent escape in the morning.

Just then, the man in the white linen suit slipped into the booth beside Baseball. 'Good morning, Baseball. Who is your new friend?' He smiled at Wiggins. The smile couldn't conceal this man's power, though. He was dressed like a picture of a wealthy young New Yorker in summer, right down to the dicky bow. His nails shone bright and neat, his teeth glistened and his hair looked cut yesterday.

'This is London,' Baseball said. 'London, beware, this is the Brain. He is so smart that he could lay you odds that the earth is flat and somehow win that bet while selling you a globe at the same time.'

'I don't gamble, at least not with money,' Wiggins said.

Baseball's cup clattered onto the table. The Brain stared, openmouthed. It was as if Wiggins had farted in front of the King.

'You do not gamble?' Baseball said. 'How is this possible, Brain? Here is a man on Broadway who does not gamble.'

'I have heard of such people,' the Brain said. 'But they are strange and unusual, like a bird that does not fly. What was your name again, sir?'

'London will do,' Wiggins said.

The Brain thrust out his hand. 'Rothstein. Please ignore my friend here. He has a way of letting his words run down the street. What's this?' Rothstein added, looking down at the stolen police badge.

'London,' Baseball explained, 'is by way of being a white knight, in the line of Camelot, et cetera. I know, I know, he is not dressed in the knightly way, but last night he saves some small children – who, I may say, are doing nothing but skipping and laughing, tee hee, as children are prone to do. London here saves them from the unwanted attentions of an officer of the law, and by way of issuing a moral corrective, he dips the said officer.'

Halfway through this story, Rothstein swiped the badge into

his hand and looked at Wiggins with an expression of growing respect. When Baseball had finished his story, Rothstein held up the badge. 'This is a big problem for you,' he said to Wiggins. 'For this badge belongs to the meanest, dirtiest cop in New York. This theft is the talk of the Tenderloin already. It belongs to Charles Becker.'

Baseball whistled.

'And he is . . . ?'

Rothstein set the badge back down and covered it with a napkin. 'You are fresh in town, I see. Let me explain. Becker is the head of a strong-arm squad, right here in the Tenderloin.'

'Tenderloin?'

'The juiciest part of Manhattan,' Baseball put in. 'It is in this part of town that you have various illegal activities. Gaming, brothels and whatnot. Others of a more Christian persuasion are known to call it Satan's Circus, on account, perhaps, of it being adjacent to Hell's Kitchen. But I digress. The strong-arm squads are like to come in and break up such activities, by way of appearing in the newspapers.'

'He didn't look like no hero to me,' Wiggins said.

'He is not,' Rothstein replied in a hushed tone. 'It's not called the Tenderloin for nothing. That's what the cops call it too, because that's how they make most of their money in this town. Becker just paid cash in full on a nine-thousand-dollar house in Brooklyn, on a two-thousand-dollar-a-year salary. His morality does not look like a good bet to me.'

'Bribes?'

'Graft,' Rothstein nodded. 'He is up to his neck in half the stuss joints in the city, and willing to fight to stay there. So,' Rothstein gestured at the table, 'while I'm very impressed with this fine piece of street work – dipping Becker is a famous move, your name will be hallowed by all the fingersmiths and pavement artists on Broadway for years to come – as I say, it is dangerous for you. The NYPD is no enemy to have.'

The waitress reappeared with more coffee, and a huge wedge of cheesecake for Rothstein. She fussed with Wiggins's now empty plate while no one spoke. Once she was gone, Rothstein ate a piece of cake and then turned to Baseball. 'Did you hear the news from downtown?'

'What news?'

'The Lower East Side can talk of nothing else. Last night someone beat up Big Jack Zelig. He is stomping all down Second Avenue, screaming blue murder.'

'What happened?'

'He sharped some old man, as he does, but the old man had a bodyguard. My accounts are all mixed up, except that Big Jack took a beating and now he is screaming for Gyp the Blood and Lefty Louie.'

Wiggins slowly raised his hand. 'That might have been me.'

Rothstein turned to look at him in astonishment and awe. Wiggins went on. 'This Zelig fella, kink in the nose? Hat two sizes too small, pigeon-toed? Works out of Segal's International Café?'

Baseball gaped, for once wordless. Rothstein shook his head in admiration. Finally, Baseball blurted out, 'First you dip Becker, then you biff Zelig – what do you do for an encore, march on Moscow?'

Rothstein considered. 'This is another bad thing to do. Jack Zelig is in charge of discipline in the Lower East Side – you might say he is the police there, for what the police cannot do. He prides himself on his fighting skills. If I were you, I would not go back there. Nor here. In fact, New York may not be the smartest place for you to be at all.'

Wiggins shook his head. 'It ain't that easy.'

'He has put your name out. Gyp the Blood and Lefty Louie carry rods, always. And they are interested parties who are very far from being scared to use such implements. In fact, I would go so far as to say that they quite enjoy firing these guns.'

Wiggins couldn't help but smile. He liked the way these people spoke. 'Thanks for the warning,' he said. 'They friends of yours, are they? Or yous just know of them?'

'The Brain,' Baseball butted in, 'knows just about everything that goes on in this city. Especially those, ahem, corners of the city that respectable, law-abiding citizens such as ourselves are wont to avoid.'

Rothstein dabbed at his mouth delicately with a napkin, then folded it up. 'Well, London, if you decide to stay in this town, and you stay alive – which is, what, 100 to 30? – then you can come work for me. Anyone who can dip Charley Becker is a good man to know. And anyone who can best Jack Zelig in a set-to is a man you would want by your side in a clinch. Now, you should sell me that – it will bring you nothing but trouble.'

'This?' Wiggins held up Becker's NYPD badge. 'I'm all right for blunt. But you can have it anyway.'

Rothstein glanced at Baseball. 'I told you,' the reporter said. 'He is a man of honour. It is a wonder this table is not round.'

Wiggins handed Rothstein the badge. In return, Rothstein scribbled down an address on a piece of card. 'As I say, you want a job, you come to this address and ask for me.' He stood up to go.

'I don't want a job, but I might need a favour.'

'A favour?'

'At some later date,' Wiggins added.

'He is taking your marker, Rothstein. For the badge,' Baseball said.

Rothstein nodded. 'You have my marker,' he said, and left.

Baseball shook his head slowly, in admiration. 'That was a very fine piece of negotiation, London.'

'I didn't negotiate anything.'

'That badge. The Brain there is the smartest man in New York. What he does not know does not need knowing. He is the best bookie there is, and will give you the real odds on anything in this town. And now, you have his marker.'

Wiggins grunted. He looked down at Rothstein's half-eaten cheesecake. 'He's scarpered without paying for his grub.'

Baseball laughed. 'Do not worry. He will have settled the account for all of us.'

'But I didn't see—'

'You do not see, but it happens all the same. That is Arnold Rothstein.'

Wiggins said goodbye to Baseball and continued his way down Broadway to Times Square. He'd got rid of the policeman's badge, but he still felt weighed down. It was careless to have made two such powerful enemies in one night, the policeman Becker and the criminal Zelig. He was getting sloppy. Ever since he'd left Dublin, he'd begun to relax. Out of Hannigan's firing line, with only really the OC to fool, he'd lost his edge. But he couldn't give up now; he still had to find Fitz's killer. He wasn't going to leave the OC just yet, and he wasn't leaving New York.

He stole a bright new boater from a gentlemen's outfitters on the strip, and exchanged his coat for a navy blue blazer – again unseen by the harassed staff. They didn't give him a second look, regardless of what he was dressed like. He'd noticed that about America, or New York, at least: they didn't really care what class he was from; he wasn't marked the same way as back in London, or Dublin, for that matter.

Most people really did treat class as just the guinea stamp, if they noticed it at all. Take the man Rothstein. He was obviously high-class. He had the duds, he had the swank and the manners, but he didn't think twice about addressing Wiggins as an equal. An exchange like that would have been almost unthinkable back in England. Even in the heat and blast and hellish dying dirt of Ladysmith, with women and children starving and his captain shitting his own life out in the dirt, with Bill holding his hand and all, still the bounds of class had stopped a true word. Even teetering on the lips of hell, the officer had still worried about social rank.

Rothstein hadn't hesitated to talk with Wiggins and, as Baseball said, the exchange had worked out well. Still, Wiggins wasn't as green as all that – he'd given up the policeman's badge easily enough. To him it meant nothing, and without Rothstein's intervention it didn't even have any value. But he'd known that doing a favour to such a man was worth more than money. Wiggins hadn't told him about the letter, however, the one he'd dipped from the copper, addressed to John J. Donohue. Again, it didn't do any harm to keep something close to your chest. It could be leverage if he were to run into Becker again.

It had contained a document in the form of a mortgage between this Donohue character and a man named Herman Rosenthal. Wiggins didn't know either name – although he assumed Donohue was an alias of Becker's – but it had an address on it. He detoured off Broadway to West 45th Street, just off Sixth Avenue. The house was a four-storey brownstone, no different from its neighbours except in one remarkable respect. Its large wooden door was split in three places and hanging off its hinges to boot. Wiggins barely glanced at it as he walked quickly past on the other side of the road.

He turned at the end of the street, then headed back for a closer look. He was hidden enough by the mid-afternoon bustle. Children flocked around great bricks of ice on the sidewalk, glistening blue and white, set out for the various vans coming and going – the ice-cream men, the drugstores, the bars. The sound of the young children echoed between the high buildings. Delivery vans rattled by. Wiggins watched as someone tossed a package of newspapers to a waiting shopkeeper, a livid green *Variety* on the top.

As he reached the house with the broken door again, he paused and peered into the hall. A policeman in uniform sat in the hallway and stared back at him. 'Whaddya want?' he called, standing up and putting his hand on his hip.

Just then, a plump man in a tight-fitting serge suit appeared behind the policeman. As he pushed his way past, he called, 'Out of my way, Officer Jones. I'm trying to get out of here. If you're at a loose end, I believe my wife has some fresh iced tea upstairs.'

'Served with razor blades? I'll take a rain check, thanks, Herman.'

'Suit yourself,' the plump man said and came out onto the street. He cast an idle glance at Wiggins. 'You looking for action? Well, we're closed – at least until I can get that monkey out of my hall.' He dabbed at his sweaty head with a handkerchief. 'I'd give you a steer, but there isn't a straight house from here to Coney Island.' With that, he sighed heavily and waddled off down the street.

Wiggins cut away in the other direction, before the cop took any more interest. The owner referred to in the letter was Herman Rosenthal, which had to be the plump man, but Wiggins had no idea why a policeman would be sitting in the hallway. He doubled back up Sixth Avenue, then swung right again, to the Hotel Metropole.

He sauntered, easy and unhurried, despite the presence of beat cops at many of the corners – he reasoned his disguise was good enough, certainly in the crowds around Times Square. He guessed that O'Connell would still be at the hotel. It wasn't yet two o'clock, and although he'd been used to heading down to the Occidental in the morning, Wiggins reasoned that the extra liquor of the night before might make the OC start late. In any case, he'd almost certainly wait for Wiggins to show before venturing down the Bowery.

There was a crowd around a hokey-pokey cart. The ice-cream seller called out in an Italian accent, 'Vanilla, vanilla. Chocolate, chocolate. Iceeeee-cold.' Wiggins inserted himself into the hubbub of kids and hot, hungry adults and took a few minutes to observe the hotel.

The Metropole had two entrances. One directly into the lobby, the other into the hotel's bar and cafe. Whatever time of night he and the OC returned, the bar was open and busy, jumping to the sound of fast and furious piano music. And filled, so far as Wiggins could make out, with gamblers and showgirls, actors and drunks, until gone 3 a.m. at the earliest. In fact, he'd never seen it shut. Even in the afternoon it buzzed and hummed with steady consumption, visible through the large corner windows.

Wiggins decided that if he stayed any longer among the ice-cream buyers, it would attract more attention than if he went into the hotel. In any case, he wasn't the kind of man who could wait outside a bar for too long. Even thinking about a pub made him thirsty.

He went in and sat at a corner seat of the bar, which gave him a view through the glass door to the lobby. O'Connell would have to come past, whether he was leaving or entering the hotel. He ordered a short beer and a large whiskey, and waited.

The barman made elaborately mixed drinks. He waved a shaker wildly. He tossed cubed ice into the air and caught it in glasses with practised ease. His hair was plastered with oil, a harsh slash down the centre that reminded Wiggins of a beetle.

'What do you call this music?' Wiggins asked the barman at last, nodding towards the pianist.

The barman gave him an odd look. 'Rag, mister, it's a rag. Where are you from, Canada?'

A glass smashed at the far side of the bar. A flame-haired old man was making a bit of a scene. He broke into song, and Wiggins recognised the Irish accent. It was a song about the Pope and King Billy, more a comic rhyme. He'd actually heard Fitz sing something similar, as a joke. But now the old man was shouted down. A waiter came over. 'Siddown and drink or get outta here!'

The flame-haired Irishman nodded, and stumbled over to the banquette by the front doors. 'Beer,' he cried, then held a hand over his mouth in a theatrical show of silence.

Wiggins was about to signal the barman for the same when a great kerfuffle erupted from the lobby. He looked up and saw the blue coats, brass buttons and swinging nightsticks of the cops – three or four at least. The bar went quiet. Even the pianist got the message. Everyone stared at their drinks. One of the cops came through the door adjoining the lobby and glanced about the room.

'Anyone seen an Irishman by the name of O'Connell?' he shouted. 'Anyone?'

No one said a word. The policeman swung his stick into his free hand at regular intervals, but didn't move. Shouts came from the lobby again. Wiggins saw O'Connell himself frogmarched past the glass doors and out into the street. The policeman at the door looked over his shoulder, then looked back at the bar one last time, and was gone.

Everyone in the café let out their breath simultaneously. Even the loud-mouthed old Irish guy had kept his trap shut. Out of the window, Wiggins saw the police wagon drive past, going north with his current boss, his paymaster, the one with the cash. As he always did when his life reached a low ebb, he ordered another glass of beer.

Maybe he should have taken up Rothstein's offer of a job. The guy obviously had money to burn, and he looked like he knew how to spend it. But it was still someone else's money, and didn't it all taste the same, wherever it came from? Sherlock Holmes, the army, Tobias Leach, Captain Vernon bloody Kell and now Patrick O'Connell – he'd run around after all of them, doing whatever they said for a shilling or two. Why add Rothstein to the list?

As he contemplated the bitter harvest of his life, Wiggins began to notice something about the flame-haired drunken Irishman currently insulting his fellow patrons from a seat by the front door. He wasn't drunk.

There was something theatrical about his movements, too precise, too obviously sloppy and showy, and every so often his quick eyes flicked to the large mirror across the back of the bar, as if the man was fixing the scene in his head, before then going on another drunken flight of fancy.

Wiggins put a coin on the bar and got up. He walked past the flame-haired man and straight out the front door. On the street, he hesitated behind one of the large pot plants standing sentinel by the hotel. Then he ambled slowly up the street. At the corner, he stopped again to check his shoelaces. He crossed the road, then stopped again and peered absent-mindedly into the window of a sports-equipment shop. Baseball bats lined up like rifles. He stood shielded by a lamp post and glanced back the way he'd come. Sure enough, the flame-haired Irishman exited the Metropole and came walking towards him.

The man was an expert tail. He'd changed his hat and pinned

his hair somehow so it was hardly visible. He no longer limped and looked about a foot taller. Visually, the change was striking. Wiggins made a great show of crossing the road once more, making sure his tail saw him. Then he dived into the chaos of Times Square at a slow amble. He hadn't forgotten that he was a marked man in this part of town, but the flow of people and mid-afternoon traffic was such that it would be a miracle if the cops pulled him up now. And he wanted to make sure his tail kept following.

He doubled back down 42nd and skirted a miserable patch of scrubland. A sign said *Bryant Park*, but Wiggins wouldn't even sleep rough in the place. It lay shadowed by the dark, clanking, dripping, smoking monstrosity of the Sixth Avenue El. Wiggins didn't look behind him as he headed up the stairs of the 42nd Street station, northbound.

The platform thrummed and creaked and sang with people crowded onto its narrow boards. A train jangled into the opposite platform, rattling and spitting and stinking of oil and grease. Great clouds of tobacco smoke hung in the air above the passengers' heads. Wiggins pushed himself to the very end so he could board the last carriage when the train came in. He lifted himself up momentarily on a lamp post that butted the end of the platform. Sure enough, his tail was on there too – showing no interest in Wiggins (and definitely not drunk). In the distance off to his right, he saw the train wiggling and wagging along the dart-straight track towards them. Dust and soot and steam swirled as it approached through the heat-hazed afternoon. The rails screeched.

Wiggins jostled his way onto the last carriage. He checked his tail had done the same, then pushed his way forwards. It was peculiar to travel at this height through a city – every now and then the trains in South London would trundle by houses, but the El ran straight down the road. Either side, buildings shook and windows rattled as the train hurtled northwards. Wiggins shuffled on into the next carriage. He caught sight of his tail in the crush. He'd changed his hat again and there was no sign of the flame hair that had so marked him out in the bar of the Metropole.

But Wiggins recognised the set of his shoulders, and the long, slender fingers that grasped the handhold above his head. He'd recognise those fingers anywhere, even from half a carriage away. The train rushed into the next station. People got off. People got on. The tail waited. Wiggins waited. The train went on.

This dance continued until the train reached the final stop up by Central Park. The tail now cut an entirely different figure – tall, thin, just past energetic middle age, his face masked by a handkerchief worn in the fashion of a high-class prig coughing ostentatiously at the bad air of the city. A health freak. The tall man got off at the last possible moment, and Wiggins followed.

He made no pretence at concealment now, and the tall man didn't turn around, didn't look back. Instead, he kept a steady pace east across the south end of the park, towards the elegant towers and brownstones of the Upper East Side. Wiggins hadn't been in town long, but he knew this was where the money was. He didn't make any effort to catch up with the tall man, and the man in turn gave no sign of being followed, nor made to stop and wait. They carried on like this for a while, until the tall man turned down one of the elegant side streets off Park Avenue. Trees grew here. Gleaming, chauffeured motor cars rolled by. The heat of the afternoon seemed less intense. And still the tall man walked on.

Suddenly, he turned a corner sharply out of view, making a move at last. Wiggins hurried over. There, parked up, engine idling, stood a covered motor car with the back passenger door open. Wiggins got in.

'Ah, there you are, Wiggins. I must say it is very good to see you.'

'Mr Holmes,' Wiggins said. 'You're a long way from home, sir.'

'Ha ha, yes, indeed,' the great old detective said. He sat in the corner of the car, the various accoutrements of his disguises discarded on the floor in front of him – from the flame-haired wig to the three hats. Now he sat smiling from beneath a smart homburg. 'Here, put these on,' he said, handing Wiggins a jacket, tie and hat. 'Drive on, Phelps,' he called to the driver.

The car pulled away from the kerb. 'I'm sorry for all the cloak-and-dagger, but it is imperative that your cover is maintained. I had to be sure you weren't followed.'

'*You* were following me,' Wiggins grunted.

'Yes, do you like the wig? I wonder if it is a little too red?'

'And I wonder what the hell's going on!'

'Hmm, well wonder on until truth makes all things plain.'

'That ain't much of an answer.'

'Phelps!' Holmes cried. 'Park up around the back. We'll go in the servants' entrance. Are you ready, Wiggins? Oh, do take that hideous expression off your face. You'll find out where we're at soon enough.'

Holmes got out first and led Wiggins down some steps and along a shadowed passage. He opened the door at the end without knocking. The two of them walked through a large, well-appointed kitchen and up the stairs into a sumptuously decked-out house. 'In here,' Holmes said as he threw open the doors into a drawing room. 'I give you my erstwhile pupil, scourge of Marylebone, leader of my Baker Street Irregulars, the man himself . . .' Holmes left it hanging there as he ushered Wiggins into the room.

Captain Vernon Kell, head of His Majesty's Secret Service Bureau, spycatcher-in-chief for the most powerful nation on earth, turned towards them as they entered. 'Wiggins,' he said to his most valuable secret agent.

'Boss.'

9

'What in God's name are you doing in New York?' Kell blurted out. 'I sent you to Dublin, man!'

Wiggins took a half-step back, surprised at his tone. Kell relented and gestured at a chair. His agent, though well dressed in the clothes Holmes had given him, looked tired and nervy. He was unshaven, and his eyes were lifeless and red. It was the first time Kell had seen him in months, and the intervening time had worn heavy on his best – and only – undercover agent.

Kell offered Holmes a cigarette, lit one himself and ignored Wiggins. He looked out of the window while he smoked. Summer leaves dappled the quiet uptown street, orange and dusty in the lowering sun. A motor car rattled by, a lone policeman strode past. The previous year and the first half of 1912 had been good to Kell. The anarchist terrorists behind the Sidney Street siege and the Exchange Buildings police murders had all been captured – in large part because of the Bureau's intervention (well, Wiggins's intervention). The fact that most of them, including the vile bomb-maker Yakov Peters, had walked free from the Old Bailey had been regrettable, but it wasn't a black mark against Kell. It was the police's fault for not arranging the evidence correctly. He, and the Bureau, still retained the credit in Whitehall for finding them in the first place.

Likewise, the biggest intelligence scandal of the previous year had left Kell personally unscathed, his reputation intact. In fact, it had burnished it, for his partner in the Bureau – Sir Mansfield Cumming, who ran the foreign department – had been tarnished, which made Kell's star shine all the brighter. The Agadir Crisis had caused great consternation in Whitehall, but thankfully had been outside his own sphere of influence and responsibility. France and Germany had got into a very heated squabble outside the Moroccan port of Agadir in the summer of 1911. For a moment, it had looked as if war might ignite from this tiny spark, with the Germans bristling and the French, Britain's ally, all set to assert themselves militarily, leading to Lord knew what else.

Panic had swept through Whitehall and the Admiralty. Cumming, whose sole job was to warn of German attack in the event of war, was hauled up in front of the First Lord of the Admiralty, the Secretary of War, the Foreign Secretary and even the Prime Minister. It was Cumming who'd had to admit, in front of such august company, that the King's entire navy, military and intelligence apparatus had 'lost the German fleet'. All 1,000,000 tonnes of it.

Of course, they'd found it eventually, floating around aimlessly in the North Sea, but not before Cumming had been so deliciously embarrassed that he'd almost lost his job. Kell's star had risen as Cumming's fell. The crisis had died down when the French finance ministry used its considerable muscle in the stock market to short German government stocks to such an extent that the Germans had been forced to withdraw their ships from outside Agadir.

For Kell's part, the work of the domestic arm of the Secret Service went on untroubled. His registry had become vast. A huge filing system with details of thousands of foreign nationals and potential discontents. It was a magnificent feat of administration, and he had an army of clerks – working in concert with local police – that ensured up-to-the-minute filing. The only task left undone from the last year was the capture of Van Bork, the shadowy German spymaster he and Wiggins had brushed with on two occasions but never pinned down.

Kell was utterly convinced that war with Germany would come at some point in the next five years. German imperial ambitions had reached such a pitch that a clash with the British Empire was inevitable. And Van Bork was the head of the German Secret Service, or if not the head, then their most active and important agent. While Kell's Secret Service Bureau had been successful in identifying and rounding up low-level German spies, the master manipulator, Van Bork, had escaped their grasp.

Other than Van Bork still being at large, there were only two problems in Kell's world. One was Ireland, and the other was Wiggins. His street agent had proved unsuited to paperwork and the rigours of life at a desk. He had an analytical mind, but he didn't like staying in the office, and he certainly didn't like writing anything down. Wiggins had tried to quit the Service the previous year, parading moral disgust at some of the methods employed. But he'd changed his mind soon enough. The pay was better than he'd get elsewhere, and the work more interesting. It had come down to money in the end, though. Kell knew he always had money on his side. The paymaster has the whip hand. But even though he held the pounds, shillings and pence, Kell knew that a disgruntled Wiggins was half the agent he could be. He had to find a use for his best man beyond tailing faintly eccentric German sympathisers around the south coast, otherwise he'd lose him for good just as the battle cries sounded.

Ireland was the answer as well as the problem. Unlike the rest of the United Kingdom, the Irish had been agitating for self-governance. As far as Kell was concerned, it was an impertinence. The Empire was the richest and most successful the world had ever seen – why would the Irish want to leave? Nevertheless, there were nationalistic factions there and the Liberal government in London – propped up by the Irish MPs – had been forced to introduce a Home Rule Bill that looked like it would eventually pass. However, this wouldn't settle the matter – for many in Ireland, Home Rule wasn't enough, while for many in the north of the country, Home Rule was a gigantic step too far. They regarded themselves as British and considered Home Rule the first step to Catholic control.

Not only was the country threatening to break away, it was also threatening to become two armed camps, implacably opposed. The only thing stopping this was the lack of the arms themselves. At present, the only people in Ireland sufficiently armed to put up any kind of fight were the British Army – and that was the way the government wanted it to stay.

Not that Kell cared about Ireland particularly. His wife Constance had family in Cork – he had even been married there – but he felt no special affinity for the place. If it were up to him, he'd never go back to that rain-drenched hellhole again. Unfortunately, this was not how his German enemies felt. He'd picked up some rumours, and a stray line in an otherwise asinine intelligence report from Dublin Castle, that various forces in Ireland were looking to arm. If this was true, it would be a gift for the Germans. They had the means to supply an infinite number of guns and would like nothing better than to flood the country with munitions, given the chance. If Van Bork and his organisation could place even as few as a thousand guns onto the streets of Ireland, it would be extraordinarily destabilising to the Empire.

So, when Wiggins had started moaning again about needing to leave the Service, Kell had instead sent him to Dublin. He'd bought him a ticket on the *Titanic* as promised, but now with instructions to inveigle himself into the Dublin underworld however he could. They'd cooked up the plan together, with the limited intelligence they had on a Patrick O'Connell. Elements around the criminal kingpin were known to have nationalist tendencies, but more importantly, he was one of the few people in Ireland who could raise enough nefarious cash to acquire a significant shipment of guns. For months, Kell had heard nothing from his agent – not until Wiggins had wired from the ship, on his way to New York.

Kell turned back from the window and addressed Wiggins once more. 'What did I say? Your job was to infiltrate the nationalist elements in Dublin, uncover links to German intelligence and – if necessary – to stop any gun shipments from falling into the wrong hands. Is this correct?'

'It is,' Wiggins grunted.

'So, I will ask again: Why are you in New York?'

'I could ask you the same question,' Wiggins said.

'How many times must I say, you work for me,' Kell snapped. Then he took a deep breath and lit another cigarette.

Holmes had draped himself over a chaise longue and lay with his eyes closed and his long, thin hands placed together on his chest. When he spoke, he did not move a muscle. 'We are here, Wiggins, to catch Van Bork – or Von Bork, as I feel sure his real name is.'

'You've come out of retirement?' Wiggins said, astonished.

'I intend to insert myself into the Irish republican community here, so that eventually I can go back and make myself useful as a German spy. I think it is the only way to truly snare Von Bork. The only way to catch a spider as big and menacing as him is to make oneself into a morsel so tasty, so tempting that he has to scuttle to the edges of his web himself. I am to be that morsel.'

'How?'

'It will take time to bait the hook, to establish my credentials as a true republican, as an ingrained hater of the British. But once this is secure, I will be able to provide Von Bork with the most prized pieces of intelligence he's ever come across. And then we will have our man.' Holmes revelled for a moment. 'I intend to call myself Boyd.'

'Not sure that's quite right,' Wiggins said, then added hurriedly, 'sir.'

'Oh, why?' Holmes opened his eyes and looked at Wiggins.

'Sounds a bit northern, don't it? Scots, even. They's very particular about where yous come from. They's also particular about your family, like. They'll think they know your cousin, if you're not careful.'

Holmes frowned. Kell stepped forward, eager to break it up. Despite the gulf in class between Holmes and his agent, he could sense the bond between them, as if they were operating in their own private world. 'Excuse me. It's a very jolly reunion, I'm sure, but I'm the head of the Secret Service Bureau, you are my under-cover agent, I've heard nothing from you in months and you are thousands of miles away from where you should be. I demand you report immediately, else I'll have you arrested, court-martialled, dragooned, shanghaied or bloody well kidnapped. Why are you here?'

Wiggins hesitated and bent his head slightly. 'A young lad was killed in Dublin, probably cos of me. Cos of us. I'm trying to find out who did it.'

'What are you talking about? You were meant to insinuate yourself into the Dublin underground. You had a *mission*. Or did you forget?'

'He has become O'Connell's bodyguard,' Holmes drawled from his recumbent position, eyes closed once more. 'Which is why he's in New York – with O'Connell. It is the perfect cover.'

'How on earth do you know that?' Kell said, and then quickly, 'Oh, don't bother.'

He had recruited Holmes to go after Van Bork in the aftermath of the Home Rule Bill, and had decided to come with him to New York after receiving Wiggins's telegram. But travelling with the man was infuriating. He'd say nothing for days, then gnomically pronounce some useful truth much too late. Holmes did have his uses, though. Once they'd arrived in New York, Kell had headed to the consulate and asked Holmes to find Wiggins. Hence the two men were in his comfortable sitting room now, slouching in their different ways, barely paying him any heed at all. He felt like a stable master with two recalcitrant horses – one a thoroughbred, one a half-breed, but both temperamental, and only willing to go out on a gallop if given the right incentives. Just then, he'd had enough of Holmes's explanations. He turned back to Wiggins. 'What is going on?'

His agent stretched out his legs and kneaded a thigh slowly. 'I'm in with O'Connell. His right-hand man tried to kill me – so did some Dublin coppers, as it happens, but that's another story. Anyway, the OC trusts me, I think. I ain't got no evidence of German contact, guns, nothing like that, but I know he's here for money, though I don't know why.'

'And . . . ?'

'He invited me to New York, so I came. I couldn't refuse – he called my bluff on my cover, didn't he? *Want to find your lady love, do ya?* Anyways, better than losing my fingers in a Dublin slum.' He looked down at his hands for a moment. 'And as I say, we've got a dead man's blood on our hands, and I want to find out who did it.' Wiggins's face hardened as he said this, much to Kell's irritation. It was his agent's perpetual problem – digressing from the fight against the Empire's enemies to fight battles of his own. As if the death of one man could tip the scale on the death of an Empire.

'I suppose I have to leave you to it. You should get back to O'Connell as soon as possible.'

'It ain't that easy.'

'What now?'

'Wiggins is wanted by the meanest policeman in New York.' Holmes chuckled. 'You do have a knack of choosing particularly nasty adversaries.'

'I don't care!' Kell tried to regain control. 'Get back to O'Connell. What's your cover story again – for the New York trip? You are searching for your lost love? "My lady love", isn't that the story?'

Wiggins shrugged. 'Something like that.'

'Search for her. Kick up a hue and cry, make tongues wag – let it be known. Then, when you don't find her and run out of money, go back to O'Connell with your tail between your legs. He'll expect that. Tell him she's dead or married or something. No, dead is better. Then you'll have a reason to stick with him, to go back to Dublin. There's a pipeline being planned, guns coming from Germany into Ireland. The cables are quite clear, although the details are hidden.'

'Cables?' Wiggins asked Holmes.

'He means the telegrams,' Holmes went on. 'It's not well known, but—'

'Ahem, yes, thank you, that's quite enough,' Kell said. 'As I was saying, we know there are plans to bring the guns into Ireland, but we don't know the details. That is why you' – he pointed at

Wiggins – 'must get back in the game and do your job. Find those German links. Find those guns. We can't let them fall into the wrong hands. If you fail, Ireland could explode.'

'What about the murder? Didn't I tell you a man died cos we botched the set-up?'

'Well, even if that is true, what can we do about it now? He's dead.' A silence fell on the room. Wiggins slumped back into the armchair. Holmes remained stretched out on the chaise, his eyes closed, his hands placed on his chest. Kell watched the old detective. Was he asleep? He barely moved, and made no sound. His thin nose flared almost imperceptibly; that great thinking machine, thinking. Was that how the magic worked?

He switched his gaze back to Wiggins, who'd also closed his eyes and shifted his head back, as if asleep. He had two of the best minds in England, both asleep in a New York sitting room. Yet for all their talent, Ireland hadn't been cracked and Van Bork still operated, undetected.

Kell had been elated when Holmes had agreed to fight the good fight and go after Van Bork; he'd been equally discouraged when Holmes had gone on to say it would take him at least a year, and furthermore, that much of the year would take place in the United States in order to establish his cover. Holmes had referred to this as his 'legend' – a story about his past that would hold up when he eventually turned to spying for the Germans. Kell couldn't help thinking it was just an excuse to play-act. He could tell Holmes liked playing roles as much as he liked solving crimes – the three costumes he'd said he needed to tail Wiggins were an extravagance, as was the whole clandestine nature of bringing him in at all.

He looked out onto the Manhattan street, now glaring with electric lamps. When he'd received Wiggins's telegram, he had been both astonished and irked. That his agent, sent to act within the United Kingdom under his auspices, should end up in America somehow affronted his sense of decency and propriety. It was one thing to pose as a criminal among criminals, to dupe those members of society who chose to flout its rules; it was quite another to act in such a manner in the home of their American cousins.

When Kell had confided in Holmes about Wiggins being in New York, the old detective had decided there and then to enact his plan against Van Bork. On the spur of the moment, Kell accompanied Holmes to America. Constance was consumed by the latest suffragist parliamentary delegation, and hadn't had any time for him in months. And when a sun as bright as Constance didn't shine on you, the days could be dark indeed. He began to wonder if the latest Parliament act, and consequently the prospect of votes for women becoming a reality, might send Constance back into his arms.

Wiggins jerked in his chair, startled awake, surprising Kell out of his own reverie. 'There's a bed upstairs,' Kell said. 'Stay here tonight. You look as if you need a rest.' And a bath, Kell did not say.

'I'll be all right,' Wiggins grunted. 'If you could spare me a nip of that bottle there.'

'Listen to him, Wiggins,' Holmes said suddenly, surprising them both. 'Undercover work is by far the most exhausting kind of investigation. You must forever be on guard, forever vigilant. Take a night to restore your vigour. O'Connell will be in jail for twenty-four hours at least. You will not be missed. Besides, I'll need you in the morning.'

'What for?'

'Something magnificent.'

Fitz's death. For Wiggins, it all came back to that. Before Kell and Holmes had shown up in New York, he'd almost forgotten why he was with the OC in the first place, his supposed 'mission' for Kell and country – chasing links to German interference in the United Kingdom. Ever since Fitz's body had spilled out of that beer barrel on the Guinness quay, he'd vowed to find his killer. He felt responsible for the boy, as an older brother might. He felt he should have saved him. But now he was dead, all he could do to discharge that duty was bring the murderer to justice – whatever that meant.

Wiggins stared sleeplessly up at the fan of pale yellow street light spread across the ceiling. Manhattan's streets were never dark. Holmes and Kell had packed him off to bed on the top floor, and he'd slumped into it gratefully enough. But the clear, deep, dreamless sleep he needed never came. Instead, his mind ran back, back over the roiling ocean, back to Dublin and that bloody quay.

He couldn't shake the feeling that in some way he was to blame for Fitz's death. Wiggins hadn't told the OC everything he'd found out. That Fitz had been taking the OC's money and slicing the revenue in two different ways. In the first place, he'd been collecting less than he should from some of the whores and the tenants. Or rather, he'd collected the full amount from the kip houses, but passed some of it back to the girls. In addition, he hadn't been depositing the full amount into the OC's bank accounts. The OC had lost thousands of pounds and he was unlikely to get any of it back in a hurry, if at all.

In this sense, O'Connell and Hannigan had the most obvious motive for the killing. Wiggins could quite believe the latter would happily murder anyone on the say-so of the former, and he had no doubt the pair of them had meted out this kind of street justice before. But the OC had been truly shocked when Wiggins told him of Fitz's death. Hannigan had been sickened, too, and Wiggins had another reason for doubting his guilt.

Wiggins was deeply suspicious of Dublin's other crime supremo, Lynch. If Lynch hadn't known that Fitz was doing the dirty on O'Connell, then he might have had a motive for killing him. He certainly had the means with his gang. But even then, it didn't really make sense for Lynch to have escalated things like that. No one, apart from Wiggins, had known that Fitz was so essential to the OC's operation, and if Lynch had wanted to send a message in any gang war, then he'd certainly have claimed credit.

Wiggins needed to find a motive that made sense, to find the person responsible for Fitz's death. It wasn't necessarily the same thing as finding the person who'd landed the killing blow. You could punish the tools of violence all day long, but that was punishing the weapon rather than the culprit. He'd had enough of fighting soldiers while the generals went free.

He and Kell had been so careful. Knowing that O'Connell was the most powerful criminal in Dublin, they'd reasoned that he would be Wiggins's best way into any gunrunning that might be going on. They'd also known his weekly routine. Kell had used a gang of 'thugs' drawn from a regiment stationed at Beggars Bush barracks and due back in Aldershot the following day. Kell knew one of their officers, and on the quiet he had instructed five big men dressed in civvies to attack O'Connell and whoever he was with at midday on the Coombe. Wiggins would then pile in and save the day, while the 'thugs' would withdraw, never to be seen in Dublin again. Meanwhile, Wiggins would be invited into the fold.

What they hadn't bargained for were the very aggressive Dublin police – if they were indeed real policemen – who'd carried off Wiggins and tried to kill him. It was only the RIC officer Captain Masters, arranged as a fail-safe by Kell just in case, that had saved Wiggins's life. Wiggins thought back to that night, to the shock on their faces when he'd spoken in his English accent. Had those men actually been sent to kill Fitz? Or had the attack convinced Fitz's killer (Lynch, perhaps?) that he had to act soon?

Just then, Wiggins heard the front door of the Manhattan townhouse close. He rose to the window in time to see a tall, elegant figure dressed in black flit in and out of the pools of light from the street lamps and across the road. Wiggins peered down as his former mentor, the greatest detective in the world, disappeared into the New York night.

He slumped back onto the bed. If he was going to solve Fitz's murder, or get to the bottom of any link with Germany, Kell was right about one thing. Wiggins had to get back in with the OC. And to do that, he had to deal with the cops. He had to deal with Becker.

'Hurry up,' Holmes cried. 'The hares are running.'

Wiggins started up in his bed. Sherlock Holmes stood in the

doorway, wearing a straw boater and a light linen suit. He pointed an ashplant at Wiggins, like an aggressive conductor.

'Wiggins. Be downstairs in ten minutes.' His eyes shone. 'We have to deal with Lieutenant Charles Becker.'

'Where's Captain Kell?' Wiggins said as he followed Holmes through the back door to the kitchen at the bottom of the house five minutes later.

'Kell's gone to the consulate. He is due back in London and has been good enough to deputise all his orders to me, so that I can pass them on to you.'

'You my new boss then? Sir.'

Holmes glanced up and down the sidewalk, then set off at a trot. For a man in his late fifties, he moved well, thought Wiggins, falling into his slipstream. 'These Americanisms don't suit you, Wiggins,' Holmes called over his shoulder. 'I am your superior, let's leave it at that.'

Wiggins let that one slide. For all the egalitarianism of New York, the feeling of equality (if your money was green, they didn't give a damn what accent you spoke in), it had only taken Kell and Holmes twelve hours to remind him of his true position in life. England's social order travelled well.

They continued through the East Side streets. Holmes swung his stick with jaunty panache, but his pace precluded any more questions. Wiggins was content enough to follow him. For all that he baulked at Holmes's superior attitude and social blindness, an aura of safety hung about him. Walking at his heels, even in a strange land, felt a little bit like home. After about twenty minutes, they neared the East River, choked with traffic. Wiggins was about to point out that they'd need to go further south to pick up a public boat when a tall figure hallooed from a motor launch moored higgledy-piggledy at the side of a private jetty.

'Mr Holmes,' the tall man cried. 'Hurry. We are going to be late for the greatest show in New York.'

Holmes waved, and took the ladder down to the boat, gesturing Wiggins to follow. The man on the boat continued: 'Or at least, the second greatest show in New York. I hope to write about the greatest show if you can give me what you promised.'

'Swope,' Holmes nodded, 'let's get there first, shall we?'

'Whatever you say, Mr Holmes, whatever you say.' Swope grinned and threw a cursory glance at Wiggins, then strode to the front of the boat, calling at the boatmen to cast off.

The small launch puttered out into the East River and slewed south. Great warehouse buildings lined the left-hand bank, while far out in front even greater ships stood at anchor. And greater still: the huge span of Brooklyn Bridge, its cables an iron webbing in the sky.

As the launch drew underneath, Wiggins leaned in next to Holmes while he looked ahead. 'Where we going?'

Holmes pointed to another island in the river. 'What do you make of Swope?' he said quietly.

Wiggins glanced up the boat. Swope was haranguing one of the boatmen about something or other. He looked like an upside-down mop, over six feet tall, without a scrap on him, flaming-red hair sticking out from under his hat any which way. He jiggled excitedly as he gave directions. His pince-nez were so thin as to be pointless, and his hands were covered by long yellow gloves. Wiggins lowered his voice. 'Newspaperman. But a liar and all. Not to be trusted.'

Holmes chuckled. Wiggins went on. 'Clever. Gambler. Social climber.'

'Ha! Right again,' Holmes said.

'But why are—'

Holmes thrust out a hand and pointed. 'There he is!' he cried, and hustled along the side of the boat for a better view.

They'd gone under Brooklyn Bridge and now saw in front of them a sizeable island. Opposite the island, on the Brooklyn banks, a crowded steamboat was chugging out into midstream. More excited onlookers thronged the bank. Sherlock Holmes's eyes danced and sparkled in the morning sunshine. 'Look, Wiggins, look – isn't he magnificent?'

On the side of the steamboat, amidst the crowd of onlookers, stood a man wearing a red swimming costume and handcuffs. Long frizzy hair fell from a centre parting. He held his cuffed wrists up to the crowd and then leaned back into the hands of an attendant. Another man began shackling his legs, while a third wrapped chains around his body.

'Happy now, Mr Holmes?' Swope called. 'A ringside seat for the ultimate fight: the battle between life and death.'

'Yes, yes,' Holmes replied, then muttered under his breath, 'Fool. It's no battle for Houdini – he's a genius.'

They watched as Houdini was bound tightly and nailed inside a large wooden crate. The boat rocked and swayed in the current. Wiggins couldn't help thinking of the Dublin quays, when he'd been bound and hooded, moments away from the Liffey and his own deep, dark, watery end. Seagulls swooped and squawked, the smell of the sea caught in his nose – the sea, and coal smoke, and Swope's cheroot. But no one took their eyes off that crate. A winch swung it out over the river and everyone watched in silence as the attendants slowly lowered it into the water.

As soon as it was submerged, Holmes flipped open his pocket watch. 'This man has much to teach the world.'

'A magician?'

'He is no magician, Wiggins, he is a man of science and dedication. I'll wager we will see him in fewer than three minutes, alive and well.'

'But . . .' Wiggins hesitated. He felt like a grown-up taking the nipper to the music hall for the first time. Was this what happened when your father got old? He turned into the child? Wiggins didn't know. He'd never known his father, and his mother had gone when he was seven. Where he came from, only the lucky ones got old. Going mad was a small price to pay for making it past fifty.

'There!' Holmes cried. Houdini's head bobbed up about two hundred yards away from the steamboat. The crowd cheered. He raised a hand in salute, then began to swim back to the boat. 'Two minutes, twenty-eight seconds.' Holmes closed his watch.

'I'll wager a ten-dollar bill that he's been free for at least a minute of that. But it doesn't do to make it look easy, does it, Wiggins. Watson taught me that. Ha!' Holmes was as bright and as pleased as that young child at the music hall.

'Why're we here?' Wiggins asked again, still mystified.

'Houdini!' Holmes clapped his hands together. 'Must be seen to be believed. Swope! Onwards.'

Swope jostled the boatmen back into action and while the boat turned towards the southern tip of Manhattan, he edged along the deck towards Holmes. 'And now, Mr Holmes, surely the time has arrived for us to conclude our business? These launches do not come cheap, and while the *World* is surely the finest paper this side of the equator, my expense account is nevertheless scrutinised like the last parchments of the Egyptian kings.'

Holmes sniffed slightly, then spoke to Wiggins over his shoulder. 'Give him the letter.'

'What?' Wiggins said, caught unawares.

'The letter you stole from Becker. Come on, Wiggins.' Holmes held out his hand.

'How did you . . . ?' Wiggins couldn't deny it. Not in front of the grand old detective. He might be past his best, but his eyes could see into your soul. Slowly, he pulled the letter from his inside pocket and held it out. Swope swept it off him, pulling it free without another word.

Holmes stepped away and whispered into Wiggins's ear, 'That letter means nothing to you. But to Swope? He will deal with Charles Becker. Mark my words, Becker won't be after you from tomorrow morning onwards.'

Swope exclaimed loudly. 'Goddam it!' he cried excitedly, and looked over the letter at Wiggins. 'This came from the pocket of Charles Becker?'

'It did. I took his badge and all.'

'My God, it's dynamite. But listen, I can't give you a byline.'

'Don't give him anything,' Holmes said. 'Just make sure Charles Becker never darkens the corridors of the New York Police Department ever again.'

'Oh, have no fear on that account, Mr Holmes, have no fear!' Swope said, and took to reading the letter once more.

Holmes gestured for Wiggins to follow him to the stern. 'Now, Wiggins, you must do as Captain Kell orders. You understand? Don't scowl, man, you're not ten years old any more. Reaffirm your cover story. Try to find this woman of yours. Or at least, make public that you are trying to find her, kick up a hue and cry – O'Connell may seem a bit down on his luck, but he has longer tentacles than you might imagine, a stronger belly, too. Once you have made your presence felt, shall we say, go back to the Metropole, go back to O'Connell. Report failure. Report contrition. Act the poor supplicant. He will take you back.'

The boat had almost reached a small pier that nestled in the lee of the Staten Island Ferry port. Wiggins could see Swope at the front of the boat, hands on his hips, looking like a regular tool. 'But what's the point, Mr Holmes?'

'Wiggins! You are in a position to do a great service to your King and country, to avert catastrophe. Not only are you trying to find German spies, you should be trying to stop the acquisition of deadly weapons. To save lives.' Holmes hesitated. The boat bumped against the small jetty and Swope jumped ashore and walked back down the wooden planks towards them. 'Besides,' Holmes went on, 'if you want to find the killer of your friend the young Irishman, then you have to be with O'Connell. The truth lies close to him.'

'How do you know?'

'Violence is O'Connell's trade. That is where you must investigate. And I can see it in your eyes – you will not rest until the murder's solved. You always were an apt pupil.'

'Mr Holmes!' Swope called. 'Let me help you.'

Wiggins glanced up. Swope was reaching down towards the great detective. Holmes looked at the yellow-gloved hand, then held out his arm instead to Wiggins, who helped him ashore. Swope affected not to notice the snub. He took off his hat, swept back his hair, reapplied the hat and bowed. 'An honour, sir, and a pleasure. I must be away, back to the newsroom, to write up this sensation.' He slapped his hand with the letter Wiggins had stolen. 'Don't forget to buy a copy.'

'When will it be out?' Wiggins asked.

Swope barely glanced at him. 'By eight tonight. Now, goodbye.' He bowed again, then sashayed away up the jetty and into the crowd waiting for the ferry.

Wiggins looked after him and opened his mouth.

'Don't say it,' said Holmes quickly. 'Now, be off with you. Find her. Or rather, pretend to find her, as loudly as possible.'

'What about you?'

'I shall disappear. I have listened to your point. Boyd is no more. A new identity – Michael Kelly, disillusioned Irish-American, republican. I will start in Chicago, act the part. Slowly and surely, I will follow the spindles of the web, all the way to the centre of German intelligence command, all the way to Von Bork. He is the spider at the centre of the web. He will think he has caught me. But I – we, maybe – will slay the beast.'

During this speech, Holmes had begun to change physically – becoming the man he was going to impersonate, the embittered, working-class Kelly. His jaw began to work, his shoulders hunched and his accent changed. Wiggins had seen it before, but he admired the skill all the same. For all his rationality, this pure thinking machine understood other men more than he'd admit. He understood how to walk in another man's shoes.

'One thing,' Wiggins said when Holmes had finished. 'Not Kelly.'

Holmes looked at him sharply, but Wiggins went on. 'You're bound to meet an Irishman named Kelly. He'll be all over you, wanting to find family in common. Nah, go for something else, something a bit out of the way.'

'What do you suggest?' Holmes said, icily.

'How 'bout Altamont? Met an old drunk in Dublin by that name. Stood out for being nothing.'

'Well, I don't know,' Holmes replied, huffily. 'I will give it some thought.'

Wiggins was struck by a sudden pang of sadness and regret.

It surprised him, like déjà vu or nostalgia, this strong rush of yearning, unfulfilled. Part of him wished he'd never offered the advice. It felt like blasphemy to question Holmes, and now he'd faltered, it felt like God had died. Was this what it felt like when you had to tie your father's shoelaces for him, or hold his hand when he got confused? Holmes must have seen the confusion on his face, for he placed his hand hard on Wiggins's shoulder.

'I could come with you,' Wiggins said suddenly. 'You'll need a hand. And you're used to having someone by your side, what with the Doctor and all. I can be your fist.'

'There's some truth in what you say, Wiggins. I am not quite the athlete I once was.' He looked past the launch and out over the water, his sharp eyes fixing on the Statue of Liberty. The huge figure held his attention, and he stared at it intently for an age. Then he swung back to look at Wiggins. 'But no, not you, Wiggins, not you. Your country needs you.'

He swirled his walking stick around in a great arc, and grinned. 'Find the gunrunners and stop them. Find out who killed your friend. Be the man we know you are.' Then he marched back up the jetty, stopping only to call out, 'The rest is nothing.'

10

'The woman worker must have bread, but she must have roses too!'

A great cheer went up and rolled through the crowd, redoubling. It was as if they'd been expecting the line, an old favourite. Wiggins stumbled through the throng. Up ahead, the speaker surveyed her audience. She stood on a temporary podium in one corner of the square. Her voice carried easily over the women – for the crowd was mostly women – and even from a distance Wiggins could feel her stage presence. She couldn't have been five feet tall if she was an inch. She wore a loose blue shirt open at the collar and she gripped the improvised lectern tightly with both hands. She wore no hat, and twists of dark hair fell over her face. She waited for the cheers to die down before she began again. 'We must all unite together . . .'

Wiggins thrust deeper into the crowd, towards the podium. He lost his footing on a cobble and was pulled straight by two or three women. 'Sorry,' he said. 'Ta.' The women recoiled and turned away. He'd been on his feet all day since leaving Holmes, dutifully filling out his cover story, but by the end of the afternoon he'd been desperate for a drink. He must have reeked of booze by this time.

After leaving the Staten Island Ferry port, he'd pulled his hat low and walked deep into the Lower East Side. Going north up Pike Street, looking across at the great 'H' of the Brooklyn Bridge looming over six-storey tenements that seemed so full and large that each of them could house a town, he'd worked again at his story. *My life, my love, my Bela. Came off the boat in 1910, had a sister. Bela's her name. Bela Grybus. Latvian.* New York was stacked full of people from Eastern Europe, he knew, and this part of town was the first stop for many of them. Italians, too, a little further up, but he was interested in the Latvians.

He started asking around, first among the women and children who hung around the tenement doorways, then in the shops and at the market stalls. He acted aggressive, angry and out of the usual, trying to kick up as much of a fuss as possible. And yet despite this, despite his threatening manner, his loud voice, his London slang; despite the fact that every third person he spoke to couldn't speak English, or looked at him askance, or bemused; despite all this, they were unfailingly helpful. It was as if each of those he asked knew what it was to lose someone they loved, literally lose them in the pitch and yaw of existence and migration, lose them to the waves and tides of time, to death, perhaps, or to another life in another country and another world, to actually *lose* someone they loved. They all knew this, even the young children, and they turned kindly eyes on Wiggins, and shook their heads slowly, and dipped their chins, and pointed up the street, or opened their arms and brought their hands together in sympathy.

After each exchange, the lie in Wiggins's heart pulled tighter, until he wondered if it was a lie at all; if, indeed, he really did want to find Bela and these kind-hearted people were leading him to what he'd wanted all along. Was the path of kindness the one true path? Should he leave behind him O'Connell, Kell and Holmes? Leave behind duplicity, leave behind Molly and Dublin and London, and all he knew? There was nothing to leave behind. And when there's nothing, why not leave?

Finally, after he'd tried most of the cross streets between Houston and the bridge, a woman with a bright red headscarf and a baby on her hip listened quietly as he spoke, stared at him with dark chocolate eyes so intense that he faltered, then put her free hand on his shoulder. She rousted a small boy who'd been clinging to her leg. He stood to attention as she barked orders at him in a language Wiggins knew to be Yiddish. The boy nodded, then looked up at Wiggins and gestured for him to follow.

Wiggins followed the boy, who kept a steady pace through one street, then the next, through a market, then on another block. The boy turned every now and then to check that Wiggins was still there, but other than that said nothing. Finally, they reached a small storefront with black glass. Emblazoned across the top, read the sign *Weiss People-Finding Union*. Wiggins looked back at the boy, astonished. 'Ta,' he said.

The boy stood for a moment, examining Wiggins again, as if anew. He had two front teeth missing and a low brow, and wore battered leather shoes and a cap half on, half off. He was all inquisitiveness. Wiggins pulled out a coin from his pocket – some of the change Holmes had passed to him that morning – and handed it to him. 'Where can I get a decent drop round here?'

The boy put his head to one side.

'You know.' Wiggins drew his hand up to his mouth and mimed glugging down a pint.

The boy smiled. 'Whaddaya want? We got whiskey joints down Pike and vodka joints all over. There's even a gin house, but the liquor is rotten, so says Levi Roth, anyways.'

'Does he?'

'He's only twelve, so what does he know, right? But I reckon you're a beer man? You a beer man? Continental Café, that's the best spot round here.'

'Ta,' Wiggins said again.

'Mind how you go, mister. You look a little green.' The little boy nodded, then ran off.

Wiggins went into Weiss's. A wooden bench ran down one wall, another under the window. People were crammed together, faces blank. An old woman in a black headscarf turned towards him as he came in, her face full of hope for an instant; it dropped on seeing him, and her hands sank back into her lap. A young girl sat at the feet of a man holding his head in his hands. She click-clacked a wooden doll against the bench leg. *Click, clack, click, clack.* A clerk in a heavy black suit sat at a table with a huge, open book. Behind him, document boxes piled high. Wiggins could hear someone on the telephone, hidden by a wooden partition.

'I'm looking for Bela Grybus,' he said in a loud voice.

The clerk jerked up, a look of surprise across his face. 'Take a seat, please, sir, there's a line.' *Click, clack.*

'It's a queue, not a fucking line,' he cried. 'I don't care about no fucking line!'

Click. A hush descended on the room. The clerk quailed. Even the person on the telephone stopped talking. Wiggins clenched his jaw and shook his neck muscles minutely. 'I said, I'm looking for Bela Grybus,' he hissed angrily.

He stared at the clerk with all the intensity he could muster. It didn't feel good. He'd never been a bully, not even when he'd been running the Irregulars and Tommy had been trying to ruin the thing. It didn't sit well. But he had to make his presence felt.

'In here, sir.' A short, round, middle-aged man stepped out from behind the partition. He still held the telephone receiver in one hand. He put the other up in a placating way to the clerk, and gestured for Wiggins to follow.

'I don't need no special treatment,' Wiggins replied, not moving. He kept his voice loud. 'I just need yous to find Bela Grybus. Latvian. About twenty-eight, thirty. Came from London in '10. One sister. Got a birthmark across half her face. I'm staying at the Metropole, name of Wiggins.' He tossed a coin onto the desk and turned to leave, then hesitated. 'I love her, see?' he said, and left.

Tired of acting drunk, Wiggins got drunk. He couldn't go straight back to the Metropole just yet. Becker wouldn't be out of action until after the news broke in the paper later that night, according to Swope. So, instead he toured the bars and cafés the young boy had suggested – and he made a big noise at each joint. He'd take a drink or two, then holler out his message – 'Anyone know a Bela? Bela Grybus? Yay high, birthmark, a peach' – before being pushed on his way.

As he traipsed from place to place, and as the sun got lower, the sounds of New York got more distinct. Mothers calling their kids in for dinner. The clanking of pans, the distant squawks of hungry gulls. Onions frying, the smell drifting down the streets, mixing with the dank stench of summertime drains. As a sweltering, sweaty pause seemed to come over this strange corner of the city, Wiggins's mood spiralled down. The unexpected kindness of people, the understanding in their eyes even as he swore and cursed and shouted. Perhaps they knew more about him than he knew about himself.

He stumbled out of a cheap grog shop by Hester Street market and thought again of his line: *'My love, my life, my Bela.'* He'd always told Kell that the best cover stories were those closest to the truth. What had he said to Weiss? *'I love her, see?'*

It was while in this confused and inebriated state that he'd come across the women's demonstration, so ably commanded by the dark-haired half-pint up on the stage. He assumed it was a suffragist gathering, but didn't give it much thought. For as soon as Wiggins understood quite how many people were in the crowd, he was seized by an idea that would put to shame all his previous attempts to publicise his mission. He looked back at the speaker, pointing, rallying, holding the attention of the crowd, and immediately set off towards her.

He pushed and jostled his way to the front, ignoring the cries of complaint. He didn't have to pretend to be drunk any more, he realised, as the figure of the woman on the dais swayed in and out of focus.

'We will march, we will strike, we will never give in to the forces of oppression,' the woman cried. 'This country is a great country. But it is our country too!'

'Go on, Rose,' someone cheered in his ear. 'You tell 'em!'

Wiggins grasped the lectern and swung himself up beside the woman.

'Hey, what are you doing?' she cried, as Wiggins loomed over her. He felt the commotion start in the crowd, a raised voice, a cry of alarm, bemusement.

'Does anyone know Bela Grybus?' Wiggins bellowed, ignoring Rose, who, despite being nearly a foot shorter than him, now had a hold of his arm.

'Get the hell off my stage!'

'Bela Grybus! Birthmark here to here, Latvian. Anyone seen her? Tell her I want her back. Tell her Wiggins wants her back,' he shouted.

He slumped forward for a moment, suddenly overcome with tiredness and drink. In his ear he heard the woman, Rose, shouting. The crowd began to boo. 'Get outta here! Ya bum!'

'Where is Sirocco?' Rose cried out. 'Jack Sirocco!' She turned to Wiggins again. 'Seriously, get offa my stage, mister.'

Wiggins tried to focus. From the near side of the square, he made out a trio of burly men making their way towards the stage. The lead man held a club up high, jostling people out of the way as he came. Wiggins glanced the other way, to the far-off corner, and saw something that made him hesitate. Jack Zelig.

The tall man with the big nose and too small hat was unmistakable, even at a hundred paces, and his intent was unmistakable too. He stood stock-still when he saw Wiggins and nodded to himself, as if confirming some report or other. Then he slowly drew a finger across his throat and pointed at him.

Wiggins tried to clamber from the stage, but as he looked up, the lead burly man ran towards him and lifted his club, ready to strike.

Rose thrust her hands out to protect him. 'No violence! Just get him the hell outta here,' she cried.

Wiggins glanced around, trying to spot Zelig. *BANG! BANG! BANG!* Three gunshots in quick succession told Wiggins all he needed to know about Zelig.

The crowd exploded around him. Screams. Women running, placards discarded. Wiggins ducked. Rose stood by his side. She tutted, amidst the chaos. The clubber and his two pals stopped in their tracks while the sea of people crashed and streamed around them.

'It's Zelig!' the clubber cried to his pals. For Zelig was clearly visible, far across the square, gun still drawn. He was now flanked by two men with thick black hair, and pistols.

The clubber and his men turned away from Wiggins and headed towards Zelig, striding slowly, seemingly unafraid.

Another bullet pinged into the lectern, just by Wiggins's left ear. He pulled Rose down by his side. 'Careful,' he hissed.

She struggled against his grip. Around them, startled suffragists fled. Someone cried out, 'Police!' Wiggins was sure he heard a chuckle. He looked back at Rose. She pulled away from him, unruffled.

'Get off me.'

Another rattle of gunfire. A wail. Above the shrieks, Zelig bellowed, 'Come out, Englishman! This ain't your town.'

Rose glared at Wiggins. He shrugged.

More shots. 'Get outta here, Jack,' the clubber shouted back.

The crowd was streaming into the side streets and alleys, and Wiggins didn't like his odds. He was unarmed. The clubber and his two men had swerved towards Zelig, shouting, and it seemed as though a stand-off might develop. The trouble was, as soon as they got to talking, Wiggins couldn't see any reason why the clubber wouldn't hand him over.

Rose must have been thinking the same thing. 'Zelig after you?' she said, her eyes darting at the women running around her.

'You know him?'

She tsked. 'You're not a hood, a bad guy? You on the level?'

Another bullet thwacked into one of the banners behind them. Rose did not flinch. She held her eyes on Wiggins.

'I just smacked him when he fleeced my boss. Honest,' he said.

'What about what you said up there?'

Wiggins glanced back. Zelig and the clubber now stood opposite each other over on the other side of the square. It was a stand-off, but Wiggins could see it wouldn't last long. Zelig was pointing over at him and saying something.

'True.' Wiggins turned to Rose. 'Every word.'

Rose hesitated, looked over at Zelig, then nodded. 'Come on.' She took hold of his hand and pulled him into the last of the fleeing throng.

'Hey!' Zelig shouted.

Wiggins glanced back. The men beside Zelig had drawn their pistols again.

Rose hustled him. *BANG! BANG!* Bullets pinged off the brick-work as they reached the corner. Rose pushed and pulled him down the street. They ran past a row of fruit carts. A Coca-Cola van idled by the kerb, its back doors wide open.

'Go, go, go!' Rose shouted to the unseen driver, and dived into the back of the van. Wiggins tumbled in after her, closing the doors as the van picked up speed.

'Take the next cross street,' Rose called out to the driver, and slumped back against the side of the van. It slewed round to the right. The glass bottles jingled and clattered in their wooden crates.

Wiggins was crouching at the doors, but crawled back and sat opposite his rescuer. She sat between two crates, knees bent, long skirt hanging down between her legs, arms perched on either knee. She stared at him intently, her dark eyes fixed and unwa-vering, but not hostile. Wiggins stared back. He noted the strength in her face, her nimble, scarred fingers, her fearlessness.

'Thank you,' he said at last. 'I'm sorry about that.'

She squinted at him. 'Sorry about what?'

'About ruining your meeting. Getting up there and all. Bit of a plonker.'

Rose was about to snap back, but she paused at the word plonker. The van slewed around another corner. The bottles rattled and sang.

'Give me one good reason why I shouldn't toss you out right here? You seize my podium, you ruin my meeting, and all for a pack of lies about some poor woman probably desperate to escape you.'

'It weren't a pack of lies.'

'And what about Jack Zelig? He sure seems eager to see you.'

'What can I say? I have that effect on people.' Wiggins tried a smile, suddenly conscious that he stank of beer. 'I don't know what he sees in me.'

Rose snorted, unamused. 'What's her name?'

'Bela Grybus, married name Marinsky. 'Bout your age, I reckon.' She looked away, then back at the circles of glass in the doors.

The van bumped and clattered. A klaxon sounded close by. Wiggins picked up an empty bottle and felt its heft. 'You don't seem surprised,' he said after a moment.

'America's full of missing people.'

'Nah, I meant by the guns and shooting and that.'

'Why would I be surprised? This is New York.'

'What about the coppers?'

'Zelig *is* the cops down the Lower East Side.'

Just then, the van pulled to a halt. They listened as the driver got out and walked round to open the doors. Rose nodded to Wiggins, and he started forwards.

The driver pulled open the doors just as Wiggins put up his hand. He sat back, surprised, when he saw her.

'Rose Schneiderman,' the woman said in a delicate Irish accent, 'I never knew your demonstrations could be so exciting. You've been hiding your light under a bushel.'

Rose laughed darkly and pushed past Wiggins. The woman offered her hand, and Rose stepped out. 'You ain't seen nothing yet. Maud, this is . . .' She waved her hand absently at Wiggins.

'Wiggins,' he said, getting out. They'd parked on one of the quieter streets down towards the river – far uptown from the Lower East Side. It was almost dark now as Wiggins peered first at Maud, then up and down the freshly lit street.

Maud put her hand out to shake his. 'Good evening, Mr Wiggins.'

'Hey, not so fast with all that nicely, nicely, how-do-you-do Britisher crap, Maud. We've got to decide whether we take this guy to the precinct.'

'But whatever for?'

'What for?' Rose barked. 'He crashed my podium. He broke up our demonstration. Hell, he almost had us all killed.'

'And yet here we are.' Maud smiled. She put her hand on Rose's arm, and left it there.

'Who were them other blokes?' Wiggins said. 'The big geezers – went up to Zelig.'

Rose squinted at him again, her mouth twisted slightly in

suppressed amusement. 'Geezers? You mean Sirocco. It was his job to protect us.'

'You need protection for a demonstration?'

'I told you. This is New York.'

Wiggins nodded. Maud still had her hand on Rose's arm, gently, softly. They looked easy together, comfortable, in a way that made Wiggins turn and examine the other side of the street. He could make out the advertisements painted on a high wall. *From All Points Hunter Whiskey. Gratifies and Satisfies.* He licked his lips, but then his shoulders slumped. He suddenly felt awash with tiredness. The day on the streets, the booze, the pounding on and on about Bela, the booze, the crowd, the bullets, and on and on. His body, as if no longer taking direction from its errant master, cried out for sleep.

'Would you like a cup of tea, Mr Wiggins?' Maud said, pulling him back to that New York street, but the Irish-tinted English accent, the idea of tea, pulled him back to Dublin too, to London, to the tasks in front of him – finding Fitz's killer, denying German spies, and halting non-existent gun smuggling. He turned back to her.

'He doesn't want tea,' Rose barked. 'Look at him, slathering over that billboard. He's soaked.'

Wiggins looked between the two women, one short and powerful, the other tall, wispy, almost floating, but both with eyes steady and true and surely hearts to match. 'I wouldn't mind a sit-down.'

Thirty minutes later, he found himself ensconced on a sofa in a one-room office above a shop. The office was stacked with papers, posters, banners, a pile of clothes, newspapers, files, ribbons, and three tottering desks, each with a typewriter. Maud sat at one of the desks in a pool of green light cast by the desk lamp. She looked over at Wiggins every now and then, but said nothing as she worked. The street lamps threw faint shadows on the ceiling. Wiggins pulled off his boots, put his feet up and closed his eyes for a moment.

The office clearly belonged to a union or a campaign or

something similar. There were newspaper cuttings pasted on the wall, a poster about forthcoming meetings, and a banner with the words PICKETS LADIES TAILORS STRIKERS hung across the doorway.

'You union, or suffragette?' Wiggins asked at last.

Rose had left the office as soon as they'd got in, leaving Wiggins in the care of Maud. She looked up when he spoke and said, 'There was I thinking I was both.'

'Sorry, it's just . . .' He waved his hand around vaguely.

She put down her pen. 'Well, to be honest I *am* more of a suffrage campaigner than a union organiser. That's Rose.' She nodded at a photograph on the far wall, and gazed at it for a moment. 'She runs the NYWTUL – think of that, a national union run by a woman. She used to be a—'

'A seamstress, yeah, I saw.'

'How . . .?'

Wiggins rubbed his fingers together.

Maud didn't press it. Her eyes drifted back to the picture of Rose. 'Pulled herself out of poverty. First woman ever to set up a union branch – for the cap-makers. She's a pocket battleship, and the whole of New York knows it, especially after the Triangle fire. I've been all go since I met her.'

Wiggins nodded gently, put his head back once more and closed his eyes again.

'We didn't make a single one!' Rose marched into the room and threw down a slew of evening newspapers. Wiggins popped his eyes open.

Maud leaned over the desk to look at the headlines. 'Maybe we'll make the mornings,' she offered.

'No, no – look at it. There's only one story in this town tonight, and it'll be in all the papers for a week. Look at the *World*.'

Wiggins stretched over from the sofa and pulled down a newspaper, a copy of the *New York World*. It had one huge sentence highlighted like Wiggins had never seen. A 'headline' that took half the page.

NYPD LIEUTENANT IN CORRUPTION SCANDAL

Swope was right. Wiggins rocked back into the sofa and closed his eyes in relief. No need to worry about Becker now. 'Bent copper,' he said out loud.

'Let's eat,' Rose said. 'Not you,' she added without glancing at Wiggins. He smiled to himself. He couldn't help but like her. She was barely four foot ten, but you could tell she commanded any space she found herself in, and anyone in that space too.

Maud stood up, straightening the desk, and caught Rose's eye. 'Now then, Mr Wiggins doesn't have to go right now, does he? He looks all-in. Didn't you tell me the first time we met that you worried about break-ins?'

'It's a campaign office, not the Federal Reserve!'

Maud pulled on a lilac shawl and looked around for her hat. 'Where are you taking me? Italian?'

Rose let out her breath and turned to Wiggins. 'You can stay one night – on that sofa there, understand? Maud here has a heart that bleeds for a steak dinner, let alone a little boy searching for a lost love. You got that?'

Wiggins nodded slowly. 'I got it.' Now that Becker had been neutralised, he could go back to the Metropole, back to the OC, back even to the dosshouse in Hell's Kitchen. And he would do, too – but not tonight. Tonight he needed to sleep alone, where no one knew him, where no one would ever know him. He closed his eyes again and settled down. He listened as the two women fussed and chided and teased as they got ready, like new lovers.

They left, but a second later the door creaked back open and Rose said, 'Hey. What did you say her name was again? Your lady love.'

Wiggins opened his eyes to peek and told her. Rose's face clouded. 'I'm gonna have to check. You come back here in a day or two, I might have something for you.'

'Roses?'

'What?'

Wiggins closed his eyes. 'It ain't just women who need more than bread. We working men need roses too.'

As Wiggins slept a troubled sleep, Captain Vernon Kell began his journey home. Out past the East River, out, out, out past Staten Island, the Statue of Liberty a distant, diminishing beacon, he settled into his berth and cursed French vulgarity and wondered again whether Holmes and Wiggins were still untethered canons likely to blow holes in his ship. Out, out, out, further, over the roiling ocean, on Dublin's streets and in its alleyways, Vincent Hannigan crushed criminal insurrection with devout efficiency. And still Wiggins slept on, his dreams full of roses, and women.

I I

'Golly, it's you!'

Wiggins flinched. He'd knocked on O'Connell's hotel door expecting to see his putative boss, only to find Molly standing in front of him, grinning.

'We thought you were dead. I'm so glad you're not,' she went on.

'Is that him, is it?' O'Connell called from within.

Molly opened her arm out to the room, and bent her head slightly. She wore a floaty cotton lace dress and a dazzling enamel brooch. Wiggins couldn't help but smell her as he went past. Clean sweat and rose water.

He'd walked back to the Hotel Metropole that morning. The atmosphere in the hotel's café felt strangely subdued. Every morning he'd come in previously, there'd been a happy buzz. The late-night drinkers had gone, but the place would be gearing up for another day in paradise: journalists off shift, looking for the fag end of the night for leads, the odd gambler who'd won big, cigars and champagne bottles splashed across the tablecloths. That morning, though, the café hummed with sullen expectation. No gamblers celebrated. The cups and glasses sounded louder in the silence. The piano lid was closed. The doorman fidgeted with his lapels.

Only one man in the joint seemed in any way animated. Wiggins recognised him from the other day – the fat gentleman who had been named on the mortgage he'd stolen from Becker; the owner, indeed, of the house with the broken front door and the cop in the hallway. He sat at a round table with a splay of newspapers around him, smiling. 'Look at that, will ya?' he said to everyone and no one. 'You see this?'

Wiggins glanced at the stories as he passed. CORRUPT COP – GAMBLER TELLS ALL. As he reached the door into the lobby, he caught sight of a young man in a yellow waistcoat, wide-awake hat and dirty boots, slumped in the corner of the bar. Wiggins thought he was asleep, but the young man's head twitched as he saw him, like the faintest hint of recognition, quickly hidden. But Wiggins caught it. He went into the lobby and up the stairs to the top floor.

Now, in O'Connell's hotel room, he found the spruce OC regarding him askance. 'Where the hell have you been?' he snapped.

Wiggins shrugged. He glanced around. He felt a surprising stab of relief that the bed hadn't been slept in. None of Molly's things seemed to be in there either. He was pleased, despite himself, and that unsettled him.

'Patrick,' Molly said, a bubble of laughter in her voice. 'Not five minutes ago you were lamenting his demise, and now here he is.'

O'Connell glowered but said nothing. He looked much better than when Wiggins had seen him last, slobbering drunk after the night at Zelig's and mooning horribly about women and money and Dublin. A couple of days in a police cell had obviously done him good. His face had lost its reddish, boozy sheen. Maybe Wiggins should try it.

'Well?' Molly went on, reminding Wiggins of her presence. It was probably she who'd put O'Connell on better form, he suddenly realised. Judging from the state of the room, and her travelling clothes, she'd only just got back into town. He found himself standing taller when she was in the room, and quietly patting away the scuff marks on his sleeves.

'Well, right enough. I would have drunk a short one for your memory, Wiggins, had you gone. Maybe.'

Just then a racket broke out in the corridor outside. Slamming doors, shouting. '*Where is he? Where is he?*'

O'Connell moved to the door, then stared wildly at Wiggins.

It wasn't the cops. It must have been the man in the café, watching out for him and alerting Zelig's men. Zelig's pockets were deeper than he thought, sending men all the way up to Midtown. That man really didn't like a beating.

Molly didn't hesitate. She ripped Wiggins's cap from his hand and threw it out onto the iron fire escape that ran down the back of the building. Then she leaned out of the window, stretched up and pulled down the ladder that led to the roof. She twanged it very hard and let it vibrate. Wiggins couldn't help but look at her as she bent out of the window. He turned away quickly, only to see the OC doing the same. She drew back in, took hold of Wiggins's hand and pulled him towards the connecting door.

O'Connell shot a glance at them but didn't intervene. Instead, he faced the door to the corridor, just as the heavy footsteps approached.

Molly pulled Wiggins through the connecting door and turned the key. She placed her finger on his lips and held his eyes.

They heard the shouts and grunts from the corridor. 'What's this then?' the OC said, his voice clear through the door. He'd obviously let them into the room.

'Where's your boy?' a harsh New York voice pinged back. 'The Englishman.'

'He heard you coming.'

'Lefty, he's gone over the top,' another voice piped up.

'I told you,' the OC said. 'He heard you coming. A deaf man could hear you coming.'

Balls, Wiggins thought. O'Connell had them. There was a long silence. 'Lefty?' the second voice said again.

'Listen, mister,' Lefty said at last. 'You tell your boy. You tell him, Mr Zelig has put a price on his head. If he does not leave town, he is a dead man.'

'Why?'

'Whaddayamean why? You were there, you dope. He beat the big man blue, and the big man does not like that.'

Wiggins and Molly held each other's looks. Her wide eyes

widened further at this news of Wiggins's fighting prowess. She looked like a big cat sensing a kill.

'Well, it's nothing to do with me, sure it's not,' the OC said in the other room.

'Sure it is. He is your boy. And if you do not leave town, you are dead too.'

'What did I do? I paid the man a dollar to look after me, and here he is this morning asking for more money. I tell him no, he hears you coming, and he's off out and away.'

'You are to leave town. Big Jack Zelig says. So that is what is. *Versteh?*' And then, 'Gyp!'

Molly kept her eyes on Wiggins as they heard the men clatter out of the OC's room. Her cheeks had reddened. She didn't look in the least frightened. She looked excited.

'Hey,' the second New York voice said. 'Where's that door go?'

'I don't know,' O'Connell replied. 'It's always been locked.'

Suddenly someone rattled the door handle. Molly twitched. Wiggins braced his back leg and tensed his shoulders.

RAT-TAT-TAT – a metallic object banged against the door.

'Leave it, Gyp,' the first voice said. 'It goes to the other room.'

'I could blow off the lock?' the man called Gyp said, musing.

'He has gone over the roof – he did the same to Becker. In any case, I do not think Big Tim Sullivan will be too happy if we shoot up his hotel. And if Big Tim is not happy, then Zelig will not be happy either. We go, but you, old man, get out of town – and if you don't take your boy with you, he is a dead man.'

It wasn't until they heard the door slam, and the two men scuttle away down the hotel corridor, that Wiggins realised he and Molly had been holding hands throughout the whole exchange. She'd dragged him into her room at the beginning and neither of them had thought to let go. Her excitement felt physical. The danger. For the first time, Wiggins began to understand. O'Connell knocked on the door and they sprang apart, the spell broken.

Molly unlocked the door and they trooped back into O'Connell's room, hangdog. For all the seriousness of the situation, the armed men after him, the cops still sniffing around, and the very fact that he was working undercover in an organisation that would rip him in two if they ever found out he worked for the British Government, Wiggins felt an irresistible urge to giggle. He could sense it in Molly, too, the giddy nervousness as O'Connell regarded them sternly.

'You were meant to protect me, not the other way around,' O'Connell said at last. 'Jaysus. I feel like your da, so I do.' He shook his head and sat down in one of the three armchairs. Molly drifted away from his side to sit at a small writing desk.

Wiggins stood. He looked between the two, feeling something pass between them but he wasn't sure what. The last twenty minutes had unsettled him. First, seeing Molly there, feeling her so close, and his own startling, irrational relief that she hadn't slept in O'Connell's bed. Then the appearance of Zelig's men. He'd misjudged Zelig and the big man's reach. What for Wiggins had simply been a barroom brawl had obviously become a matter of honour. A matter of honour for a man who had gunmen on the payroll.

At that moment, as O'Connell worked on his fingernails and Molly began writing on hotel paper, Wiggins was most troubled by what O'Connell had said to the men after him. He'd protected Wiggins, sure, but he'd lied with such facility, such conviction, that Wiggins was rapidly reappraising his view of the man. Specifically, Wiggins wondered as the OC dusted non-existent lint from his sleeves, was this the man who'd killed Fitz?

O'Connell looked up at Molly. 'Is it time?' he said.

She stopped writing, inclined her head slightly, glanced sidelong at Wiggins and nodded.

'Right, you, sit down.' He pointed to the chair opposite. 'You're an idiot, so you are. Not only have you set the polis on us, you've got every gunman in New York on to you. What the hell have you been doing?'

'It weren't me that got us into trouble with Zelig, was it?'

O'Connell flicked his eyes at Molly, who was bent over the desk. 'Yes, well, you didn't have to beat the bejaysus out of him. But what's done is done. Why the hell was I arrested?'

'That was a mistake.' Wiggins shifted his gaze. The room had a sink with hot and cold taps, and he picked out the various soaps, brushes and grooming apparel that the OC took with him everywhere. The silence continued.

'Tell me!' O'Connell shouted. He hadn't moved from his chair, and he looked outwardly cool – despite the rising heat – but the cold fury in his voice was clear.

Wiggins dipped his chin and avoided eye contact. Molly's pen scratched away at the desk. He could hear her breathe out. 'I set the wrong man straight is all,' he said at last. 'Turned out to be a bent copper with big fists. But we don't need to worry 'bout him no more, he's in shtuk of his own.'

O'Connell clucked his tongue, then spoke in his normal voice. 'That's what I heard. Becker fella.' He considered, then nodded. 'Good. Never lie to me, see-ho? See-ho?' he repeated, more loudly.

Wiggins nodded.

'Right, to business. It's time you knew what the business here really is.'

'Ain't Hannigan keeping things sweet?'

'Ach, Dublin's dandy. Or it will be when I get back. Lynch is a pipsqueak, with a cock to match, and we'll soon make him happy. Didn't I tell you about little Becky up at the Talbot? She'll make him happy, so she will. No, we're here for money.'

Wiggins shrugged again. He could sense the seriousness in the OC now, that this was the moment when the door might be opened – but he didn't want to let on that he cared. 'I know,' he said. 'Ain't we been lapping at Big Tim's door near a month, looking for the scraps?'

'Shut up,' O'Connell said. 'You're clever, but you're ignorant, son. We have been paying homage, so we have, and you don't do anything in this town without homage. It may be called New

York, but these people rule like ancient kings, and you need to pay your tribute.'

The OC rested his hands on his knees once more. Wiggins shifted in his seat. 'But why's you need the cash anyways? Ain't Dublin sweet?'

'Because of the amount we need, see-ho? The amount Fitz stole – the amount you can't fucking find.'

The word 'Fitz' hit Wiggins like a hammer. It hung in the airless hotel room like a suit of forgotten clothes. Yet Fitz wasn't a suit of clothes – he'd been a crumpled, broken, grey corpse in a barrel, and now a rotting body out in the pits of Glasnevin. Wiggins thought of those lies slipping out of O'Connell, and wondered again whether he'd misjudged his man. Certainly, O'Connell wouldn't baulk at killing a man; he'd done it before and he would do it again. Your average thick-skulled policeman – your Lestrade or Jones from the old days – might have assumed that any criminal killing was designed as a message. That if O'Connell had wanted to punish Fitz for stealing, he would have murdered him out in the open, for all to see. But Wiggins wasn't so sure. The OC was cute and the OC was vain. Such a message would have been a tacit admission of failure, an admission that it was possible to steal from him. O'Connell wouldn't have wanted anyone knowing either how important Fitz was, or that he'd been able to dupe him. O'Connell was omniscient.

And now, as the older man leaned slightly forward in his chair, Wiggins realised he was finally going to be trusted and that if he broke that trust, he too would be a dead man. Most of his life he'd lived close to death; from the Irregulars' first base in Paddington arches, to the dust and pity and shells of the veldt, to the streets of London, Death had stalked everyone he knew. But never before had this real threat taken the form of the by turns genial and volcanic, pristine Irishman now eyeing him closely from across a Manhattan hotel room, while his mistress scratched and tutted as she wrote.

'All right then,' Wiggins said at last. He forced himself back into character. Stay as close to the truth as possible in your backstory, and stay as close to who you are as you can. He reck-oned he knew what it was for, but there was nothing like getting someone to tell you in their own words, seeing the whites of their eyes, to find out if they really meant it. 'How much do you need, and what the bloody hell is it for?'

Before O'Connell could answer, Molly interjected. 'Guns,' she said simply. Wiggins couldn't see her face.

~~

They never did get to see Big Tim in the end.

Molly and O'Connell left Wiggins in the hotel for most of the day. It was clear to Wiggins that the bellhop was somehow reporting to Zelig's men and thus he couldn't move before 8 p.m. Wiggins had made a point of learning the staff rota at the Metropole as soon as O'Connell had moved in. Hotel staff knew every detail of every guest; sometimes they knew more about a man and wife than the couple knew about each other. He assumed Zelig would use the bellhops as a source of information.

'I'll slip out after eight,' he grunted.

'Good,' the OC replied, pinching his cuffs. 'We're due at the Occidental at eight thirty. Stay here until then. Your men there won't be back in here any time soon, not unless you're spotted downstairs. Is that understood?'

Wiggins grunted again. The OC might have been dead drunk and at rock bottom when he'd carried him back from Zelig's the other day, but he'd reasserted his control now. Wiggins was his boy, and he wasn't going to let him forget it. Especially in front of Molly.

'Molly?' O'Connell said, breaking into Wiggins's train of thought.

'Ready,' she said brightly, as if about to embark on a Sunday-morning ride down Rotten Row rather than a gunrunning plot designed to strike a blow at the most powerful empire the world had ever known. Wiggins frowned involuntarily, and from Molly's reaction he knew she'd registered his unease. She collected her bag and a parasol, humming a jaunty air and refusing to catch his eye. Yet he felt her talking to him through her movements, the way she bent away from him, the arc of her neck as she pinned her hair, even the rhythm of her humming, which shifted from one tune to another, ending on a soft, lilting refrain. And when she and the OC left, her scent remained, talking to him still, in the empty room.

That scent came back to him as he and O'Connell sat in the café of the Occidental Hotel later that night, waiting for word of Big Tim Sullivan. Wiggins had slipped out of the Metropole when the bellhops changed shifts and made it to the Occidental just in time to meet O'Connell on his own.

Wiggins gazed up at the frescoes on the ceiling, lurid pink nudes bathing in a turquoise sea. 'Not here,' a voice suddenly addressed them. Wiggins looked down to see a short man with brilliantined hair and bottle-thick horn-rimmed glasses. He handed O'Connell a visiting card. 'Go to Jimmy the Priest's at ten. Ask for a Mr Doyle.'

O'Connell squinted at the address. 'You mean Little Patsy Doyle? A bloody Duster? You kidding me?'

'Just ask for Doyle.'

'But I was told Big Tim—'

'And Big Tim is telling you to go to Doyle, at ten.'

The address turned out to be a bar on the Lower West Side, facing the shambling docks and warehouses on the Hudson River. The bar took up the whole ground floor of a four-storey terrace, but it was a long way from the swank and bustle of the Occidental and its naked frescoes. Wiggins could just make out in the last of the evening light the words *The Williams and Wells Company* in black on the brickwork above the bar front. The walls were a sickly, choleric shade of yellow and the whole place stank of beer, cheap whiskey and the perpetual weather-beaten decay of a dockside dive. It was a sailors' bar. Sailors, hookers and drunks.

Wiggins went in first, while the OC took a turn around the

block. From outside, the bar had looked like the arsehole of the island – and the inside lived up to that description. For the first time since he'd arrived in New York, Wiggins felt something like home. He clambered on to a bar stool, signalled for a beer from an avuncular, heavyset barman and scoped the joint. A few scattered tables, bar stools, little forests of empty glasses here and there. This was a place for drinking and not much else. A large ledger lay open behind the bar, beneath a rack of keys, next to a set of stairs. It was a boarding house, too, and Wiggins reckoned that at least half the people in there, once they'd reached sufficient levels of stupefaction (or penury), would stumble up those stairs to bed.

Further down the bar from where he drank, a group of obvious regulars were engaged in the kind of rambling, six-way conversation that Wiggins had witnessed all his pub-going life. The barman dropped in and out, refereeing, placating and deftly avoiding requests for credit or a free drink. The four men and two women lamented their lot, cracked old jokes, repeated complaints and shouted out lewd endearments to the young woman bussing the glasses.

One end of the seating area was partitioned off by a wooden screen with frosted glass. He could make out through the open door a large round card table, where two or three men sat and smoked but did not play. Undoubtedly, this would be where Doyle conducted his business, and they'd be expecting the OC there.

'Hey, Dolores,' one of the regulars shouted at the busgirl as she fussed behind the bar. He rattled the last of the ice in his empty glass. 'Has the iceman come yet?'

'No,' the girl said wearily. 'But he's breathing real hard.'

The regulars at the bar cackled, willing themselves to find an oft-repeated joke funny one more time.

Just then, O'Connell came in. Wiggins indicated with his eyes to the partition, and waited. The OC strode straight to the marked-off area, but made a point of leaving the door open. Wiggins watched as the OC shook hands with one of the seated men and sat down. One of the other men had got up and was now leaning against the far wall, just in Wiggins's eyeline. He thrust his hands into his pockets, revealing a holstered pistol nestled against his ribs. A display. You could go months in London never seeing a gun, even down the dodgy boozers. All Wiggins had ever seen, except for the semi-automatics Peter and his lot had cut about with, was the odd service revolver. Old soldiers hanging on to their irons. Every second American seemed to carry a gun, as if their cocks didn't work proper.

Wiggins signalled for another beer and pulled his shirt away from his shoulder. Manhattan was hot, and down by the docks it stank too. He glanced along the bar. A young man with an angry pinch mark between his eyes and a beakish nose stood with his hand on a whiskey bottle, pointing. 'Damn it, ain't it time to forget about God for the moment? What's He ever done for us?'

'Easy, Gene,' the bartender said.

'Sorry, Harry, but really? There's these Europeans have the right idea. Anarchists.' He necked a large slug from the whiskey bottle, then glanced over at Wiggins. 'Hey, mister? You from Europe?'

'London.'

'See, you know about anarchists. Tell 'em they ain't all bad, are they?'

Wiggins considered. 'The only anarchists I know burned to death in a fire of their own making, after shooting dead four coppers and an eight-year-old kid.'

Harry the barman let out a bitter laugh. The angry man eyed Wiggins carefully, poured a shot of the whiskey and pushed the glass towards him without saying a word. Wiggins nodded, and said nothing. He didn't need to say anything. That one gesture was enough. You looked at politics too closely when you were at the bottom of the pile and the answer always came back 'Drink'. He shot the booze back and shivered as it burned his throat. Everyone had brighter ideas for the future, for the world – Peter, Jakov, Molly, too, it seemed. In his experience, political action made things worse; certainly, it rarely made things better, at least for those that needed the help most.

Still, a small part of him did hope for something better, could almost glimpse it in the reflections of these flawed revolutionaries, though in their words rather than in their deeds. If they could only rise above their own flaws, fears and egos, maybe their ideas might change the world for the better. Was Molly that woman? Was the cause of Irish nationalism that cause? Would it turn around the Empire, and by extension the world, such that the workers would finally get their dues?

'See-ho!' the OC hissed across the barroom. He stood at the open door to the partitioned room and gestured Wiggins over.

Wiggins downed the last of his beer, nodded at the barman and sauntered over. It never did to show the boss you were eager. The only thing eagerness led to was more work.

'Jaysus,' O'Connell whispered. 'You're slower than a priest in the chair, so you are. Now listen, I want you to—'

'O'Connell!' a male voice boomed from inside the partitioned room. 'Is that your man there, is it?'

'It is.'

'Then bring him in. I want to see the fella.'

Doubt flashed across O'Connell's face, followed quickly by resignation. The face of a supplicant. Wiggins had seen it often enough. You come from the streets, you serve in the army, you work for a living, you're a supplicant – you feel *lucky* to be a supplicant, cos that normally means you're gonna get something when the alternative is nothing. Still, Wiggins felt with a lurch, it wasn't comforting to see the OC in such a position. He stepped past him into the room, towards the owner of the voice, his new boss of sorts.

The man, Doyle, did not get up. He swayed back in his chair, hands clasped behind his head, elbows jutting, the bright buttons of his waistcoat agleam. Fresh sweat darkened his shirt at the armpits, but Little Patsy Doyle obviously didn't care. He smiled at Wiggins, a wolfish smile. 'So, *you're* the Englishman?' His eyes shone bright and huge and wide awake, despite the cigarette smoke swirling.

'London,' Wiggins said.

'He don't look up to much, does he, Meath?' Doyle said to the large, heavy man leaning against the wall. His eyes looked fat and glowing too.

Meath grunted. 'He smells of booze.' Then he stepped forward, looming over Wiggins like an avalanche.

'I use it when I can't find cologne. You know, to cover the smell.'

Doyle laughed. 'I hear about you a lot, fella. A lot. You are making trouble all the way from the Lower East Side to Hell's Kitchen and back.' As he said this, he opened a small metal box on the table in front of him. It contained white powder and a little spoon.

'I'm from London,' Wiggins replied. 'I'm not used to these small towns.'

'New York?' Doyle clapped and leaned forward, laughing again. 'I wouldn't get a price for you, fella.' He held up the small spoon, scooped a tiny amount of the powder and with one violent snort took it up his nose.

Wiggins stepped back involuntarily, astonished. 'New York ain't bad, I s'pose,' he said quickly, to cover his surprise.

It was, in fact, true. Ever since he'd been in the city, he'd noticed how everyone owned the streets. Germans, Eastern European, Italians, Irish – they strode around like they owned the place, or at least like they owned a part of it, their little polished patch of sidewalk. New Yorkers belonged, and they were happy to let anyone know it. Not like Belgravia or Hampstead or Kensington; a poor immigrant – Bela, say – would tread those wealthy London streets with care. America was open. It would be the greatest country in the world, Wiggins thought, if it continued to remember this. Anywhere that could attract the best of us would one day be the best of us.

But just then, with the swollen Meath next to him and the staring, buzzy Doyle acting the big man, Wiggins held his front, put out his chest and did not buckle. 'But it don't matter what price you get on me. I ain't for sale, not to you or your nose.'

'Hey!' Meath stepped forward.

'Why am I here?' Wiggins went on, looking at Doyle.

O'Connell coughed from behind. 'Mr Doyle here—'

'Patsy, please. We're among friends.'

'Yes,' the OC said. 'Patsy would like to . . . er . . . like to meet Miss Lansdown-Smith. You're to get her from the hotel, see-ho!'

Wiggins turned to O'Connell in astonishment. 'Now?'

The OC nodded and set his features hard, not a flicker of concern about Molly coming to such a place, or for Wiggins having to get back into the Metropole, for that matter.

'But why?' Wiggins said.

Slam! Slam! Slam! Doyle brought his hands down on the table. Everyone turned to him in surprise. 'Listen, you streak of English – sorry, *London* – piss, I don't give a goddam what you think or why. I am here on behalf of Big Tim Sullivan – Big Tim, no less – who wishes to help out the old country in any way he can. Which means he has asked me, as the leader of the Hudson Dusters, to lend you some money, but I don't like bankrolling anyone until I know why and—'

'I told you why.' O'Connell stepped forward.

Doyle held his hand up and went on. 'Until I know why said party is so interested in borrowing the money. And so . . .' he glared at the OC '. . . I want to meet the mysterious Miss Lansdown-Smith, or there's no deal.'

Wiggins glanced again at the OC, up at the monstrous Meath and back to Doyle. The little man's eyes still glared big and bright, but now he looked around nervously and shrugged inside his too big suit. His hands fidgeted with the dust box on the table.

'Now, Meath,' Doyle said, pulling himself together, 'bring us in a bottle of Harry's best. Me and the OC here will talk over the details, while you fella – ' he pointed at Wiggins ' – you will do as you're told. Tyrone!' he called. A door behind him suddenly sprang open and a small young man appeared. He wore a cap with a high peak and had dark skin. He shot quick, shy glances around the room. Doyle didn't even look at him. 'Take him up to the Hotel Metropole on 43rd in the automobile,' Doyle said. 'Can't have a lady waiting on the streets, can we?'

'On you go,' O'Connell muttered, and pulled up a chair. 'She'll be as good as gold, you'll see.'

12

Wiggins sat next to Tyrone as the open-top Packard glided through the Village and up to the Metropole. 'What kind of name is Tyrone anyway?' he asked at last.

Tyrone's hand fidgeted on the wheel. He glanced sidelong at Wiggins.

'Don't worry,' Wiggins went on. 'I'm staff. I'm just doing as I'm told. No one cares a stuff what I think.'

The kid nodded sharply and blinked. 'My name's Petey. But the boss fella likes to give us all Irish names. You know, the counties or something – Tyrone, Galway, Kilkenny. There's even a Tipperary.'

Wiggins thought again of Fitz. The man-boy Tyrone was a similar age, and probably had a similar job. The boy had a fearful air to him, though, like he expected death at every corner. And those nerves were nothing to do with the driving.

'Swimmer, are you?' Wiggins asked idly.

The car swerved. 'How you know that?' Tyrone gasped.

'I never learned,' Wiggins went on. 'Almost killed me, that. How did you?'

'What else you know about me?'

'Easy on, fella, I ain't being fly – your hands tell me most things. Like you were a canner?'

'Right again,' Tyrone said. But then he looked at his hands on the wheel, the old cuts and scars. 'Near cut off each of my fingers, one time or another. But you is right, I swim whenever I can – I'm a wharf baby. I could swim like an eel before I could walk.'

They moved into Midtown, where the buildings got higher,

the cafés got louder and the lights, the lights seemed brighter than the sun. 'And what's the boss's business?' Wiggins said.

Tyrone shrugged. 'This and that.'

'And what's the white powder? Is it cocaine?'

'It is.'

'Thought so,' Wiggins said. 'I knew someone once, stuck the stuff in his arm with a syringe. I ain't never seen no one stick it up their nose, though.'

'Why do you think we're called the Hudson Dusters?'

Wiggins laughed. 'You like it, do you?'

Tyrone shook his head. 'Not me, mister. I gotta keep sharp.' His eyes slid back to the road. Wiggins knew his type, the flotsam and jetsam of a big city, knew that nervousness, the feeling of never being able to say you were safe. The boy pointed. 'The Metropole. You want me to pull up out front?'

'Nah, drop me here.' Wiggins gestured to a spot on the corner, sheltered from the Metropole by a rubbish cart. 'Keep an eye out. I'll turn left out of the hotel and walk fast. Come up behind us dead slow, but don't stop. We'll step on the board.'

'What's the big noise?' Tyrone said.

Wiggins looked at him carefully. 'That's just the way things are, Tyrone. Ain't that the world?'

He got out of the car and slipped a pebble into his boot. Then he pulled up his collar, took out a new cap, stooped his shoulders and turned his cuffs out. 'Hey, can I borrow that?' he asked. Tyrone handed him down a brilliant yellow silk handkerchief. Wiggins tied it around his neck in a raffish style and limped towards the hotel.

The Metropole café teemed. Chorus girls lined the bar while sweaty gamblers cruised or drank strong drinks from tall glasses and smoked bitter cigarettes. As he limped through, Wiggins caught the fag end of a heated conversation. 'Get out, Herman!' A wide-shouldered man in a check suit pointed a stubby finger at someone sitting down.

'I'm in the papers!' the sitting man protested, looking down at the newspapers splayed across his table. 'Ain't it grand?'

'You better shut up.' The man in the check suit waved his hand and strode away, past Wiggins.

Wiggins kept his head down as he passed the distracted bellhop in the lobby and took the stairs two at a time. But it wasn't the exertion that made his heart beat faster as he rapped on Molly's door.

'It's you,' she said, delighted. 'Again. You can come in, if you like – if your sense of decorum allows.'

She was fully dressed, as if she'd been expecting him. She even had her hat on, and a bright blue sash over her shoulder. Wiggins stared at her for a moment. She stared back, taking him in, grinning. 'Well? Do you want to come in?' she said at last.

'Er, we . . . um . . . Yes, no,' Wiggins stuttered. 'I mean, we've got to go. The OC . . .'

'That yellow looks good on you. It suits your eyes.'

Wiggins's hand went to his neck involuntarily. 'O'Connell, he needs you there to help close the deal,' he said, holding his eyes low.

The easy grin left Molly's face as she picked up her bag and went to close the door. She hesitated, searching his face until he met her eye. 'Are you all right, Wiggins? You look . . . unsure.'

Wiggins turned his head aside. 'It's a dodgy old boozer is all. It ain't no place for a lady. It ain't no place for a gent neither, if I'm honest.'

'But you'll protect me.'

They moved sharply through the hotel lobby, Wiggins a stride behind Molly, playing the servant as ever. He moved forward to open the door.

'Hey, you there!'

'Keep going,' Wiggins whispered.

'You,' the voice boomed through the room, causing heads to turn. Wiggins had no choice but to stop and angle his body slightly, hand on door. 'Your name Wiggins? It says "Wiggins" here – you Wiggins?' The bellhop scuttled across the lobby.

Wiggins took a step towards him, clenching his fist at his side. He was close enough to the door to down the man with a straight right, then run for it. Tyrone would drag the car up alongside in a clinch. He picked a spot where the bellhop's hat strap pinched his chin, set his legs ready for the swing—

'Is this you?' the bellhop said angrily. He held up an envelope with *Mr Wiggins c/o the Hotel Metropole* written across it in black ink.

'Yes,' he replied, dropping his arm.

'This ain't a mailroom, mister,' the angry bellhop said, handing him the note. 'I've got a good mind to charge you for this. What do you say about that?'

'I say put it on Mr O'Connell's bill.'

A volley of shouts burst out of the café, the piano music halting for a moment. The bellhop turned towards the commotion. 'Let's go,' Wiggins muttered to Molly as he put the note in his pocket.

They hustled out onto the street, turned sharply out of the exit and didn't look round. A few moments later, Tyrone drove up from behind them and slowed the car. 'Look lively,' Wiggins said to Molly.

He put his arm around her waist and together they leapt onto the running-board of the Packard. He bundled her into the back, whistling for Tyrone to speed up. Molly whooped as the car slewed around the corner into Broadway. Wiggins squeezed in beside her. She did not move away.

'This is jolly,' she said, as the lights of the theatres and cafés swept by, night-time New York on show. The car picked up speed and the hot wind rippled their clothes. 'How marvellous.'

Wiggins grunted.

Molly bent her head towards him, close enough to smell her. 'You look nervous,' she said quietly. 'Don't be nervous.' She pulled her gloves off slowly.

'These fellas are armed,' he said. 'I don't like guns.'

'But think of what they'll be for,' she said, missing the point. He could feel her hot breath on his cheek, but didn't dare look at her. 'You're a working man. We're doing this for Ireland, for the working people. Ireland will be a beacon.'

As she began this speech, Molly slipped her hand into the pocket of Wiggins's trousers. 'The working people of the world will look to us.' She ripped out the lining of his trouser pocket in one swift jerk and took hold of his cock. 'They'll be excited,' she went on, looking straight ahead, her hand working. 'They'll be emboldened that a country like Ireland can *rise up* and defeat the mighty, mighty British Empire. Does that not excite you?'

Wiggins nodded, but could not speak. She let her strong, soft, small hand do its work. Bright lights flashed by as the Packard slewed away from the main streets towards the docks and Jimmy the Priest's. When it was over, as the car bobbed to a halt, Wiggins couldn't suppress a loud sigh. Molly pulled her hand out just as Tyrone yanked the brake stick.

'I find it exciting,' Molly said brightly. 'This chance of freedom.' She put her gloves back on, and continued, seemingly unaware of what she'd just done to Wiggins. 'I find it exciting that we are on this journey together, that you are here to help us free Ireland, that you are here with us. With *me*.'

At this, Molly looked him straight in the face. Tyrone had jumped down and was opening the door beside him. And as Wiggins shifted and moved to hide the evidence of his own excitement, he looked into her eyes and saw it there too – in the half-knowing, half-amused but always dazzling eyes, caught in the glaring electric lights that danced and swung outside the Priest's. The colour up in her cheeks, the slightly parted lips, the eyes like saucers.

He wasn't the only one who found New York exciting.

'Gene! Gene!' a voice cried from the heavens. 'Whaddaya doin'?'

Wiggins looked up. Sounds of a scuffle drifted down from an open window above him. He could just make out a figure shadowed against the window, then suddenly hauled back in. 'You crazy sonofabitch!' the voice went on. 'It's only two floors, you dope. Get back here.'

'I can't,' Gene cried. 'I can't, I can't, I can't.'

'You're not going to save anyone by breaking your ankles, are you? If you really want to kill yourself, we'll go up to the El tomorrow, when it's light. Here, have another drink.'

More scuffling, then the voices receded into the room above Jimmy the Priest's and Wiggins returned to his toilet.

He had delivered Molly into the pub, as far as the partition. The OC had leapt from his chair at the sight of her and she'd shot him and Little Patsy Doyle a languid smile. In that moment, Wiggins didn't exist and he'd slipped back to the bar.

Only then did he realise how sticky he was. 'John?' he said to the bartender.

'Now ya talking like one of us.' He grinned. 'And you can piss like one of us too. It's out the back.'

The bartender had meant this literally. The backyard ran into an open drain, and drinkers simply leaned against the wall and pissed. Wiggins had jostled his way into the corner when he'd been distracted by the shouts from above.

Now that the suicidal Gene and the drunken Samaritan had retreated inside, Wiggins tried to clean himself up. His mind was aflame with Molly. He counted to ten, then looked up into the sky once more. Gene reappeared in the window above, but this time he was singing a gentle, happy song, a not quite lament about requited love.

Wiggins dipped his hand into a hanging bucket – someone working at Jimmy's was a real gent, to have water to wash in and all – and it was only when he was patting his hands dry that he remembered. The note left for him at the Metropole, the one the bellhop had handed him.

'Isn't she the cream, eh, Wiggins?'

Wiggins bent his head back slightly. 'Eh?' He was sitting up front in the motor, next to Tyrone at the wheel, as they drove back uptown. O'Connell sat behind the driver, while Molly sat behind Wiggins. He felt her eyes on his back, but he couldn't bring himself to turn to her.

'This woman here by my side – the absolute cat's whiskers, so she is. She's the best.'

Wiggins finally twisted round to look at O'Connell. In his eyeline, Molly flinched, impatient for something, though he couldn't tell what. Wiggins nodded. 'Are we in with Doyle then? Are the Dusters going to dish?'

'By God, and there was me thinking you're a romantic. I'm heaping praise on my lady love, singing like the angels on high, and all you're on to is the business. Isn't that the English all over?'

'But is it on?' Wiggins persisted, avoiding Molly's eye.

'Of course it's on!' O'Connell cried in exasperation. 'I am just halfway into my hosannas about Molly here, you see? She's the best, so she is.'

Wiggins nodded again, and craned his neck around further to see her.

'Who was the note from?' Molly asked suddenly.

Wiggins shook his head slightly.

'What's this?' the OC asked.

'It's nothing,' Wiggins grunted. He pointed past Tyrone. 'Pull up here, same as before.'

'Oh no, we won't,' the OC called. 'We'll drive up to the front like everybody else. You don't like the Metropole, Wiggins, it's not up to scratch?'

'It's . . . you know – I'm known.'

'Ach, shall we go to the Waldorf tomorrow, shall we? Molly?'

Tyrone pulled the motor up outside the hotel and leapt to Molly's door, all nerves and twitches. 'That would be wonderful, darling Patrick,' she said, then added loudly, 'I'm going to turn in. I am absolutely bushwhacked. Is that what you Boer veterans say, Wiggins, when you need to go into a long, deep sleep?'

'Something like that,' he said, avoiding her eye again. She went into the hotel without another word. Wiggins got out and stood with the OC, who wore a troubled look. Wiggins warily checked out the corner of the café through the glass. He hadn't forgotten those thugs of Zelig's. 'Can we get into the lobby, boss?' he muttered.

The OC barely glanced at Tyrone as he waved off the motor. He marched into the hotel, Wiggins by his side. 'It's too hot for me here,' Wiggins said, stepping into an alcove partly obscured by a large palm plant.

'And you meant to be a bodyguard?' O'Connell hissed. He cast his eyes up the stairs, where Molly had just disappeared.

'We was both warned off here, weren't we?' Wiggins persisted.

'Ach, Doyle's seen to those pretty-boy Jews. They won't be bothering me again.'

'And what about me?'

'You?' O'Connell fixed him with a stare. He dropped his voice. 'The only person you've got to worry about is me, the stupid bloody bastard who pays the bills. You want a way out of here? New York too hot for you? Then do the fuck as I say.' He paused, checked the empty lobby and put his hand on Wiggins's shoulders in another one of his unsettling attempts at intimacy. Or an intimate attempt at intimidation, more like. 'Listen, son, get yourself a flop tonight. You'll be dandy. And tomorrow, tomorrow night, we'll be on the big boat out of here, with the money from Doyle. You help me with this and get us on the boat, you'll get your big bonanza. You'll get your compensation.'

Cash. Money. Did it always come down to that in the end? It was what all these men had over him – Holmes, the army, Leach, Kell and now the OC – it was what everyone had had over him his whole life long; it was what he always needed, to live, to buy the next day's meal. It was what the rich never understood, why Molly had asked him the reason he was working for the OC, why Holmes contemplated what he, Wiggins, might do in the future, as if he'd ever really had any choice in this world: he had to work to stay alive, and that normally meant the first job that came along, until that ended on the whim of the boss, and then another job, and another, until your muscles wasted and your eyes grew weak and your hands shook, and all for what? When would it ever end – just in death? Did the contents of the note weighing heavy in his pocket change that? He didn't know. But he did know what to say to O'Connell.

'What do I need to do?'

After the OC had finished, Wiggins turned away. There was a knot of people at the lobby door, so he strode into the café, head down, troubled. The OC had whispered the briefest of hideous instructions in his ear and it was all he could do to nod mutely. He was to meet O'Connell in the Waldorf Astoria late the next afternoon, and then carry out the plan.

As he entered the café, his senses prickled into life. Something wasn't right. A hush where no hush should be. It was packed, but no one made a sound. The fat man from earlier sat in front, perusing his papers still, his rumpled pink shirt billowing around him like a ball gown. As Wiggins was about to walk past, a small, thin man, dappered up, approached the table. 'Hey, Herman,' the dapper man said to the fat guy. 'There's someone wants to see you outside.'

Herman got up, grasping the last of his cigars. Wiggins blurted out, 'Don't go.' Through the window he could see the empty street, brilliantly illuminated by the arc lights that dazzled down from the Metropole. It shouldn't be empty, even at two in the morning, not so close to Times Square. The silent café, full of singers and gamblers and actors. Fucking actors. And it was grave mute. Everyone knew something was going to happen. Everyone but Herman.

'Fuck off, mister,' Herman said to Wiggins, and followed the dapper man to the exit. The glass doors swung open. Wiggins stepped forward, almost mesmerised by the situation, the dread he felt.

He saw Herman standing alone on the sidewalk. Suddenly, a Packard pulled up and three men got out. One of them raised a pistol and fired. The shots crashed and boomed and echoed in the empty street, shattering the quiet of the café. The chorus girls lining the bar screamed. The silent gamblers scrambled under their tables, composure gone.

As the shooting stopped, Wiggins watched through the swinging glass door as one of the gunmen stepped towards the body. He was supremely unconcerned by what he'd done. He bent over Herman's body for a second and said, 'Bye-bye, Herman,' then looked straight up at Wiggins. Wiggins started – he was one of Zelig's men. And beside him, out on the street, the other men were Zelig's too – Lefty Louie and Gyp the Blood, perhaps, if they were the men who'd visited O'Connell's hotel room. Certainly, they'd been with Zelig at Rose's demonstration.

The killer gasped in surprise, and an angry frown etched on his face. He brought up the gun again.

Wiggins, shocked by the moment, still shocked by what O'Connell had just asked him to do, stood mute.

The killer squeezed the trigger *CLICK, CLICK, CLICK* – out of bullets.

'Louie, let's go,' someone shouted from the Packard and Louie turned and jumped onto the running-board. The car accelerated away in a screech of rubber.

Wiggins rushed out into the street, the shocked café regulars close behind. Herman lay at his feet, his fat white body bleeding onto the sidewalk. Wiggins gazed after the Packard as it raced towards Broadway and off into the distance. A police whistle burst the night air at last.

He looked down. He had blood on his shoes.

Wiggins picked his steps carefully. Dawn broke, beautifully, over the East River, a blueish light that coloured and mottled the tops of the tenements, leaving the north–south streets cool and nightly still.

He felt safe enough at this time in the morning. There were few people around. He looked up at a tenement, 141 Essex Street, and hesitated. Laughter broke out, startling him. It was a seagull, laughing like the policeman. The bird plucked at the detritus outside a shuttered saloon, then took off, flapping and squawking away towards the birds circling the peaks of the Brooklyn Bridge, like the new flying machines in the newsreels. One, two bumps and then away, free.

The note in his hand read:

A Miss GRYBUS, late of Europe, arrived New York City before 1911, currently resides at apartment 22, 141 Essex Street. We have kept the money you so graciously advanced us.
    With compliments,
    A. Weiss, People-Finding Union

Wiggins looked up again at the building, and then entered.

Poverty was poverty wherever you went. It had a smell, a reek, that wasn't just squalor – it was almost elemental. This is where you are, and this is who you are, and ain't that the shame. As he walked through the hallway and up the stairs, he could see all the familiar signs of over-occupation – the lack of sanitation, small, bleary-eyed kids spilling from the doorways, every wall too close.

He finally reached the fourth floor and knocked on the door marked 22.

Last time he'd seen Bela, she'd been running away from the police in London. He'd caught her just as she was about to blow up a bomb and he'd let her go, even as the detritus of the explosion flew through the air. He'd even given her all the money he had. This despite his conviction that she was involved in the death of his best friend, Bill – albeit possibly indirectly. And there it was, he thought bitterly as he stared at the door, that 'albeit', that 'indirectly' – had he already forgiven her? Did he even care if he couldn't forgive her? Would it be enough to see her again, to hold her hand once more, to cradle her in his arms? Was the lie he'd been peddling all this time, to Molly, to O'Connell, about his lady love, even a lie at all? Wasn't it actually the truth, this complex lie? Wasn't his heart beating fast, his limbs aching, his head throbbing with the desire to be with Bela once again?

She opened the door.

She did not open the door.

It was Bela. It was not Bela.

'Yes?' she said. Where had the birthmark gone? Same voice, same eyes, wide, piercing – she seemed the same in every way to that idealised image in his head. More beautiful, if possible. Except she had no birthmark spread across her face, her harlequin face. And the strands of hair that fell about her ears, escaping the tight headscarf, were much lighter than he remembered. It was her sister.

'I'm looking for . . . Bela,' he said at last. He raked his memory for the sister's name, whispered to him once in the bed off another Essex Road, in Islington, after they'd made love, when he'd still believed what she told him, when he'd felt that together they were whole, when he'd felt at home for the first time in his life, when he'd felt at peace. 'You're her sister, Sarah, ain't ya?'

She nodded, half surprised, half scared. By this time, two young children clung to her legs. A little boy and a little girl, two or so, with round dark eyes, fat cheeks and shoeless feet. 'And you are Wiggins,' she said simply, like it was the most obvious thing in the world.

His heart lurched. Bela had not forgotten him. Sarah stepped back and gestured for Wiggins to come into the room. He noticed then her slightly swollen belly and wide-hipped gait. Another baby on the way.

She pointed him to a single wooden chair up against one wall and shooed the children from her legs. Wiggins recognised the one-room home. He recognised it from the slums of Lambeth, from Dublin, from all over: barely a pot to piss, as clean and tidy as the poor woman could make it, but sweaty and damp and dusty, and musty and foul as five folk living in a ten by ten is always going to be, when the outside crapper's four floors down and there's no running water. He thought of the optimism on the *Titanic*, he thought of those Dublin pubs: America was the big, bold escape, the road to freedom, the land of the free. But only money made you free, whatever patch of ground you chose to call your home.

As Sarah rooted around in a small box of possessions, the two children stood and stared at Wiggins. They looked at him like he was a god, a giver of life, not a taker, their eyes wide, mouths open, hoping for something good to happen, for him to make a miracle. Wiggins's eyes were drawn to the little girl; something about her hair and the cast of her brow drew him in. She could easily have been his, he thought idly. But any of the kids in the building could have been his. Poor kids. Poverty makes you look the same, it flattens you out. The toffs couldn't tell you apart. When he was in the Irregulars, the coppers who'd harassed them, the toughs who'd kicked them, the do-gooders who'd pursued them into iron orphanages – you was all the same to them. It was only Sherlock Holmes who'd picked him out.

The little girl frowned, seemingly unsettled by the intensity of Wiggins's scrutiny. Then she stuck out her tongue at him.

He laughed. 'Twins?' he asked.

Sarah shook her head quickly as she turned towards him. She handed him a sheaf of newspaper cuttings. 'Bela. She worked here.'

Wiggins pulled out the first cutting on top of the pile and began to read.

140 DIE AS FLAMES SWEEP THROUGH THREE STORIES OF FACTORY BUILDING IN WASHINGTON PLACE

Wiggins read on in horror.

> *Nearly one hundred and fifty lives were lost as a fire swept through the upper stories of a ten-storey factory building in the northwest corner of Washington Place and Greene Street, yesterday afternoon.*

His eyes swept back to the date: March 26, 1911. 'Was she . . .?' he asked hopelessly, and grasped another cutting.

Fifty women jumped to their death down the elevator shaft, desperate to escape the flames . . . Doors blocked up . . .

Wiggins felt an iron taste in his mouth as he read on. The

Triangle Shirtwaist Factory had gone up in flames, its fire escapes (apparently) blocked by bosses eager to deter absenteeism, and despite the heroism of the elevator operators many of the women had either fallen to their deaths or been burned alive. Barely two months before this happened, Wiggins himself had escaped the inferno of Sidney Street by a whisker – and yet here in New York, not two miles away, Bela had burned to her death, or had she . . . ?

'I do not know.' Sarah saw the question in his look. 'She did not jump, so . . .'

He looked back at the clippings, could not stop the slight flutter of the papers in his hand, his muscles shaking. He tried to hold steady.

Organised Labor Calls for New Laws.
Rose Schneiderman's Union.
Rose Schneiderman Calls for Register.

Rose. That was why Rose had recognised Bela's name, he thought vaguely, clinging on to facts.

He'd broken into Rose's campaign office the night before, to sleep on her sofa. After witnessing the murder outside the Metropole, he'd reasoned it was the only place in New York he was sure no one would be trying to kill him. As soon as dawn had tipped the skyline, he'd come down to try to find Bela.

Rose's name was in the cuttings again and again, fighting for justice, for rights. But that fight didn't help Bela. Just like Peter's gang, who'd died in the furnace of Sidney Street the year before, she too had burned to death, burned for her sins.

After a while, he handed the cuttings back. 'I'm so . . . I didn't know.'

'You must go,' she said, waving his condolences away. 'My husband will return from work soon.'

'Will he beat me?'

'No, he will beat me. He is this kind of coward.'

Wiggins stood up. He pulled the last coins he had out of his pocket and handed them to her.

'No,' she said.

'Not for you – for them.'

As he went through the door, the young girl padded after him and stood at the threshold to watch him walk away. He paused. Again, that frown on her face, the clear blue eyes piercing into him, finding his.

He took hold of his pocket watch – the battered watch that had saved his life from Peter the Painter's bullet and still had the dent to prove it, that Dr Watson had gifted to him many years ago. He swung it on the chain, then gave it to the little girl. 'Give this to your mama. Tell her to take no less than five dollars. To mama,' he repeated, then held up all the fingers on one hand. 'Five dollars.'

And with that, he was gone.

13

'It's a nothing job, boy. You're a gunner, aren't you? Do it in your sleep, then onto the big ship by night, and we's home and free.'

'I don't like it,' Wiggins said levelly. 'It's murder.'

O'Connell threw his hands up in frustration and strode towards a table laden with bottles. Wiggins stood in O'Connell's new hotel room, in the lavish Waldorf Astoria. His boss had recovered all of his vigour and now paced around the large room in his shirt-sleeves, holding court to an audience of one. Early-evening light filtered through the half-drawn curtains, facing west, and Wiggins edged towards them to take a look at the view down the street.

He listened to the clinking of glasses. A line of jagged traffic stretched into the distance, the pavement still clogged with people. O'Connell was obviously pouring both of them a drink, working the charm. He needed to.

The night before, in the lobby of the Hotel Metropole, as Wiggins was fretting about detection – and just before he'd witnessed the sensational sidewalk killing – the OC had whispered to him the clinching elements of the deal with Little Patsy Doyle. In return for the sizeable loan that the OC was taking out from Big Tim (funnelled through Doyle), O'Connell had agreed to take care of a certain job for Doyle, the kind of job usually undertaken by out-of-towners.

Now, as O'Connell poured drinks and sauntered around his Waldorf room, he pressed upon Wiggins the merits of the task. 'It's the way they do things here. It makes a lot of sense,' he said, handing Wiggins a glass of something strong and brown and Scottish. 'Use outside help for your dirty work – keeps the kitchen clean.'

Wiggins took the drink. 'We don't even know what he did wrong.'

'We don't need to know,' O'Connell snapped, then checked himself again, took a sip. 'Listen, you'll be well paid. They've planned it all out. Shoot him down there, out in the docks, the body drops down into the deep, and you'll be home free. We'll all be home free, with money to burn. You'll get your cut. Besides,' O'Connell downed his drink, 'the boy's a thief.'

'Tyrone can't be any older than Fitz.'

'And he was a thief too!' O'Connell bellowed.

The door behind him swung open and Molly stepped into the room. She wore a red dress that rustled and sparkled as she moved. Her eyes flicked between the two of them, summing up the moment in a second.

O'Connell shot out his cuffs. 'Hello, dear. Wiggins and I were just discussing our travelling plans.'

'We're all booked on the *Olympic*, aren't we? Pier 88, weighing at one thirty in the a.m.?' She smiled at them and carefully took off her hat. Her hair dropped suddenly around her shoulders, by accident or design, Wiggins couldn't tell. He didn't need to; the effect was just the same. Wiggins gripped his glass tighter.

'He is a little bit after wavering, my dear,' O'Connell said. 'Whether it is the sea air that disagrees with him, or the shit-streaked Liffey, or maybe it is the lure of America, I'm not to know.'

'Do you not want to come, Mr Wiggins?' Molly said as she ran her hand through her hair in a vague effort to re-pin it.

Wiggins felt the heat rising to his face. He couldn't speak. He leaned against the window frame and failed to appear nonchalant. He hadn't seen her since hearing of Bela's death earlier that morning. And yet here she was, so different, in front of him, half smiling, fully alive, so different in so many ways. He could hardly hold on to his feelings, let alone name them, or make sense of what they might mean. He gulped down the last of his whisky. A knock at the door saved him from having to answer.

'Enter,' O'Connell cried, swinging his arms into a serge smoking jacket – which looked new, Wiggins noted. Spending the money now.

A bellhop stood at the door, his brass buttons gleaming like electric lights. 'Package downstairs for a Mr O'Connell, sir.'

'Bring it here, would you.'

'No, sir, sorry, sir, cannot do it, sir. The gentleman is most insistent, sir. His package is for your hands only, sir. He sent me up to get you, sir. He is waiting. Sir.'

O'Connell hesitated. 'Right,' he said at last, glancing at Wiggins. 'That would be . . . yes, lead on, son, lead on.' He placed a gentle hand on Molly's arm and nodded. 'I shall be back in a moment.'

As soon as the door closed behind him, Molly strode across the room and pushed Wiggins up against the wall. She pressed her lips against his, almost too violently for a kiss, but then her mouth opened and he submitted. Her hand reached for his cock and she held it there, even when she broke from the kiss.

She whispered into his ear, 'One more day. We will be on our way back to Dublin. You can come with me. It's for the poor, for the country. Ireland will be free. *We* will be free.' Her breath tickled his ear, her hand worked gently at his trousers.

Wiggins closed his eyes, breathed in her scent, his face in her unpinned hair, his mind racing, whirling, soaring, falling. He could hear his heart beating in his ear, he could see Bela's upturned face, her eyes closing; but what he could feel was Molly's hand on his cock, he could feel the burning, surging excitement, the hope of something more.

'Do you know what he wants me to do?' Wiggins whispered, his throat dry.

She squeezed his straining cock hard, almost pinched it, then stepped back, eyes gleaming, lips open. 'They call them rods here, don't they?' she said.

The door opened and they turned to see O'Connell come in on his own. He looked back into the corridor for a moment, then closed the door. He held a brown paper shopping bag under his arm, wrapped tightly. Without a word, he marched over to the room's writing desk and began to unwrap the parcel. Molly fluttered to O'Connell's side to look, her hand maddeningly on his shoulder. Wiggins waited.

'Here it is,' O'Connell said, pointlessly, as he turned towards Wiggins. In his hand, a silent black metal object; a heavy, dull, latent thing: a gun.

~~

Wiggins waited. Across the street, the electric lights outside Jimmy the Priest's crackled and fizzed. Wiggins stood fifty or so yards away, in the darkness of an alcove under a faulty street lamp. It buzzed and sizzled but cast no light. Away to his left, the brooding darkness of the Lower West Side docks. The wharf houses cast slate-grey shapes against the night, and even from this distance gave off the chilly air of desertion. Wiggins had never seen anywhere in Manhattan that seemed as deserted as those docks just then, at eleven o'clock at night. It was as if something had been planned. And still he waited.

More than twelve hours earlier, he'd stumbled away from Sarah's tenement in shock. It wasn't shock that Bela had died; even the manner of her death, like some sinner in a hellish furnace in the sky, didn't surprise him the way that it might have. What shocked him was first of all the surge of emotion as he stood waiting at the door, his racing, thumping heart, his twitching fingers, the sheer uncontrollable emotion. He didn't think he could feel like that again, that's what shocked him – that his heart still worked, like it worked when he was a kid, like all our hearts are born to work, as a vessel for love, a generator for love until life's reverses clog up the system, the pain blocking the emotion, until it just beats and beats and beats until it beats no more.

As he walked from the Lower East Side, Wiggins – still dazed, emptied yet energised by the surges of conflicting feelings – had stopped outside a large corner shop selling gentlemen's clothes. In the window, a small boy stood and demonstrated how to tie a bow tie. Hair plastered to his head with a gleaming white parting, soft, shining cheeks, he tied and untied the bow tie in an endless loop. Ties hung down each side of the window and across the bottom. *Forms 10 cents each – 3 for 25*, read the sign. Wiggins watched, entranced.

Later, he walked across Manhattan, down to the West Side, then up Broadway. He went to the docks. He went to a couple of gaming rooms but did not play. He made a telephone call at the first, but not the second. He ate ravenously at a roadside food stall, the pretzels piled up on sticks and bursting out of buckets, shiny dark brown like vulgar shoes.

Finally, he'd gone up to the Waldorf to see O'Connell and receive the instrument of his terrible commission, and now – as he stood watching Jimmy the Priest's late at night, waiting for Tyrone, touching that cold iron gun strapped to his hip – he couldn't help thinking of the little boy diligently tying and untying that bow tie all day long.

A figure came out of the bar, hesitated and then lumbered down the road towards him. It was Meath, Doyle's man-mountain of a right-hand man. He swivelled his head round, unsure, distracted. Wiggins hissed out of the darkness.

'Jesus, Mary and the other one, you scared the shit out of me,' Meath gasped, clutching his side momentarily. 'You're a ghost, so you are.'

'Is it on?' Wiggins said, staying in the darkness of the alcove.

'Of course it's on. It's all as we settled. Your man is in Jimmy's, waiting on the boss. When he comes out, chase him into the docks and fulfil your commission.' Meath glanced around. 'Make sure the body goes in the river, you follow?'

Wiggins nodded, sickened.

Meath peered at him through the darkness, a burning cigarette by his side. 'You follow! Good. Now, I'm off to get our favourite patrolman from the corner – he is coming off duty in ten minutes and as is natural, he will repair to our Jimmy's fine establishment for some light refreshment. It will just so happen that he'll see a whole lot of friends at the bar, including myself and anyone else that might be under danger of the frame for such a deed. You follow?'

'I follow.'

'Good boy.' Meath exhaled and a beery, rotting-beef smell wafted towards Wiggins, mangled up with the smoke. Off to his left, between the road and the docks, a long slow train rattled by. The goods train, running straight through the streets. It clanked and hissed and screeched into the night – led all the way by a man riding a horse and waving a flag. Wiggins was momentarily distracted by the sight. He'd recced well enough to know the tracks were there, but it was still odd to see a large goods train rumbling through the city streets.

'Does that run all night?' he asked, nodding into the darkness.

'What? Nah, that'll be the last one, down and back. Now . . .' Meath threw his smoke to the ground and crushed it under foot '. . . I'll be off collecting my wee alibi witness. Once we've gone back in, Tyrone will be out. He'll be off on an errand that way.' Meath pointed to the warehouses on the other side of the train tracks. 'With you. Good luck, Englishman. Make sure you finish the job this time.'

'This time?'

'Huh?' Meath had turned to go, but he hesitated.

'You said finish the job *this time*?' Wiggins said.

Meath walked away, but muttered over his shoulder, 'The whole town knows what you did to Big Jack Zelig.'

'What did I do?'

'You didn't kill him, ha ha ha!' And with that he was gone, ambling towards the corner and his date with another of New York's bent coppers.

About thirty minutes later, once Meath and the policeman had gone back into the bar, Wiggins saw Tyrone come out of Jimmy the Priest's. He wore a white shirt, sleeves rolled up to the elbows, a huge flat cap, but no jacket. He looked both ways, then set off at a jog in the direction of the docks. Wiggins watched as the small young man bobbed along the other side of the street, in and out of the lights. This was the moment.

Tyrone reached the corner, still at a steady jog. Wiggins walked fast, but let the boy stretch a lead. Tyrone did not turn round, but instead flitted across the train tracks and down an alleyway between two warehouses, into the darkness leading down towards the pier.

Wiggins broke into a sprint over the tracks. He checked his stride to pull the gun clear from his hip, then set off once more. 'Tyrone,' he shouted.

The boy turned, startled. Wiggins could just make out the white dash of his shirt. He'd been standing at a doorway – obviously the supposed 'errand' – but on Wiggins's shout he ran. Wiggins held the gun out in front of him. Meath had clearly chosen the spot well, for the tight alleyway only opened into the wide, deserted pier. Tyrone hared across it, towards the Hudson River. He'd ignored the right-hand turn that would have led him back to the gates and instead ran on, as if in a blind panic.

Wiggins pounded on. A light twinkled at the end of the pier, marking the extent of Tyrone's dead end. Cases, cargo and barrels lined the dock, but there was no hiding place now – not for the boy. He slowed, glanced back, checked what he'd seen earlier, then sped on.

Tyrone veered right, out towards the dark river. He shuddered to a halt on the edge, the slow, stinking water beneath him. Wiggins approached, gun still drawn. He could only just make out the boy, now capless. Tyrone thrust his half-white, half-black arms into the air.

'Don't shoot,' he whispered.

Wiggins was close enough to hear his breathing now. He hesitated.

'Don't do it, Englishman.'

'Speak up,' Wiggins hissed.

'Please, don't kill me,' the boy shouted and wailed. 'This . . . this ain't your battle. Please help. Help, Lord, help!' His cries reverberated into the bleak night. 'Please, Englishman, have mercy.'

Wiggins nodded slightly. 'The name's Wiggins,' he said and

squeezed the trigger, double time. The boy let out a great scream and tumbled backwards into the deep.

'It's done!' Wiggins shouted into the night, perhaps to no one, or to himself, or perhaps to God Almighty.

Except he did not believe in God.

14

Wiggins had killed before. What gunner hadn't? He knew manning a ten-pounder, loading, siting, firing, was all part of the process of killing. Those guns could take out twenty people at a time, and he hadn't thought too much about it, not with the flies and the dust and the heat of the veldt at his back, and an angry sergeant hollering in his ear. If you didn't get them, they'd get you was about the size of it.

The army wasn't the end of it neither, nor the start. But hand-to-hand was different from the cannon. It had started with poor Sal and the bastard who'd tried to rape her. (That was if Wiggins didn't count his mother – but self-killing weren't killing in the same way, whatever the law said.) Sal had plunged the knife in then, but he'd have done the same. Peter the Painter last of all, when they'd both tumbled to their deaths off a factory roof and Wiggins had managed to cling on to the flag line. But all these killings, all these deaths, at heart had been a matter of one or the other. Kill or be killed – self-defence, he'd heard Dr Watson call it once – no court in the land would convict. And truth be told, in his heart he hadn't convicted himself either – that was the way of the street.

New York was different. He'd already seen a man shot dead on the street like it was a punch-up. They did guns here like they did fists and shivs back home – but there was no coming back from a gun. You didn't even need any skill or balls to kill a man with a gun. At least with your hands you had to feel the death, you had to mean it; with a knife into the flesh, too, you had to live that violence, you had to steel yourself for the kill. A gun was just nothing, a gun was easy, you could kill without even feeling it.

He held his own gun by his side as he strode back down the pier towards the city.

'Good shooting, Englishman.' Meath's voice pierced the darkness. He stepped out of the alleyway. Wiggins could only just see his bulky form as he loomed towards him. Meath held out a bright white handkerchief like a smother. 'Here, hand me the rod.'

Wiggins did so. 'Shouldn't we get out of here?'

'Nah, the cops are happy at Jimmy's,' Meath said. He slowly turned the gun in his hand, stepped back and then pointed it at Wiggins. 'Now, could you just walk back to the edge of the pier there? With your hands up.'

'What?' said Wiggins.

'I don't want to have to carry your body all that way out to the river, now do I?' Meath twitched his gun hand, gesturing Wiggins back down the pier.

Wiggins turned instinctively. 'O'Connell's not gonna be happy,' he said over his shoulder.

Meath laughed. 'What's he gonna do about it?'

Wiggins continued to walk to the water's edge with a slow, deliberate stride. 'But why?'

'Why?' Meath replied. 'I told you why already.'

'Zelig?'

'Smart kid. You should've killed him, though, so not that smart.'

Wiggins slowed as he came to the pier's edge. He'd walked to the other side from where Tyrone had gone into the water, but far enough from the alleyway that they were almost out of sight in the darkness. He kept his hands high. 'But I thought yous and Zelig's mob were different – Jews, Irish, at it.'

'Oh, we're at it, but not like you think. The town works on favours as well as guns. We get rid of you, we get a lot out of Zelig. You get me, mister?'

'I get you.'

Wiggins was now positioned, at Meath's gesturing, on the very edge of the pier, the water at his back. As soon as the bullet struck, he would topple backwards into the depths. Even in his manner of killing, the huge Meath wanted to go light on the manual labour.

'So, goodbye, English.' Meath took aim with the gun.

'I don't think so,' Wiggins said and stepped towards him.

Startled, Meath squeezed the trigger. *Click click click*, went the bulletless gun.

Wiggins grasped the muzzle, yanked the piece clear and smashed Meath on the side of the head with it before the huge man could even cry out. He slumped to the floor groaning, shocked, defeated.

In a second, Wiggins grabbed him by the collar of his jacket and half dragged, half carried him to the water's edge. Then he hissed in his ear, 'I told you, I ain't English. I'm London.' He threw him into the water with a great splash.

'Hey,' Meath cried out from below. Wiggins could hear him splashing and spluttering in the water, but he ignored him. People like Meath didn't die in a place like this. He'd crawl his way along to one of the access ladders, and so Wiggins let him shout. He picked up the gun and hurled it far into the Hudson River. He took from his pocket the gun's bullets – filched from the revolver as he'd walked back to meet Meath – and tossed them aside as he walked away.

As he approached the alleyway, he heard Meath's faint shouts again – the big man must have climbed out. A shadow flitted ahead at the entrance. Wiggins ran at it without stopping.

The shadow moved towards him. Wiggins slammed a fist into his face and burst past, into the dark alley. 'Cork! Cork!' the felled man cried, as if giving chase. 'He's coming at you!'

Wiggins sprinted on fast, fast like he'd run on the street as a kid, away from the coppers or worse, when you'd nicked something and they were crying blue murder. It never did to think too much when you ran like that. 'Cork!' the voice called again.

A smaller man was hunched at the end of the alleyway, illuminated by one of the warehouse lights. He'd drawn his gun and made shaking aim as Wiggins ran towards him – *BANG! BANG!*

The sound echoed down the tight alleyway. Wiggins heard brick chip by his right ear. He ran on.

'Jesus, Cork!' a pained voice sounded from behind.

Cork, gun up high, hesitated. Wiggins bent and barrelled into Cork's midriff. The momentum lifted the smaller man up and Wiggins tossed him over his shoulder. He let out a great roar as he did so, in anger and exhilaration. As he ran on, he heard Cork scream out in pain. That's his shoulder gone, Wiggins thought. One less pursuer to worry about.

Off to his right, he could make out the huge shape and rumbling of the goods train returning north for the night. He upped his speed. If he didn't get to the other side of the tracks before it passed, Meath, Cork and the rest would surely have him – but if he did, he'd be home free.

At the head of the train, he made out the warning guard astride the horse. He even wore a cowboy hat and boots. In his hand he waved a red flag. The lights of the train engine dazzled sharply at his back as Wiggins ran on.

'Hey, mister,' the cowboy shouted. 'Outtatheway!'

Wiggins was running too fast to reply. He ran towards the horse, his lungs bursting, his newly healed rib stinging like a bastard.

'Mister,' the cowboy cried again as Wiggins neared. 'This baby don't stop.'

Wiggins pulled the cowboy's nearest foot out of its stirrup.

'Hey,' the cowboy cried, as Wiggins tipped him up and off the horse. The cowboy rolled away, off the tracks, as the train screeched towards him.

Wiggins leapt up onto the horse and dug in his heels. The horse bucked and neighed, and then galloped off up the tracks. The train let out a furious barrage of whistles and bells, grunting and straining at the horse's heels. Wiggins wheeled the nag away, onto the city side of the tracks. The train rushed past, shutting out his pursuers, leaving him to gallop on alone into the Manhattan night.

It was only when he was two blocks east and north that he

felt it was safe to slow down to a canter. Adrenaline coursed through him, and he'd yet to catch his breath. But the presence of the horse comforted him. He was a London boy, brought up under the old Queen, which meant he was as familiar with horseflesh as he was with the Thames, or the Underground, or the smell of soot-thick fog in the morning. Horses always felt like home, though God knows he barely came across them any more. The London he once knew was now in thrall to the motor.

And so was New York, he thought – the motor and the gun. He turned the nag's head back north, towards Pier 88 and his ride across the Atlantic – the *Olympic* was set to weigh anchor within the hour. He didn't pause to think of the oddity of it, that he'd stolen a cowboy's horse in the middle of Manhattan. He didn't think of the oddity of the cowboy being in New York at all.

The sea. Lashed by a summer storm, peaks and dips and swells and rearing tunnels of foam. The sea, blacker than a miner's snot. The sea, rearing up to meet the gunmetal sky, falling to its depths, salt-flecked cheeks, sodden arms, in the very middle of a world untouched by man and machines, by comfort, by morality, just in and of itself immense, unstopping, eternal. The sea.

Wiggins gripped the rope that ran along the inside of the rowing boat. Eight silent boatmen pulled at the oars, oblivious to the lurching of the boat, intent on their oars, the sea and nothing else. Across from him, Molly sat and grinned, despite the rain, despite the pitch and yaw, despite it all. Pinned between her legs, a leather holdall, holding all the money from New York, Little Patsy and Big Tim's money. Wiggins was supposed to be guarding both of them.

The journey on the *Olympic* had been entirely different. Wiggins had made his berth, in steerage, only minutes before the gates closed. The ocean had been billiard-table flat from New York to Mizen Head, but as soon as Ireland came into view, the seas had taken on a life of their own, the skies had grown angry, and the horizon had disappeared.

Wiggins had boarded the *Olympic* in New York with the expectation of staying put all the way to Ireland, and thence Dublin, with O'Connell and Molly. The ship had dropped anchor off Cork, just like the *Titanic* earlier that year. The three of them had boarded the tender that would take them into Queenstown. But as it rounded the bend into Queenstown harbour itself, the tender had veered off and a large, eight-man rowing boat had drawn alongside.

O'Connell obviously had the complete cooperation of the sailors aboard the tender, and they did as he said. All in a quiet, non-demonstrative silence – as if this stopping of the tender, this mid-sea transfer, wasn't even happening. Or if it was happening, it was being commanded by an unseen force. It was a reminder to Wiggins that the OC was a powerful man, and now that he was away from New York and back in Ireland's orbit, that power extended into every area of life. A man who could cause the ferry from the prize ship of the world-famous White Star Line to detour, was a man who could commit dark deeds unchecked.

First Molly had climbed down the ladder to get into the rowing boat, and then Wiggins. The OC had handed him the holdall of money and said simply, 'Look after them both.'

Now Wiggins sat opposite Molly, soaked through, as the men rowed on and his stomach heaved and lurched violently in the swell. He looked away from her, out across the tumult, and thought about all that had passed between them (and between him and his own soul) in New York. It felt sour, very sour, yet she smiled at him still. They had barely spoken on the passage over – the classes didn't mix on the big ships, and Wiggins was never left in any doubt where he belonged. He'd never been in any doubt where he belonged even when Molly had her hand clamped on his cock; he was still the horse and she the rider. They'd only met alone once on the whole journey. He was swaying back down one of the service corridors after a heavy liquid supper, and she'd placed herself at the bottom of a staircase leading up to higher things (the first-class lounge, Wiggins guessed). She was obviously waiting for him.

He said nothing, but as he reached her, she put her hand onto his side – under his jacket – and he stopped. The hand flitted downwards and she bent forward to whisper in his ear, 'Not long now,' as her hand travelled and stroked and made its presence felt. He closed his eyes for a moment. He couldn't help but enjoy it.

'Quick smart,' she said in a loud voice and stepped away. 'The master needs you up in his quarters in fifteen minutes.' She grinned wickedly and he turned around.

A waiter bearing a crate of bottles clunked his way down the corridor towards them. Suspicion flashed across his face. A servant and a lady standing too close together, beneath decks, disrupted the order of things.

Molly chuckled. 'Righty-ho,' she said, and turned to go back up the stairs. She swayed her hips as she went up each step, perfectly aware that Wiggins was watching her all the way to the top.

Later on, as the crossing neared its end, O'Connell had indeed genuinely summoned Wiggins to his cabin and outlined the plan and the role Wiggins was to play. He'd insisted that Wiggins must go with Molly – and the money – as a guard, a heavy, he said. 'I can't risk landing all that cash in Ireland, in any case. If it's found, they'll take the lot and jail us all.' Wiggins was trusted now, not just with the money but with Molly too. He was trusted because he trusted no one and because of Tyrone.

Wiggins was under no illusions about where this trust had come from. The OC knew he had Tyrone's murder on him now. That ultimately was O'Connell's guarantor; crime forges bonds and the OC had made Wiggins a murderer, would always have that heinous crime over him. Wiggins felt sure this had been one of O'Connell's motives in ordering him to commit the crime in the first place. There was another possible motive too, though, an even darker one. Wiggins was troubled by something Meath had said before he tried to kill him: 'What's he gonna do about it?' Had Meath meant that the OC was impotent, that he *could not* protect him? Or did he mean the OC didn't want to, didn't need to protect him – even that the OC was in on the deal?

Not that it mattered in the end. Wiggins could hardly accuse O'Connell of double-dealing, given the situation he was in, doing the bidding of Vernon Kell and the British Government while pretending to be a helping hand and bodyguard in the Irish nationalist cause. In this, his own secret cause, he felt he was nearing the end. From the very beginning, when he'd first started working for Vernon Kell and the Secret Service, Wiggins had told Kell to follow the money. Even in a world of revolutionaries, or of national pride, or defence of the realm, the surest way to root out a conspiracy was to follow the money.

And so, there was the money, in between the slightly parted legs of Molly Lansdown-Smith as she grinned at him through the flying spume. 'There!' she suddenly cried, and pointed. 'The *Santa Clara.*'

Off to their left, lilting to and fro in the wind, a two-masted white yacht tacked and swayed about a buoy. A caped and hatted figure waved, one hand above his head, as he held on to a mast. It took a while for the rowing boat and its silent rowers to haul alongside. As they got closer, Wiggins examined the figure on the yacht until he could see him quite clearly. It was the man Molly had met in the flat off Grafton Street, and again at the vegetarian restaurant back in Dublin. Not her lover, her co-conspirator. The Civ.

He was wrapped in oilskins, but Wiggins recognised him for certain when he hauled up first Molly, then the money, onto the yacht. He held the line firm while Wiggins clambered aboard. His face was even more drawn than before, his eyes hollowed, his black moustache now flecked with spume.

The silent oarsmen stayed silent and turned their boat for home. Molly hugged the Civ. 'There's waterproofs below,' he shouted. He glanced at Wiggins. 'I'll need you to work,' he called

again. 'Get a coat and take a line.' He handed Wiggins the bag
of money and gestured to below decks.

Molly grabbed hold of the wheel as the yacht lurched. She
laughed, and Wiggins stumbled towards the hatch.

The cabin was much larger than he'd imagined, with six bunks,
a small stove, cupboards and even a fold-down table. It was wider
than he'd expected, too, and felt solid, for all that it lifted and
ducked in the swell. Polished dark wood slates lined each side
and the floor felt heavy underfoot. It stank of gas – from the
primus stove, no doubt – and the faint mould of the forever wet.
At the far end, with a bucket between his legs, sat a hunched
figure vomiting violently. As Wiggins clattered in, the figure looked
up: Hannigan.

The night was fierce and long. A storm raged, the *Santa Clara*
tossed and tumbled and lurched, as small as a cockleshell. At one
point, Wiggins had fallen asleep only to be woken by the Civ
yelling, 'All hands, all hands,' and then he was out on the deck,
holding on to a rope, hauling and yanking and clinging in the
near darkness as a swinging lantern flung flashes of wet light
among them. Molly, Wiggins and even the wretched Hannigan
worked as the Civ held the wheel and shouted commands into
the whirling mist.

The next morning was like another world. The sun shone, the
wind was briskly blowing in the right direction and Wiggins could
sit at the back of the *Santa Clara* and gaze at the choppy surf it
left behind. The Civ was again at the wheel, but, for the moment,
had found nothing more for him to do. Molly stood in the fo'c's'le,
fiddling with the primus stove and trying to butter some eggs.

Hannigan swayed down the deck towards Wiggins and thrust
his head over the back of the boat. He vomited, an empty, hollow,
foul retch. Wiggins watched as he drew his hand across his mouth.
'So. What the fuck are you doing here?'

'Taking the sea air. It's bracing,' Wiggins replied, as breezily
as he could.

Hannigan almost retched again. His eyes were bloodshot, his

hair awry, and the anger pulsed off him. 'This isn't your fight, *Englishman*. This is for Ireland.'

'Moved on then, have ya?' Wiggins responded angrily. 'Murdered Fitz, tried to pull out my fingernails, now you're a fucking freedom fighter?'

'How dare you say his name, how dare you? I know you killed him, probably for that Proddy bastard, Lynch,' Hannigan cried. 'And yes, if it means getting the fucking British out of my country, then I'll do what the fuck it takes.'

'You really think that's gonna make a difference? They're all fucking toffs, mate, whatever the colour of the flag.'

'Breakfast?'

They both turned. Molly stood behind them, hand up on the rigging. 'Eggs and biscuits, I'm afraid, boys, but better than nothing.'

Hannigan scowled but got up and pushed past her back down the deck. Molly stayed looking at Wiggins. Her long arms were stretched high up on the rope she was holding on to, emphasising the curve of her body. She still wore the white and blue dress she'd had on when they left the *Olympic*, but now it was ripped and torn and generally bedraggled. Her hair was held in a loose bun at the back, but strands fell all about. She looked the business. She couldn't help it.

'Is that true?' she asked. 'Did you kill Fitz?' She said this in such a matter-of-fact way – 'Did you buy a ha'penny bun for your tea?' – like she didn't care either way. Then Wiggins remembered with a nauseous flip in his belly that she hadn't even tried to talk him out of killing Tyrone. She hadn't blinked an eye. She probably thought it meant nothing to him. What was one more cold-blooded killing to a born killer?

He looked up at her as she bobbed and swayed with the movements of the *Santa Clara* and waited for him to speak. 'What's the plan?' he asked finally, ignoring her question about Fitz.

'Buttered eggs,' she said.

'I know you treat me like some hunk of meat, but I'm not having that.'

She bit her lip, amused. 'But what a hunk of meat.'

'Molly,' he hissed. 'Where are we going?'

'Where do you think? We're starting Ireland's march to freedom, we're riding the waves of a new tomorrow. We're going to buy guns.'

The *Santa Clara* travelled south, then turned east around the tip of Cornwall and into the English Channel. Wiggins knew this in detail mostly because the Civ, who was otherwise taciturn, took obvious pleasure in pointing out where they were. His only other interest seemed to be the good running of the yacht – or ketch, as he referred to it – and through this he and Wiggins formed a fragile bond. For Wiggins, so used to following orders, to using his body and mind in quick conjunction, was a fast study when it came to seamanship. He became the Civ's right-hand man, especially when Molly took the wheel and he and the Civ would scuttle around the deck, or haul at the sails and tie and yank and sweat. Hannigan was handless on the deck, and it was left to him to man the stove.

Only once did the easy manner between Wiggins and the Civ become strained. The ketch was making good speed, with the south coast of England close by on its port side, and the two men were checking the fastenings at the stern. Molly held the wheel while Hannigan mangled some ingredients for lunch. 'The Civ – that stands for "civil servant", right?' Wiggins said, glancing out at the coast and back. 'You're government?'

'How did you know that?' he rasped under his breath.

'It's not hard.' Wiggins shrugged. 'Her up there always calls you such, the cut of your clothes back in Dublin, your accent.'

'I am on vacation.'

'It don't bother me,' Wiggins said. 'You could be the King of Siam for all I care.'

'What else do you know?'

Wiggins looked carefully at him for a second. The Civ's hollow cheeks highlighted the size of his eyes. Wiggins knew that he must have been army, which probably meant South Africa and the Boer War. Soldiers who'd seen action, real action like he had, carried it with them – no one who'd fought the Boer could ever forget it. Not just the fighting, but the thousands of needless deaths, the women and children, the inglorious, pitiless camps. It didn't surprise him that anyone in that war might take a different view of empire, if that was what empire meant.

But as he looked at him, he didn't need the Civ to know that he knew – it was cruel, if nothing else, to remind a troubled man of what troubled him. 'What do I know?' Wiggins said after a pause. 'I know that you skipper a canny boat – which is about all I need to know right now.'

The Civ nodded absently and turned away, yanking hard on a complex knot. Wiggins had lost his chance to ask anything more, and the moment never came again.

They took turns to sleep, always two and two about. The Civ slept least of all, and would only ever entrust the wheel to Molly. As they tacked and sailed up the coast of England towards the Isle of Wight, Wiggins found himself enjoying it. The chalky cliffs of Dorset, like craggy waves, the freshness in the air, the freedom of the sea. Yet it also felt claustrophobic and constrained. The yacht's clock ticked relentless loud, and plagued all their nights. Hannigan continually raged against it. The cabin itself smelled of creosote and damp, and was airless when the sun was out; the weather infected Wiggins's mood so completely that, just like the *Santa Clara*, he felt always at its mercy. And all the while that big bag of money sat under Molly's bunk. No one was going to steal it – they had nowhere to go – but its power almost throbbed. It wasn't the money that mattered, though; it was what that money meant, what it would turn into, that kept them subdued.

All apart from Molly, Wiggins noted, who maintained an almost ecstatic mood regardless of the weather or the time of day or even of when she had to sit with Hannigan. Wiggins would catch himself staring at her, wondering where such fervour came from – the revolutionaries he knew came from nothing, had nothing to start with and were fighting for a piece of the pie. Molly already had pie, yet here she was, fighting for what she called justice.

Strangely, he slept better on the *Santa Clara* than he had for months, despite the noise and the heat and the constant lurching on the waves. He dreamed deeply, often of Molly. On the fourth night, as they approached Cowes, he woke from a pleasant dream to find her pressed by his side, her hand gently massaging him where it counted, where it always seemed to be now.

'Don't say anything,' she whispered into his ear with hot, wet breath. He heard the Civ and Hannigan clumping about above deck. 'This is what freedom feels like,' she said. 'Just enjoy it.'

And he did.

They put into Cowes the next morning. The Civ expertly piloted the boat through ranks of pleasure yachts and working boats and Royal Naval pinnaces flying the ensign. From a distance, the crowded harbour reminded Wiggins of the Thames, and he felt a pang for London, where everything seemed simpler than it did now. But when they got close, and after he had jumped onto the boardwalk while the Civ threw out a line, he realised it was an entirely different town. This was a place where money floated; a place far away from his London, or from the shit-streaked streets of slum Dublin, or even from the quay where Fitz's mangled body stared up at him still. He'd gone to Dublin in the first place to root out who might be buying guns and to stop them; now here he was, trying to find Fitz's murderer and – in the end – helping those very gunrunners, while standing amidst the boats and staff of some of the richest people in England.

He made the boat fast, then went back aboard to find Molly and the Civ arguing in undertones. 'If we take everything on the list, we can make a clear home run, without stopping at Milford,' the Civ said.

'No, no, no, Civ!' Molly said. 'We need the space. It's why we're here. Oh, hello.' She'd finally noticed Wiggins, who stood waiting on the wooden jetty and looking up at the boat. 'What do you think? Will I cut the mustard on Marine Parade?'

She'd been below decks on the approach to the mooring and had changed into a new dress, a white cotton thing ruffled at the shoulders and hemmed with sharp blue. She'd even found a hat and umbrella to match from somewhere, and she held her chin to one side, inviting comment.

'I wouldn't know,' Wiggins grunted. He looked at the Civ, who shrugged on a naval blazer and patted his pockets. 'You want me to guard the boat?' he went on.

Hannigan clambered from behind them and pointed a large finger at him. 'No fucking chance,' he rasped. He stared down from the edge of the yacht, as if he owned the thing.

'Steady on,' the Civ said sharply. 'This is Cowes.' He clambered onto the plank, then held his hand out for Molly, who followed him down.

Wiggins squinted up at Hannigan. His rough features were twisted in a heated scowl, his sailing jumper was torn across the belly, his large, square frame backlit by a sudden sunbeam. He didn't look like he was in Cowes at all. 'I'm staying right here,' Hannigan said, pointing to the deck.

The Civ and Molly turned to walk towards the town, but then Molly called back to him. 'Wiggins – could you get my bag? Bring it, will you,' she commanded, as if to a servant. And of course, he went back aboard for it; it was the cover story he, best of all, knew how to play. Every time he'd walked the streets with Kell, he'd kept a pace behind, the hired help. Now Molly expected the same of him here, in sun-dappled Cowes.

As he retrieved her bag – not the one with the money in it, Hannigan made sure of that – the angry Irishman grabbed hold of his arm and hissed into his ear, 'Just so you know, when this is done, I'll kill you.'

'Thanks for the tip.'

Hannigan squeezed harder. 'Now that's you laughing at me again, when I'm not sure that's altogether wise, you know. You did for Fitz, you've fooled the old man, you've got his missus making moon eyes, but I still see straight and true. And what I sees is a wrong 'un.'

Wiggins took hold of Hannigan's hand and slowly prised it off his arm. 'I'm not sure where that hand's been, to be honest,' he said, suddenly struck by another thought, an echo from old Dublin, from something said months ago. 'Have you got the time?' he asked.

Hannigan was surprised by the question, so surprised that he obeyed the request without thinking and pulled out a watch from his pocket. It was a very small watch, totally out of keeping with Hannigan's whole demeanour and style. It looked like a woman's watch. A lovely little thing.

'It's bust,' Hannigan said to himself thoughtfully. A shadow passed across his face and his eyes closed a fraction. Then he recovered, looked up at Wiggins and said, 'Now fuck off.' He stepped back and let Wiggins clamber down the plank. 'Remember, Englishman,' he called, all soft and blarney and under the wind. 'I will kill you.'

15

The wind had dropped. The bank of rolling fog had stilled. And now the *Santa Clara* drifted into the near darkness of evening, as if halfway across the Styx. Molly stood at the bow, eyes straining into the gathering gloom. Hannigan hung off one side, Wiggins the other, the Civ at the wheel. The gentle *slap*, *slap*, *slap* of water kissed the boat's hull. Wiggins squeezed his eyes and brushed his salty cheeks.

'There!' Molly shouted and suddenly, like the weakest of suns penetrating a black Lambeth smog, a ball of yellow light flashed away to their left. It flashed again.

'The Ruytigen Lightship,' the Civ said simply, and turned the wheel twenty-five degrees.

It had taken them two days to traverse the Channel from Cowes, out into the North Sea near Hamburg. They'd only spent one night on the Isle of Wight, a night in which Wiggins had got drunk. He'd carried Molly's bag, always dutifully two steps behind her and the Civ, as they made their way from the *Santa Clara* into Cowes proper. The Parade was crammed with parasol-toting women, small children, men in ducks and blazers, tourists in boaters and all manner of servants running errands to and fro. Seagulls swooped and dived and rose again, in haughty exaltation. Molly in her fine white dress, the Civ with his blazer, and even Wiggins as a put-upon factotum, didn't raise an eyebrow.

Molly stopped at the gate to the Gloster Hotel, a castle-like building set back from the Parade and flying a St George's cross on a high pole. The Civ took her bag and she gestured him forward, before turning to Wiggins. 'Thank you, my man,' she said brightly as a couple of chattering young women squeezed past, casting half an eye at Wiggins. And then more quietly, 'Courage. Patience. Not long before we can be alone. Once we're back in Dublin, I've got some very special plans for you. Very special.'

'Should I stay back on the boat?' he mumbled, acting part truculent schoolboy, part rebuffed lover.

She laughed. 'With Mr Hannigan? No, no, I don't want to share you.'

'Molly?' the Civ called from the hotel doorway.

'Righty-ho,' she called back loudly. Then she handed Wiggins a coin. 'For a bed – and a bath.'

Wiggins had taken the money, and taken a bed, and used the spare cash on one telegram and many pints of ale. He'd already reckoned on Hannigan's hostility the moment he'd realised he was aboard the *Santa Clara*, but until that morning when they'd arrived in Cowes, he hadn't banked on being without protection.

In Dublin, before going to New York, he'd relied on the OC to keep Hannigan at bay. In the intervening time, though, it was clear that his hatred had only curdled and soured and grown stronger. Not only was Hannigan now continually averring that Wiggins was Fitz's murderer, he'd also acquired a higher purpose than simply being O'Connell's right hand. Wiggins had seen it in his eyes, heard it in his voice – Hannigan was a paid-up Irish nationalist, member of the Brotherhood, or whatever it was called. You couldn't fake that kind of fervour, not a man like Hannigan. And paradoxically, it was that very fervour that was keeping him from trying to kill Wiggins – at least until the job was done, until they'd delivered the guns back to Ireland. Wiggins didn't need to think what would happen to him if anyone found out he was working for the British Government.

Since they'd got back on the *Santa Clara* at Cowes, Wiggins had been consumed by thoughts of Fitz, by who might have killed him and if he was ever going to bring them to justice. It was one thing to *know*, but it was another thing altogether to do something about it. That was what separated the analyst from the street man. And Wiggins was a street man.

It was these thoughts that had been interrupted by the appearance of the lights in the mist, and Molly's cry. The Civ steered the *Santa Clara* close by the Ruytigen Lightship, and then they gently tacked around it in a great arc. Finally, as the night began to close completely and all that lit their way was the *swish swash* of the revolving light from the Ruytigen, a great shape appeared out of the blackness, stately as a coffin. A tugboat.

The Civ hauled on the wheel excitedly and manoeuvred alongside. A lantern hung from each mast of the *Santa Clara* and the tugboat – *Gladiator Hamburg* picked out in white paint along its side – heaved to. Small oil lamps ran all along its gunwales. A line of chattering German sailors in naval togs came to the side to take a look.

The Civ threw the lines up to the sailors, and they made the yacht fast between them. Then Molly and the Civ – armed with the bag of money – clambered aboard. Hannigan went at their heels and Wiggins made to follow until Hannigan turned and spat, 'You're too fucking English.'

'What about Lord and Lady Muck there?' he said.

Hannigan kicked at him and Wiggins stepped back. He didn't want to create a scene here. He suddenly realised that although he wasn't entirely sure what Van Bork looked like, that might not be true the other way round. He still didn't know what Bela had told her handler two years previously.

He watched as a tall but indistinct figure in a German military uniform ushered the three of them into a cabin. Something about the German figure made him flinch, an almost recognition, not of someone seen before but someone described before. Was that Van Bork, the spymaster who'd got a man inside Woolwich, who'd been paying Bela to stir up revolution on the streets of London? It sent a chill down his spine that had nothing to do with the dank night.

Shortly after, a series of shouted commands in German echoed through the mist. The sailors, who'd been openly staring at Wiggins on the *Santa Clara*, jumped into action. Molly, the Civ and Hannigan reappeared in the gloom and within minutes the work had begun.

Wiggins soon realised why they'd had him along, for the work was fearful hard and any chill he'd experienced vanished in seconds. Box after box of Mauser rifles came out of nowhere, handed down onto the deck by the sailors, whereupon Hannigan and Wiggins (and the Civ and Molly too) had to break them open and stow them any old how. It took hours, working ceaselessly by the light of the lanterns, to load the rifles. At about 1 a.m., Molly went to each of them with a shaking cup of water, and they drank what they could. She held on to Wiggins's arm as she served him, and then it was on with the work once more. The deck was strewn with straw, their hands and faces plastered in grease and Vaseline. Molly's dress was ripped and filthy.

The cases came down in a continuous line, passed from hand to hand as the German sailors sang a deep-throated humming song. Hannigan smashed the cases so that they could fit in as many rifles as possible, keeping just one or two for the deck. Smaller boxes of ammunition followed.

At one point, Molly went to each of them and placed a chunk of chocolate in their mouths. 'Is this how those silly priests do it?' she muttered to Wiggins as she gave him his chocolate. He bowed his head, and stuck out his tongue like he'd seen the Catholics do.

The loading went on deep into the night, until the *Santa Clara* felt so low in the water it was like a drowning man barely keeping his mouth in the air. Wiggins felt for the boat, but he didn't feel much else, other than exhaustion. As the last box of ammunition was stowed, he – like the others – crawled over the tightly packed rifles and fell into a spent slumber, their heads inches from the cabin roof, the only sound the ever-ticking clock. As he closed his eyes and fell into a dead sleep, his mind snagged briefly. Did someone whisper in his ear? He twisted and turned and opened his eyes. Three other slumbering shapes in the confined space, but no one close. He shut his eyes once more.

He woke to the sound of German shouts. The boat rattled along way too quickly, and the cabin jolted around him with the speed. He squeezed out onto the deck to see the German tug, the *Gladiator*, out in front, giving the *Santa Clara* a tow through thick morning fog. The Civ held the wheel, almost laughing with the speed of it, and Molly stood at the bow, arms outstretched, back arched, her hair flowing freely in the wind. The sea tipped the very edges of the deck, so laden was the ketch. Wiggins noticed a couple of the wooden crates that they hadn't broken up, *Patronen für Handfeuerwaffen: Hamburg* written on the sides. Greasy straw was stuck all about and the whole boat reeked of metal and grease and firepower.

The Civ shouted something Wiggins didn't catch. Hannigan, crouching near the front of the boat just behind Molly, crabbed forward and worked on the towline. 'Let her go,' the Civ shouted louder. 'Let her go!'

In a moment, the line went slack and the great tug wheeled off to the right. The *Santa Clara* caught a tailwind and skimmed on, westward. Molly waved at the *Gladiator* as it disappeared into the fog. The Civ shouted once more, this time to Wiggins. 'Set the spinnaker on the bowsprit. Mind the boom.' Wiggins got caught in the hurry and the work and the exhilaration of a yacht under full wind. He looked up at Molly, now swinging back towards them, her giddy face agleam.

'We're going,' she cried. 'We're going.'

And just behind her, Hannigan crouching still, crouching like a demonic ape frightened of water, waiting for dry land to find the killing blow. For just then Wiggins remembered what Hannigan had whispered to him the night before: 'Your work's done now, Englishman . . . Sleep well on it.'

By the afternoon, the wind had dropped and with it the spirits of the crew. The *Santa Clara* drifted on the tide. The Civ stood at the wheel, staring off at the far horizon. No time was as dead as a windless day at sea. Molly tended to Hannigan's torn finger. Wiggins hadn't noticed before, but it was bloodied and crusty from the night before.

As the hours passed, the normally cool Civ fretted. His glance continued to jag between the horizon, the coast and the heavens, searching for wind. Every now and then he'd regard the limp sails with unconcealed dismay. Wiggins tried to rest his aching limbs, tried to sleep stretched out on a patch of clear deck, but that succour would not come.

'Are you asleep, Wiggins?' Molly said, as she held up her hand against the lowering sun. 'Sleeping like a babe. I wish I had a conscience as clear as yours,' she teased, but did not say more because Hannigan was in earshot.

Wiggins grunted. He had to keep reminding himself that this flirting, joking Molly thought he'd killed Tyrone.

Except that he did not kill Tyrone.

He'd never had any intention of killing Doyle's lad. On his last day in New York, as he stood staring at the small boy tying and untying the bow tie in the shop window, he'd decided what to do and had then worked out how to fake Tyrone's death. It was, he reasoned, the only way to save the boy's life while simultaneously keeping his cover secure with O'Connell and Molly. It had taken him the rest of the day to arrange, but the plan was simplicity itself.

First, he'd contacted Rothstein. Baseball, the journalist, had already told him that Arnold Rothstein was one of the most powerful men in New York, and Wiggins had his marker. Finding a man like Rothstein wasn't too difficult. It took two telephone calls, using the calling card Rothstein had given him, and a short walk into Midtown, where he found himself in one of Rothstein's stuss joints. He was treated with respect, reverence almost, when he turned up and waited for the great man to arrive. The marker was a powerful thing; it had to be repaid, and everyone understood that. And an unpaid Rothstein marker was rarer still. An unpaid marker was a stain on his character that Rothstein would not countenance.

He had agreed to supply a boat and handler to pick Tyrone out of the Hudson River and then put him on a train out of town. 'I will have my marker back now, London, if you please,' Rothstein said. 'And in return, may I take yours?'

'You may,' Wiggins said. 'Though I ain't sure I'll ever be back here again – if I even make it out alive.'

'Oh, you will make it out alive. And you will be back in New York. There is no other town in the world that can accommodate a man like you. I am a lucky man, for I have your marker. And believe me, London, I will keep it.'

Next, Wiggins had to stake out Jimmy the Priest's until he spotted Tyrone, sent out to polish the windscreen on the motor car. He explained to him that the only course of action open to them both, if they wished to stay alive, was to do as Wiggins said.

'But I ain't—'

'They think you're a thief, Tyrone. And it means you'll always be dead in this town.'

Finally, Wiggins had sent a telegram to a post-office box in Chicago for the attention of Mr Altamont: ASSISTANT ON WAY. UNION STATION, LOST & FOUND. NEXT 3 DAYS. BLACK SWIMMER. W.

Wiggins was still so pleased with this plan – and its apparently successful execution – that he almost told Molly there and then, as she gently tried to tease him up from the deck. Instead, he cocked his head sideways and called out to the Civ, 'Anything?'

The Civ just shook his weary head.

All the life and energy had gone out of the four of them, only to be replaced by nerves and anxiety. It was one thing to be sailing off the English coast in an empty yacht – it was quite another to be carrying enough firepower to start a war. There were near on a thousand rifles packed into the boat, and ten times as many rounds. As the hours wore on, the anxiety spread way beyond fear of capture (in fact, Wiggins was not scared of capture) to the pit of the cabin.

Molly had removed the stove and the lanterns, and Hannigan and the Civ had taken to smoking cigarettes only off the very stern, for a spark could blow the boat, the cargo and all four of them sky-high. They were a floating tinderbox.

Hannigan strode the deck, muttering and jumpy. He'd cut his finger badly, and Molly had bandaged it up like a bloodied paw. He picked and gnawed at the dressing as he smoked off the back of the boat.

'What's wrong with him?' Molly asked, pointing at Hannigan. 'He won't say a word to you.' She sat next to Wiggins at the bow, the two of them searching the horizon for danger. They'd seen a lightship, and a couple of steamers, but no one had given them a second glance.

'He wants to kill me,' Wiggins said.

'Golly, he's not still on about that, is he?' She shrugged, and pushed her leg next to his.

He looked down at it. The brilliant white dress of Cowes was now grease-stained, ripped and damp at the hem. Her strong, thin hands were flecked with cuts and grime, but still this contact touched him – with the Civ behind them and all, he couldn't stop his heart beating faster. 'He was in love with Fitz, you know,' Wiggins said. It had taken him a long time – too long – to reach this conclusion, but when he'd asked Hannigan the time at Cowes, it had been to confirm his suspicion, the final sign. Hannigan had Fitz's watch, had taken it some little time before he died, a keepsake, a memento.

'Golly again,' Molly gasped. 'Vincent doesn't strike me as a romantic in, ahem, that sense.'

Wiggins thought again of Fitz, and how he'd never joined in when Wiggins had criticised Hannigan, how he'd all but defended him. 'Love does funny things,' he said to Molly.

'Does it?'

'It makes you do things you don't want to do, could never do, if you weren't blind, if you didn't have the fever.'

'A fever, is it? I thought love could make you do things you never had the heart for before, that it makes you brave, it gives you courage for the things that need to be done. Isn't that why we say "take heart"?'

Take heart for murder? For mayhem, for death? Wiggins felt the anger rising in his gut, a burning rage. He tried to suppress it. 'Maybe not a fever. A fire.'

'I like that better.'

A horrible scream broke up their conversation. Hannigan bellowed from the cabin and suddenly appeared, brandishing the clock. 'Shut your bastard noise,' he screamed. He'd obviously ripped the clock from its housing, and now he smashed it repeatedly against the deck.

Wiggins hustled back and grabbed his arm. Hannigan swung the clock at him. He ducked, but the clock flew into the water, then Hannigan was on him. Wiggins dodged a right, then a left, and they closed.

Hannigan thrashed wildly, enraged. They toppled over sideways. Wiggins's temple crashed into the wheel, but as he fell he caught Hannigan's collar and tipped him over too. Molly screamed. The Civ said nothing. Hannigan cried out in pain.

Wiggins, dizzy with the head wound, managed to pin Hannigan to the deck. He clamped his free hand around his neck and began to squeeze.

Hannigan kicked out and plucked uselessly at Wiggins, but he squeezed on. Hannigan's eyes began to water, his mouth open, noiseless. And still Wiggins squeezed on, roaring, in pain, in anger, in exaltation.

'Wind!' the Civ cried. 'Wind!'

Wiggins relaxed his grip for a second. He looked up. The boom swung. Hannigan squirmed away, gasping. 'The sails, man, the sails,' the Civ bellowed, pointing. 'We're away!'

Once the *Santa Clara* caught the sudden, punishing westerly, it was one mad headlong run down the coast. Wiggins's vision swam, his head pulsed, but he joined in the work nevertheless, hauling at the sails, ducking the boom, urging the boat on. Molly worked at it too, shouting at the Civ, hollering at Hannigan to lend a hand. An illusion of team spirit glimpsed amid the thrill of speed.

The sails stiffened and fluttered, the boat tipped the very waves and still she flew on, skimming the south coast until nightfall and beyond. Wiggins worked in a daze as the Civ shouted and cajoled them on through the night. No one dared stop, or sleep, for fear the wind would fail. For hours on end the *Santa Clara* and her crew sailed on, until finally, just as the light was fading again, the wind began to drop. The Civ, slumped over the wheel, bade Molly into the cabin to sleep. He called out to Wiggins to make fast. Hannigan crawled into the cabin.

Wiggins did not go into the cabin. Instead, he hauled a tarp around himself and nestled into the stern. The Civ set the wheel and sat, head between his knees, and let the boat drift a little in the swell. Far off to their right, the coast of Devon, then Cornwall darkened and disappeared.

They slept. Later, how much later Wiggins didn't know, he was roused from a dreamless, heavy, aching sleep by the sound of the Civ fidgeting on the deck. He cursed mildly a couple of times.

'What time is it?' Wiggins muttered. A moonbeam kissed the deck, then disappeared behind the rolling clouds.

'We can't wait long,' the Civ said. 'We must push on for Milford Haven. Blast it!' Something clattered to the deck.

A few distant yellow lights pinpricked the coast off to their right. Pubs on lock-ins, Wiggins imagined, and licked dry lips.

The Civ found what he'd dropped, a lantern, which he began to light as he went on. 'We must take fresh water, and we mustn't be at sea for any longer than necessary.'

'Why Milford Haven?' Wiggins coughed. 'Can't we stop anywheres?'

'I have connections there. We should be safe.' The lantern flickered into life, and Wiggins caught sight of the Civ's face, shadowed and drawn. 'How far it is to this blessed Milford,' he said softly, the light dancing in his eyes.

'I ain't being funny or nothing,' Wiggins said, shuffling over to the lantern. 'But what are you doing here? You don't fit.'

'At sea?'

'Nah. You handle the boat like it was part of you, born to it you are. Sails for nappies.' They both stared at the flickering lantern now and cupped their hands, like old down-and-outs hunkering around the dying embers of an ash bin on the streets. The yacht creaked and yawed beneath them. The smell of gun grease hung in the air, and the rigging ruffled and snapped in the light breeze. 'You don't fit in with all *this*.' Wiggins thrust a boot at one of the rifle boxes on the deck. 'You like the sport of it all, I get that. I can see the spark in the eyes, the joy of the chase. But what's in those boxes ain't your style.'

'I see you're an amateur psychologist. Are you of the Vienna school?' he joked.

'Where I come from, that's what we call a dodge.'

The Civ hesitated. He rubbed his long, thin hands together slowly, and never took his eyes off the lantern. 'I love my country. England, that is. I love England. But England is not the Empire. I used to think it was, and then . . .'

'The Boer War?'

'Not the war, the camps, the camps . . .' He lost his thread for a moment. Wiggins waited, feeling the boat's gentle rise and fall beneath him. He'd seen those camps, too; tented towns, full of the dead and dying. Not prisoners, not fighting men, but women and children, all but left to die of dysentery and cholera and worse, while the Empire squeezed the Cape for all it could. He was young then, but old enough in heart not to be surprised. A life on the streets taught him that London was no place for the poor or the vulnerable, that England, Britain, the Empire didn't give one fag end for the likes of him or anyone beneath the bottom rung. But looking at the Civ now, he realised that such a thought would have been a sickening shock to such a man; a man groomed for Empire from his first boiled egg to his last dying day. He'd known young officers, and older ones – even Kell – convinced the Empire was God's tool, and that they did good work in its service. As if bowling up to another man's country, taking all his money, taking all his honour, taking his religion and taking his self-respect too, was something they should be grateful for. Should they, bollocks. But the Civ would have been one such man, once. Wiggins felt sorry for him.

The Civ clapped his hands together suddenly, as if he sensed Wiggins's pity and wished to dispel it. 'But we are here, now, for Ireland. She must be free, a nation unto herself. And Ireland's national freedom is a great enough reward for me to suffer, what – a happy nautical jaunt in a fine vessel such as this?' He rapped his knuckles on the deck, and laughed. 'Fisticuffs and broken clocks excepted, of course,' he added, then lit a cigarette.

The rigging creaked and flapped above them, just as the Civ's first puff enveloped Wiggins. They looked up, then at each other. 'Set the bowsprit,' the Civ said. 'We're off.'

Wiggins clambered along the side of the *Santa Clara*, but suddenly out of the darkness a huge grey shape appeared on the water, large enough to crush the yacht entirely. 'What the—' he shouted.

'A destroyer!' the Civ cried, pulling hard to port.

The *Santa Clara* scraped the side of the huge ship's metal hull. Wiggins held on to the boom as the boat jagged and bobbed in the wash. The loud scratching shrivelled his very soul, and as he looked up at the destroyer's hull – like a New York building it was so high – he felt as small as he'd ever felt in his whole life.

Molly thrust her head up out of the cabin. 'What's going on?'

Up ahead, one, two, three huge lights appeared looming in the darkness, high above them. The small about to be crushed by the big, a country crushed by an empire, a worker crushed by the system itself. 'It's the fleet!' the Civ cried. 'It's the bloody fleet.'

In the darkness and the drift, they had stumbled onto the British fleet, clearly engaged in night-time manoeuvres. The lights of the huge, dark ships hung above the tiny *Santa Clara* as they went past. Molly used her blankets to cover the two stray gun cases on the deck. The Civ clung to the wheel and tried to steer a silent path through the mechanical monsters of the sea.

After a few minutes, they heard the *chug chug chug* of a motor-boat. A startling white beam of light raked over them – the boat's searchlight. The patrol boat came towards them, and a naval officer with a loudhailer began to shout at the Civ for his details.

Wiggins crouched beside the entry to the cabin and waited. He could blow the gaff right there and then and his duty to Kell would be done. He'd have stopped the guns in their tracks, Molly, Hannigan and the Civ would be arrested and he could finally go home and have a proper drink – a London porter half-and-half, with a Thames gin chaser. He glanced at the Civ, calling out sharp, precise responses to the snotty-nosed rating's barked questions, Molly by his side, her perfect form silhouetted by the patrol boat's searchlight. Her perfect form.

His eyes dropped down to the cabin door. It was in darkness, but in the scant light from the lantern in the Civ's hand, he could make out the long thin shape when it moved – a rifle, poised to shoot. Wiggins thrust out his hand and grabbed the muzzle, pushing it aside.

'Hold it,' he hissed to Hannigan as he gripped the gun tight. 'You'll kill us all.' Hannigan silently tried to wrestle the gun from his grip, 'And we'll lose the guns,' Wiggins hissed again. Any thoughts of turning the boat in had been dispelled. Hannigan would never go quietly, and going loudly meant death for them all. Up above him, he could hear the Civ's cut-glass accent holding steady.

The seconds ticked on. Not with the loud, incessant irritation of the lost ship's clock, but in Wiggins's own heart. He struggled silently with Hannigan for the gun, a noiseless stalemate.

Then Hannigan relaxed his hands with a grunt. The Civ's manner of command had done the trick. The snot-nosed petty officer was wishing him a good night. Wiggins thrust his head back through the cabin door to see the patrol boat wheeling away, taking its searchlight with it.

Wiggins gently took the rifle from Hannigan and laid it down with the rest. Hannigan said nothing, but Wiggins heard his breath, heavy with anger and frustration. Wiggins went out onto the deck and sat down aft. Molly, too, sat on the deck. Wiggins could see her unpinned hair flashing red and black in the light from the dancing lantern. Hannigan came up on deck too, and felt his way to the stern.

No one said a word as the Civ picked the *Santa Clara* through the fleet, nor for hours after as they manned the boat. Any thoughts of a jolly cruise were gone. The only successful outcome for them all was getting the boat back to Dublin undiscovered and in one piece. All other outcomes meant death. The wind picked up again, and with the dark shape of the coast off to their right, they gathered speed, and sailed on into the dawn.

It wasn't until the mainsail ripped that Wiggins thought he was going to die.

The *Santa Clara* had rounded Land's End with all hands in an endless routine of setting and resetting sails. They had made it past Longships, north, towards Milford Haven by nightfall. But as the wind picked up, the swell grew, and great fat dark clouds rolled in from the Atlantic west. They'd all but run out of food and had scant fresh water, but the Civ and Molly had decided not to put in on the Cornish coast. So, instead, they'd beaten on into the growing wilds. Wiggins had fallen asleep on the guns, his nose now immune to the gun-grease stench and foetid cabin air. Even Molly, who squeezed in beside him for a moment, didn't have the energy to do more than kiss his ear. He'd felt it as he drifted off, and even in his state of exhaustion he'd been surprised by the tenderness, the soft edge of affection – a chasteness, almost, that touched him more than anything she'd ever done.

He was woken by her cries. The Civ was shouting. Wiggins jerked, his head crashing against the side of the boat as it slewed violently to one side. He scrambled up and out of the cabin just as the bow steepled into the air. 'The boom,' the Civ screamed. Wiggins ducked as it swung violently towards him.

The yacht was in total confusion. The lanterns flicked and dipped and cast a chaotic glare. Rain lashed horizontal, the sails roared in protest, the gun crates slid across the deck. The Civ held the wheel. Hannigan jumped on the crates and cowered in the stern, while Molly, rope lashed around her midriff, tried desperately to get hold of the boom. Wiggins leapt to help her.

He jumped onto the boom to try to hold it firm with his weight, but the boat then lurched over the top of another wave and it swung away, backwards. Molly let go but he held on as it slewed out above the maelstrom in a sickening lurch and dipped into the sea. In a second, it wheeled back and Wiggins landed on the deck with a thud. But he had hold of the boom long enough for Molly to secure it.

'Get a tether line,' the Civ called, pointing astern.

That was when the sail ripped. It made a sound like thunder itself. The boat jerked crazily again and Wiggins slithered to the stern on his front, landing right by Hannigan.

'Pass me the line,' Wiggins pointed.

Hannigan, who had a rope tied around his ankle, stared, round-eyed. He shouted something, but Wiggins couldn't hear and shouted back, 'The line!' The boat lurched again and suddenly the sky was lit with a flash of lightning. A tableau of hell. The ripped sail tailing wildly, the half-drowned crew, the lurching waves.

Wiggins crouched and again edged towards Hannigan at the very back of the boat. Finally, Hannigan held out his hand and gestured him on. Wiggins reached for it, and for a second felt the instinctive reassurance of holding another person's hand, however hated.

And then Hannigan threw him into the sea.

16

Wiggins clung on.

Not to the boat, but to Hannigan. The two of them tumbled into the wash at the back of the *Santa Clara* as it rose into the waves. Hannigan had taken Wiggins's hand and slingshotted him over the side. But Wiggins held on to his hand and pulled Hannigan in with him.

The tether snapped tight on Hannigan's ankle. Wiggins held on to Hannigan's arm under the water. Then they jerked up out of the sea. Wiggins gasped and gulped for air, but hung on. The rope whipped them back into the wash, then out again. Hannigan pawed at him with his free arm in a desperate, soaked tussle.

Wiggins got hold of Hannigan with his other arm and clung to him like a lover. Tossed and turned in the rushing waves, a star-crossed suicide pact, embracing.

The water rushed in his ears, the salt in his mouth, his arms shaking with the effort of holding on, the fatigue, Hannigan's free hand clawing at his face: *Let go, let go*, his mind screamed out. *Just let go!*

He did not let go.

They were thrown out of the water and up into the air as the *Santa Clara* lurched downwards on a wave. For an instant, the two men hung high in the air above the boat, tethered by the rope around Hannigan's ankle, suddenly stock-still in that second between ascent and descent, cleaved together in a deathly grip. Wiggins had a handful of Hannigan's braces around the man's back.

Just then, a lightning bolt split the sky, a photo flash from the heavens. Wiggins felt the stillness in his belly, Hannigan breathing open-mouthed in his face, ghastly in the lightning flash.

And then they came down, back to hell, upended and whipped towards the stern with dizzying speed. Hannigan's head smashed against the corner of the boat with a sickening thud. They bounced away, back into the water.

Wiggins clung on. Hannigan did not. His body went limp, but his ankle was still attached to the rope. And the rope was still attached to the *Santa Clara. Let go, let go*, the voice in Wiggins's head screamed on. *This is the end*.

But he did not let go.

He twisted and turned and caught hold of the rope in one hand, his body close to exhaustion, gasping and gulping at seawater, Hannigan now a deadweight, the darkness of the sea, the fear, almost overwhelming.

Finally, with a great effort, he got two hands on the rope. Tossing and turning, his arms shaking, he dragged his body closer to the *Santa Clara*. Hand over hand, he rode the snaking line until his arms sang with pain, but still he pulled himself on. He could barely make out the boat as she rose and fell and slithered wildly about the sea. He concentrated on the rope, each handhold, nothing more.

With one titanic effort, he got an arm over the bulwark at the stern. As he lifted himself up, he caught sight of Molly – lit by the swinging lantern on the mast. She was crouched over something, hacking away with the sea axe. She looked up when she saw him, wild-eyed with surprise. 'It'll send us all over,' she bellowed through the sheet rain. 'We must save the guns.'

Wiggins hung there, one arm over the bulwark, his legs trailing the boat, his energy spent.

But then Molly suddenly leapt into action. She scuttled across, grabbed his arms and hauled him over the edge. He slumped onto the deck.

She turned back to the rope, picked up the axe and hacked it clear with one final swing, consigning Hannigan's body to the deep for ever.

The *Santa Clara* stayed afloat. Through luck, or God's fell hand, or the Civ's skill, or Molly's quick thinking, Wiggins didn't know.

Maybe God was an Irish nationalist. Certainly the Irish nationalists thought so. But then God was also a unionist, according to the unionists. And also a supporter of the Empire – Wiggins had heard that one too. He was good 'un, was God, supporting everyone against everyone until they tore themselves to shreds in His Good Name.

The storm broke sometime before dawn. On the next morning they patched the sail as best they could and limped north towards Milford Haven. The three of them were hollow-eyed and dead beat. All of them but Hannigan, who was simply dead.

Wiggins hadn't killed the man, and he shed no tears for his demise. Wiggins wouldn't have pulled the trigger on him, but as far as he was concerned, Hannigan had brought it on himself. Molly appeared almost completely untroubled. The Civ, on the other hand, looked deeply disturbed. 'I didn't sign up for this, Molly,' he said, a mile or so outside the port. 'You know that.'

'It was an accident, Civ.'

'Did he have a family?'

'He must have had a mother, once,' she said, then quickly, 'Look, I'm sorry, I really am, Civ, but what's to be done? What do they say – worse things happen at sea?'

Terrible things happen at sea. Wiggins scanned the harbour walls, as if searching for the end, and pondered the night before. It wasn't the first time he'd touched his own iron soul, his will to live that – despite everything, the bottom of the pit, the fires, the ocean, the hopelessness – trumped all other desires. Even when he had nothing to live for, his instincts told him otherwise. He would never have made it out of London in the eighties, alone and motherless, if he hadn't had the desire; he could have given up so many times, and yet here he was, still clinging to the flailing tail of life's serpent, clinging on as another endgame approached.

They dropped anchor a couple of hundred yards from the quay. The coastguard had come to see what was what, but when the Civ shouted out that he was to take tea with the harbour master (a man called Stanhope) and would they mind pointing him to a decent spot to park the old girl, they waved the *Santa*

Clara on easy enough. People like the Civ never had any trouble fooling those down the social scale. Who'd ever think a gentleman would smuggle guns? Or who'd ever risk inconveniencing a gentleman on the off chance that he might be smuggling guns? Stand up to a man like the Civ and get it wrong, and that was your job gone. And so the *Santa Clara* sailed into Milford Haven serenely, unchallenged.

Miraculously, the dinghy had remained intact throughout the storm, and as the Civ readied it for the short trip to shore, he prattled on to Molly. 'I can get a patch for the mainsail at Wilson's,' he said. 'And we'll need fresh water and food. It shouldn't take more than a few hours to supply.'

'Get us a couple of rooms, Civ,' she replied. 'We can stay tonight.'

He nodded, then absently looked about the boat. 'Don't worry,' Molly went on. 'Wiggins will stay aboard.'

'Right you are,' he said and clambered down into the dinghy. 'Who's coming with me now?'

'I'll stay for the moment,' Molly said. 'Wiggins can collect me before it gets dark and I'll come to the hotel.' She then pulled Wiggins aside, out of earshot, while the Civ settled down. 'Go ashore,' she whispered. 'Have a bath.'

'I ain't got no blunt.'

She handed him a coin and leaned in close to his ear. 'I want you to have a bath, and then come back alone. And then I want to fuck you here, among the guns, on the deck. I want you inside me, I want us to be free. I long to be fucked by you.'

'Are you coming?' the Civ yelled from the dinghy.

Molly stepped back and held Wiggins's eyes. 'One second,' she called back. Then she held out her hand and took his, suddenly chaste. She nodded.

Wiggins clambered into the dinghy and settled opposite the Civ, who took the oars and struck out for the town. Wiggins looked back once, as they beat into a tide, looked back at the *Santa Clara* and Molly, who stood watching. She waved her hand in a single sweep, then held it aloft until he turned away.

By the time they got on dry land, Molly had disappeared into the cabin. The Civ made fast the dinghy and the two men wandered away from the seafront, towards the town.

'I'll meet you back here at eightish,' the Civ said at a small crossroads. 'We can take over the supplies and pick up Moll— I mean, Miss Lansdown-Smith.'

Wiggins smiled slightly at the *Miss*. Bit late for that. 'You're a good man, Civ,' he said.

'I'm a dirty man. I need a bath, a shave and a hot meal.'

'You need to get the train home. Back to London.'

'What's that?' the Civ said absently. 'The job's almost done.'

Wiggins squeezed his shoulder, not unkind. 'You need to get the train home. Now.' He patted him on the back and walked away, leaving the Civ speechless and bewildered.

The road looped around, back to the seafront. Wiggins did not intend to get a bath. Instead, he headed back to the dinghy. He looked out across the harbour and, as he suspected, Molly already had the *Santa Clara* under sail. The mainsail was a tawdry and ragged thing, but there was obviously enough wind or tide or whatever else it was (Wiggins had had his fill of all things nautical) that she felt she could get away. He'd seen that she was an accomplished seawoman on the way over – she'd tried to hide it, but she could handle the boat almost as well as the Civ. He had no doubt she could handle it fine on her own.

He leapt down into the rowing boat and within seconds was heading to the *Santa Clara* at a fair clip. It wasn't until he'd nearly reached the yacht, now completely unanchored and eddying away from the port, that Molly noticed him. She hesitated, and even from a distance Wiggins could see indecision in her body language. She reached her arm out to him, but it was unclear whether she was trying to shoo him away or beckon him on.

In an instant, he'd got hold of the tail rope and had hauled himself and the dinghy alongside before she could reasonably object.

Molly held on to the wheel and stared at him as he clambered aboard.

'What are you doing?' he said.

She leapt into action, busying herself. 'We have to be off.' She made the boom fast and grabbed hold of the wheel again. 'Chop-chop.'

'Chop-chop? Why the fuck are we going now?'

'The tide, the tide.'

Wiggins flung his arm back towards the disappearing quay. 'What about the Civ?'

'The Civ will thank me one day,' she said under her breath, then gestured to him. 'Will you fix the bowsprit, please? Oh, don't look at me like that – there's plenty of time for fun. We'll be cosy enough in the cabin later.'

Wiggins shook his head slightly, but did as she asked. The sky had gone from red to a dark purple and now, as they passed out of sight of Milford proper, onto the more open sea, it was getting dangerously dark. Off to their far right and ahead lay a commercial shipyard that looked deserted. As they drew alongside, it was little more than dark shapes.

'This is madness, Molly,' he said at last. 'We're running blind.'

'Not long now,' she said, lighting the lantern on the mainmast. Out in the mist ahead of them, a white searchlight shone. It was on a boat, a steamer, Wiggins judged by the speed, and it had obviously seen them.

'Here they are!' Molly cried. She flashed the lantern on and off twice. 'They should have been waiting at Milford, but I couldn't wait.'

'What's going on, Moll?'

She turned to him, her eyes gleaming with excitement. 'It's my men of Ulster,' she said. 'Come to take us to Larne.'

The sea had stilled somewhat, and they stood and stared at each other. The light of the lantern yellowed her face, while above them the sky had turned an angry purple. 'Oh, come on,' she said as the *Santa Clara* rose and fell with the swell. 'You didn't really believe all that guff about Ireland being free, did you? A nation free unto herself.' She laughed. 'I know you don't believe that. You're here for me. You're here for this . . .' She gestured vaguely at her body. 'And look. I'm still here.'

He glanced behind him, into the darkness. 'I didn't know what to think,' he said at last.

She looked back out at the approaching steamer. 'They're arming in the north too, you know, my people – an Ulster Volunteer Force. But we are arming to keep peace. We will fight if we have to, fight to the death to defeat Rome Rule.'

'What about that stuff, you know, down with the Empire?'

'Down with the Empire?' She almost laughed in his face, then pushed her hands out wide. 'The Empire's the sea, it's the ocean, it's the world. You don't fight the sea, you rise and fall with it, you ride its currents, you surf its waves. I'm not here to leave the Empire, I'm here to keep Ireland, my Ireland, British.'

As she said this last word, her head flinched in alarm and she gestured over Wiggins's shoulder. 'What's that?'

Wiggins glanced round. The navy patrol boat that he'd been expecting had darted out of the deserted commercial docks. As he looked, he could see the glare of its searchlight come haring towards them at three times the rate of the more sedate steamer up ahead. He turned back to Molly. 'They're here for me,' he said. 'For us.'

He wondered whether Kell himself would be on the boat. When he'd cabled from Cowes, Wiggins had made it clear that the capture should happen after Milford, out at sea, so that – if necessary – he could maintain his cover with the OC. He didn't want to waste all that work with O'Connell on a one-shot deal. He didn't want to go back to Dublin, either, but it didn't make any sense to burn bridges unless they needed to be burned. Dublin wasn't a city that was going to stay quiet for long.

Part of him also had a soft spot for the Civ, and he hoped he'd taken his advice to get on a train at Milford and not come back. He was a genuine man, helping a genuine cause, unlike the shapely snake in front of him.

Molly simply gaped at the oncoming vessel, then swivelled to look for her own boat, now seemingly stalled in its approach. 'But how's the navy . . . what? You peached?'

'Fitz found out, didn't he?' Wiggins said. The naval patrol was closing now and someone hailed them through the mist. 'I thought he was just sweet on you, but actually he *knew*. It weren't sex that made him shy about you, it was treachery.'

'Your sainted Fitz? Do you really think he's a hill worth dying on? Yes, he overheard something – probably when I was on the telephone in O'Grady's. He followed me in for some reason, the damned sneak. And yes, he let me know about it. The snivelling little blackmailer.'

Wiggins ignored the slur and went on. 'You put the DMP on him, didn't you? You hired some coppers to do him in, but they went for me instead.'

'That fool Donovan!' she cried in exasperation. 'He was meant to take Fitz on the quiet one evening, but when he heard O'Connell's bodyguard had been arrested in a dust-up, he thought he'd save himself the bother and take you straight from the guardhouse. They assumed *you* were Fitz.'

Wiggins shook his head. She was talking about murder like it was nothing.

'It would have worked if you hadn't strolled into our lives,' Molly went on, and then craned her neck to look past him at the nearing patrol boat, then back to the steamboat behind her. 'They got scared after that. Pathetic. And then you didn't leave Fitz's side again. You and he were joined at the hip – we couldn't get to him easily.'

Wiggins shook his head. 'Which is why you got me following you all over town.'

'I had to get you out of the way,' she said. She fixed him with a look. 'But don't tell me you didn't enjoy it? I know you enjoyed being with me. I *felt* it.'

She smiled at him, trying her charm again. And she had charms all right. But Wiggins shook his head, almost spat out his words. 'Then you did a deal with Lynch. I've seen his men, one of them used to be a bloody cooper – I seen them. They barrelled up the poor fucking kid, and then tried to make a play for the OC's business,' he cried, suddenly very angry. 'Not that I give a stuff about that, but Fitz? You had the boy killed to keep yourself safe.'

'I didn't have a choice,' she said.

'You could have left.'

'He was trying to blackmail me!'

'For money,' Wiggins said. 'Just for bloody money, and you've got enough of that. Money ain't worth anyone's life, is it?'

She looked at him then, speechless, processing who Wiggins really was and the mistakes that she'd made in trusting him. 'So, you're a hero, are you?' she said faintly, sardonically, but with regret too. The truth of who he was – a British spy – and what he'd done had quietened her. A double-crosser doubled-crossed.

By this time, the navy patrol boat had drawn alongside and a couple of ratings were pulling the yacht to with large hooks. Molly looked at them, all the fight gone, literally hooked. She shook her head slightly and said, 'I thought . . . I really thought you loved me.'

'I can't love a killer,' he said, like he meant it. 'It ain't right.'

'But you . . . That boy in New York?'

'Tyrone *is* his name. And you didn't bat an eyelid at his death,' Wiggins said. 'You didn't even blink. I knew then you were a stone-cold killer. You don't have to plunge the knife to take the blame.'

'Wiggins!' Kell bellowed from the patrol boat. 'Lend a hand, will you?'

'Can't you see,' Molly said quietly, 'it was such a good plan. We would have gained the firepower at the exact moment our enemy would be denied it.'

But Wiggins had turned away, sickened. He looked on as Captain Vernon Kell, head of the internal Secret Service, resplendent in yachting togs, boarded the *Santa Clara* with the air of an all-conquering king ready to accept a surrender. By his side, a naval rating swung a torchlight around the deck and called out instructions to his fellow crew on the patrol boat. A naval lieutenant followed Kell aboard.

Kell looked from Molly to Wiggins and back again, then peered into the darkness at the steamboat, which had stopped its approach and now idled in the gloom. 'Find out who they are, will you, Cairns? Use the semaphore if necessary.'

'There's no need,' Wiggins grunted. 'They're Ulster Volunteer Force – UVF – ain't that right, Molls?'

Kell nodded, unsurprised. 'Signal them anyway, will you? Get me a name or two. Who's the skipper, and who's in charge. Very good.' He turned his attention back to Wiggins and Molly. 'Good evening, ma'am,' he said, tipping his cap.

'Less of that,' Wiggins growled. 'She's a murderer.'

'Indeed.' Kell regarded her again. 'And a gunrunner too . . .'

'And a British patriot,' she said, jutting out her chin. 'I have been working to save the British Empire, not diminish it. And I am not here to be questioned by the likes of you, whoever you are.'

'I do beg your pardon,' Kell said. 'I am Captain Kell, head of the British Secret Service, though not, as it were, at your service, ha ha.' Wiggins glanced askance at Kell's nervous manner – he'd obviously just realised quite how beautiful Molly was.

She was in no mood to flirt. 'Dirty spies,' she spat back, and glared at Wiggins, then shook her head. 'You should be thanking me. I fight for Britain.'

'Like I say, she's a murderer.'

'We are not the police,' Kell said mildly. 'Murder is not necessarily our business.'

'And she powwowed with Van Bork,' Wiggins went on. 'She's dealing with the Germans, so she's a traitor an' all.'

'*That* is our business,' Kell nodded, as ever playing the big man. Wiggins was too tired to protest. Kell called out to one of the navy men. 'Take her down, aft. We will talk more on this subject, you and I,' he said, still trying on the charm.

Molly glared some more, but she did not protest. One of the sailors led her onto the patrol boat and down below decks.

Kell peered at the deck and nodded his head, looking into the cabin with a torch. 'My, my.' He whistled. 'You weren't wrong. What a haul she had.'

'I'm not wrong about murder, neither,' Wiggins said.

It was the moment in New York when Molly had revealed not only her excitement at the thought of violence, but also her desperation for the deal to go through – that was when she had truly come into focus as the killer. Her blithe acceptance that Tyrone had to die, the way she'd reacted when Fitz's name was mentioned, her word-for-word renditions of the nationalist slogans – like she'd learned rather than felt them. Worst of all, her lust had betrayed her.

Wiggins had known in his heart that it was manufactured, knew that he did not hold so much allure for such a woman, knew he was a tool to be used. She had used him to help O'Connell secure the deal, and wanked him off because she thought he was losing his nerve, then led him on to keep him under control. Maybe she did fancy him, he didn't know. It didn't make any difference. She'd needed him to be in love with her so he wouldn't discover the truth: the truth about who killed Fitz, and the truth about what she was up to. She'd used him.

He had been used all his life, like everyone he knew – that was their lot. First by Holmes, on call for a shilling if you were lucky, for nothing if you weren't; then the army, a shilling there, too, and though he'd worked the cannon he could equally have been its victim and no one would have cared, another Whitechapel scruff would come along just as desperate for the King's shilling; then by the bailiff Leach, a fucking bailiff, who'd pay him if he recovered a debt and wouldn't if he couldn't, taking money off the dead poor an' all, like they could afford it; and then by fucking Kell, fighting for an empire that didn't give a toss, selling out poor dead Jimmy Milton out of Woolwich, and Martha in the bloody brothel in Brussels, doping up girls for gossip, for the British Empire, and all that he got out of it was pay, fucking pay, because he couldn't fucking live without fucking pay; and then O'Connell had thought he'd kill a man for pay, for fucking money, and maybe he might have done, too, if he'd been hungry enough; they all used money, that leveller that could never be denied; Sal, too, her red raw hands raw to the fucking bone, and Bela and all the girls, burning to death in a shirt factory for the twenty cents a day cos they'd fucking die without the job and fucking die with it too, just like most of the folk across the world, hanging by such a thread, and all for what?

'Can we pin anything on O'Connell,' Kell asked, breaking Wiggins's bitter reverie. As if O'Connell was to blame for all the world's ills. *Can we pin it on him? Is he the devil?*

'What's the fucking point?' Wiggins said, exhausted.

'I beg your pardon,' Kell cried, sharply. 'I will not be addressed in such a fashion.' It was a flash of real anger, such that Wiggins hadn't often seen in his boss. Angrier at swearing than at murder – fucking toff all over.

Wiggins closed his eyes, took a breath. 'There ain't much we can pin on O'Connell. Not for treason anyway, and not on home soil.'

'Shame. His name isn't on any of the cables either. He's a sly dog, for sure.'

'What cables?'

'Oh, didn't I say? We can read all the telegrams coming in and out of Dublin from abroad. The British Government owns most of the underwater telegraph cables in the world – we can read them all.' He thought for a moment, then rubbed his hands together. 'Still, she's the one, is she? At least, we've stopped these guns getting into the wrong hands.'

At that moment Lieutenant Cairns climbed back onto the *Santa Clara* and handed Kell a written note. 'Here's the semaphore, sir.'

The officer held up a lantern so that Kell could read the message. 'Right. Oh . . . ah, I see, yes. UVF Tollington's on board, is he? Very good, Cairns, prepare to cast off. Wiggins, are you ready?'

'What about this lot?' Wiggins gestured around him, at the *Santa Clara* and its lethal cargo.

'Sorry? Oh, we'll leave it for those chaps over there.' He pointed over his shoulder at the idling steamer.

'Them lot? I thought—'

'Look, Wiggins, this mission has been a great success. You've prevented an enormous gun cache falling into the hands of dangerous nationalists, intent on breaking up the country. It's not our concern that elements loyal to Empire want to maintain their freedom, is it? We in the Service need to know which side we're on.'

Wiggins cursed in disgust. 'But—'

'Our job is to allay threats to the Empire, to the country, not to stop decent citizens from defending their rights. Think about it, man,' he urged. 'They're fearful of being ruled by the Catholics, of an all-Irish government. We can't stand in the way of that.'

Wiggins hesitated, looked his boss up and down wearily and nodded. 'I'll see you on there.' He gestured at the patrol boat. 'Gi' us a mo. I'll just get my stuff.' He pointed at the cabin.

Kell nodded slightly, then turned away. Cairns followed in his wake. Wiggins waited for them to get off the boat, then swiped the lantern from the mast and entered the cabin. But he did not gather his 'stuff'. He had no stuff to gather, that was not the way his life was led.

Instead, he reached out and prised from its housing the sea axe that Molly had used to cut Hannigan free. He stumbled forward, by the head, the only patch of hull left exposed by the packed guns.

John Coffey's advice rang in his ears from that night on the *Titanic* – 'Any ship is sinkable . . . if you put a hole big enough into the hull, say here or here' – and with suppressed and controlled rage he took the axe to the wooden slats.

One, two, one, two, the blade flew straight. The planks split and splintered and still Wiggins swung. The overladen *Santa Clara* sat so low that within seconds seawater came pouring in around his feet. Wiggins waited to make sure, then crawled back over the guns. He could hear the gushing, rushing sea and the creaking, complaining boat around him as he struggled to get back up the stairs.

Water sloshed across the deck as he pulled himself out of the cabin. The *Santa Clara* was almost done. He heard the shouts and cries from the patrol boat – the ratings cutting away at the ropes so that the *Santa Clara* didn't drag them down.

Wiggins felt free at last. Free from the cursed job, free to disobey Kell. And free from obligation, too, from the debt owed to the dead man, Fitz. He felt free from Bela's memory, free from Molly, free finally to do as he wished. As the *Santa Clara* pitched forward and the sea sloshed about his knees, the weight of months and years seemed to float away. He would do what he would, and the rest was nothing.

Kell stood on the deck of the patrol boat, astonished. 'What have you done?' he cried out at Wiggins, waving his hands uselessly. 'What have you done?'

Wiggins grabbed hold of the mast as the water rushed about his waist and the *Santa Clara* tipped and swayed towards its doom.

'Cairns!' Kell was shouting now. 'Get a line out there. Get the lights. Cairns!'

'It's not that easy, sir.'

'Wiggins,' Kell cried, pointing at the rope flung out to save him. 'Grab hold of the line. Really, I insist. This is no time for theatrical gestures.'

The sea was up to Wiggins's chest now, calming, enveloping, welcoming him into its arms. 'I told you,' he shouted up at Kell, as he finally let go of the descending mast. 'I don't like guns.'

HISTORICAL NOTES

Charles Becker, Herman Rosenthal and Jack Zelig

In 1915 – three years after his disagreement with Wiggins – Charles Becker became the first and only American policeman to be executed for murder. The murder, in fact, of Herman Rosenthal, which took place outside the Hotel Metropole, as witnessed by Wiggins. Becker was accused of colluding with underworld notable Big Jack Zelig and of using his men – in particular Lefty Louie and Gyp the Blood – to eliminate Rosenthal. The whole scandal erupted after a series of articles in the *New York World* by reporter Herbert Bayard Swope, the first-ever winner of the Pulitzer Prize for Reporting.

The trial was poorly conducted, and Becker's guilt is by no means certain – although he was surely guilty of much by way of corruption. Jack Zelig was murdered in October 1912 – not long after his altercation with Wiggins – while riding the Second Avenue streetcar. An angry rival, revenging some slight, shot him in the back of the head as he travelled north.

The Triangle Shirtwaist Factory Fire and Rose Schneiderman

The Triangle Shirtwaist Factory fire is one of the USA's most devastating industrial accidents, and the details in the book are derived from contemporary reports. While the owners of the business escaped prison, the fire itself proved an important moment in the development of the union movement and worker safety. Union organiser and suffragist Rose Schneiderman was heavily involved in organising labour – especially women's labour – in and around New York at the time, and the fire was a rallying point for her cause. She became one of the most important figures in the history of trade unionism in America and she was a founder member of the American Civil Liberties Union.

Irish Republican Gunrunning and Erskine Childers

The journey of the *Santa Clara*, as described in this book, is very similar to one undertaken two years later – in the summer of 1914 – by a British civil servant, Erskine Childers, and his wife, Molly Spring (among others). They sailed on the Childers' yacht *Asgard* from Dublin to a rendezvous in the North Sea outside Hamburg, and collected a huge cache of rifles and ammunition. That time, they managed to deliver the cargo back to Howth, north of Dublin, thus arming for the first time the nationalist elements in Ireland. Two months later, sympathisers of the Ulster unionist movement ran a similar amount of guns into Larne in the north, thereby ensuring that both sides of the independence argument on the island of Ireland had guns with which to make their point.

Erskine Childers was most famous for writing the huge best-seller – and forerunner of modern spy fiction – *The Riddle of the Sands* in 1902. This book launched a slew of copy-cat spy thrillers, which themselves led to a 'spy fever' that forced the British Government to investigate claims that the German invasion of Great Britain was imminent. It was not, but the government nevertheless felt it prudent to open the Secret Service Bureau (the precursor to MI5 and MI6), with Captain Vernon Kell as the head of its domestic operation.

Childers fought in the Boer War and went on to serve the British in the First World War (after his gunrunning exploits), but he passionately believed in the Irish nationalist cause. However, in 1922 he was executed during the Irish Civil War at Beggars Bush Barracks in Dublin for possession of a gun (that had been given to him by Michael Collins), in contravention of the law. His son went on to be president of the Republic of Ireland.

The Baker Street Irregulars

In his own accounts of Sherlock Holmes's work, Dr Watson briefly acknowledges the role of the Irregulars on three occasions. Young Wiggins is cited as the leader of the gang working on two cases – *A Study in Scarlet* and *The Sign of the Four* – while in a third case, Wiggins is mistakenly identified as 'Simpson'. Dr Watson's accounts are notoriously hazy on dates and names, however, and most historical sources are convinced that the Irregulars, and Wiggins in particular, played a far more substantial role in Holmes's work than Watson credits. This would be in keeping with the mores of the time, when it was rare for lower-class people – and street 'Arabs' or urchins in particular – to be given prominence.

Sherlock Holmes did indeed travel to America in 1912 in order to establish an undercover identity – an embittered Irish-American republican called Altamont – as is documented in the story of 'His Last Bow'.

ACKNOWLEDGEMENTS

I'd like to thank my editor at Hodder, Nick Sayers. His patience lasts years, his advice lasts forever. He and the team at Hodder, in particular Eleni Lawrence, have been such stalwart supporters of Wiggins and his creator. I'd also like to thank my agent Jemima Hunt for continuing to fly the flag, again, over years and drafts. Likewise, thanks again to Caroline Johnson for such a sympathetic and forensic copy edit.

I once wrote a PhD and doing the bibliography for that almost killed me. So I shall invoke the privileges of a novelist, and will not list all the books I used to write this novel. That task would finish me off. However, it would be remiss if I did not mention some of the Dublin books that helped bring that city's history alive for me: James Joyce, in particular *Dubliners* and *Ulysses*; James Plunkett's *Strumpet City* and Iris Murdoch's *The Red and The Green*.

As for New York, much of the detail of the city at the time, and the Charles Becker story in particular, I found in Mike Dash's *Satan's Circus* – a brilliant history of a crazy case. And I could never have written anything about New York without Damon Runyon, who is in a class all of his own.

Finally, the closing chapters of this book were inspired and deeply informed by Mary Spring Rice's *Diary of the Asgard*, which I first came across on *An Phoblacht*'s website.

As I write these acknowledgements, London is still in the midst of its first (and hopefully only) lockdown. It's helped me to confirm, more than ever, that my family gives me so much as a writer: life, energy, distraction, nits, focus, a social life. I couldn't ask for anything more, especially from my partner, Annalise Davis, without whom none of this would be possible.